Praise for *The Night in Question*

"*The Night in Question* is a unique and totally compelling mystery chock-full of desperation, greed, scandal, and murder. A smart and compulsive read with a thrilling ending to boot."

—Mary Kubica

"An engrossing tale of desperation, opportunity, and how one voyeuristic moment leads a woman down a rabbit hole of lies, blackmail, and ultimately murder. Fast-paced and gripping, *The Night in Question* is not to be missed."

—Haley Harrigan, author of *Secrets of Southern Girls*

"Who said only bad people do bad things…? In *The Night in Question*, Nic Joseph weaves an expertly paced and intriguing tale packed with lies, deceit, and sizzling tension. It'll certainly have the reader wondering how far they might go to protect what's most important to them."

—Hannah Mary McKinnon, author of *The Neighbors*

THE
NIGHT
IN
QUESTION

A NOVEL

NIC JOSEPH

sourcebooks
landmark

Published by Sourcebooks Landmark, an imprint of Sourcebooks, Inc.
P.O. Box 4410, Naperville, Illinois 60563-4410
(630) 961-3900
Fax: (630) 961-2168
sourcebooks.com

Library of Congress Cataloging-in-Publication Data

Names: Joseph, Nic, author.
Title: The night in question : a novel / Nic Joseph.
Description: Naperville, Illinois : Sourcebooks Landmark, [2018]
Identifiers: LCCN 2018010353 | (trade pbk. : alk. paper)
Subjects: | GSAFD: Suspense fiction.
Classification: LCC PS3610.O66896 N54 2018 | DDC 813/.6--dc23
LC record available at https://lccn.loc.gov/2018010353

Printed and bound in the United States of America.
VP 10 9 8 7 6 5 4 3 2 1

For GUYCONJ

PROLOGUE

I DECIDED EARLY ON THAT telling the truth—the whole truth—was out of the question.

I wouldn't lie about the important things, of course, since only liars do that, and I'm sure I don't deserve such an unforgiving label.

I would, however, lie about the things that mattered little in reality but significantly in perception. I'd lie about those things because I had to, because there was no other choice, and because doing so would not, in the end, make me a bad person.

That's what I would do.

I would lie about the tiny, unimportant things.

I would tell the truth about all the rest.

They wanted details.

Things like where I (allegedly) picked him up, what we (allegedly) talked about, and if I saw him with the victim when I (allegedly) dropped him off.

They kept tossing the modifier around as if I didn't already know they didn't believe me. The woman's name was Detective Claire Puhl, like *swimming pool*, and she could barely hide the mistrust in her big, bored, brown eyes. We were in the back of the 18th District Police Department in downtown Chicago, in a room with flickering fluorescent lights, folding metal chairs, and a very noticeable camera up high in the far-right corner of the room. The other cop with us was a skinny, awkward man who'd introduced himself only as Detective Greg. I'd wanted to ask him if Greg was his last name or his first, but the question felt too cheeky under the circumstances.

Sit up, Paula.

Make eye contact.

Now, *breathe*.

The questions were coming fast, and I was trying to answer them as calmly as possible. I wasn't doing well. The alcohol, of course, didn't help. I could still smell it on my clothes and taste it on my tongue, which meant they could probably smell it too. I'd apologized for it right off the bat, since it seemed that might stop them from holding it against me.

"Thanks for seeing me," I'd said when we first sat down. "I hope you'll forgive me. After the break-in, I had a couple glasses of wine to fall asleep, and when I woke up, I came straight here, so I'll admit, I'm a little bit…"

Detective Puhl had held up a hand. I'd quickly learn that she was the type of person to stop you midsentence if she didn't feel you were saying something of value. She'd shared a look with Detective Greg and then leaned forward.

"What, exactly, can we help you with?"

She'd paused, just like that, around the word *exactly*, fair warning that she wanted me to be precise about the next words that came out of my mouth.

I'd taken a deep breath and launched into my story. When I finished, they both sat back in their chairs and watched me with expressions I couldn't read.

"Ms. Wilson—" Detective Puhl finally said.

"Mrs.," I said, and she paused, her eyes narrowing at the interruption. I cleared my throat. I didn't correct about my last name (it's Wileson), because that detail didn't feel so important, and even under the fog of red wine, I remembered that *they didn't need to know too much*. I'd said my real name when I'd arrived, but she'd misheard me, and that simply did not feel like my fault.

The fact that I was married, though—that part was critical, since it was both the reason I was here in the first place and proof that I wasn't some crazed, tipsy fan who made a habit of calling in false tips to the police.

I was married, and I loved my husband.

That mattered.

"Okay, Mrs. Wilson," Detective Puhl said crisply. "Is there anything else you can tell us about what happened on the night you dropped him off? You said you thought Mr. Hooks seemed nervous when he got into your car. Do you still feel that way?"

The question made me angry, but again, that could've been the alcohol. I wanted to ask her why my story would have changed in the half hour since I'd arrived and demand to know why she was treating me like a criminal.

I was the one who'd been attacked. *I* was the victim here.

Though, in all fairness, the man *hadn't* been nervous. On the night he slid into the back seat of my 2013 Hyundai Elantra and muttered the words "Rideshare for Lotti?" the first things that struck me were that (a) he seemed incredibly confident and very much in control; (b) his voice was deep and warm, like the voice in an advertisement for some cologne that smells like a spice drawer; and (c) he was almost certainly not "Lotti."

But those weren't the kinds of things you told two cops when they stared at you, a week and a half later, suspicion dancing behind their eyes. So, for this tiny thing, this unimportant part of the story, I lied.

"Yes, he was so…" I looked down at the table for a moment and paused, then drew my gaze back up to the cops. "Fidgety. I guess you could describe it as nervous. I can't really explain it, but I could tell something was wrong."

Detective Puhl leaned forward, placing both elbows on the table between us.

"I really wish you *could* explain it," she said.

I froze. It was the first time since I'd arrived that she'd voiced her skepticism, even though it had been there all along—in her body language, her expression, her shared looks with Detective Greg.

She tilted her head and spoke slowly, as if there was a chance I might not understand her.

"So why exactly are you sharing this information with us?" she asked. "If you're insinuating that Mr. Hooks had something to do with the incident on West Oak Street this past weekend, you must realize how serious of an accusation that is."

I swallowed and tried to stave off the sick feeling in my stomach, the one that had been there for days but was still managing to grow worse by the minute.

Of course I realize that, I almost snapped. Sort of accusing someone of murder is not the kind of thing you don't realize you're doing. The cops looked at each other again, and I got the impression they were silently having a conversation with each other, right in front of my face. There was suddenly too much saliva in my mouth, and I wanted to swallow, but I didn't, since it seemed it would make me look nervous.

"Are you okay?" Detective Puhl asked.

This wasn't working.

"Mrs. Wilson?" She seemed to let her tongue linger over the syllables. "Are you all right?"

I shouldn't have come here.

"Mrs. Wilson?"

"Yes," I said, my voice shaking, and I straightened up in my chair. I cleared my throat. "Look, I think maybe we got off to a bad start. I'm not…"

"Not what?" Detective Puhl asked, leaning even farther across the table.

It was an intimidation tactic, I knew, yet I still couldn't find the right words.

"I didn't…"

"Didn't what?" Detective Puhl said again, her voice louder.

I was losing control of the situation. "No, you don't understand," I said. "It's not what it seems like. I have a—"

"Husband?" Detective Puhl said.

The single word, said so knowingly, catapulted over the table and slapped me across the face. I locked eyes with her, unsure how to respond, but then I didn't have to, because she kept talking.

"I know you do, Mrs. Wilson," she said, and there was something like satisfaction on her face. "You've been saying that since you arrived."

Had I?

I finally swallowed and looked up at the clock.

Maybe I'd mentioned it once or twice, but certainly not more than that.

Right?

The sick feeling continued to grow, and she stared at me with a knowing look in her eyes. I began to recognize, beyond a shadow of a doubt, that coming here had been a mistake.

A big mistake.

Detective Puhl leaned back in her chair and shared another glance with the strangely silent Detective Greg before looking back at me.

"That's the reason we're supposed to believe everything you're saying, right?" she asked, and she actually smiled a little bit. "We should believe you because you have a husband, and let me guess— you love him very much?"

Maybe I shouldn't have rehearsed so much.

I'd gone over my story several times before I walked into the police station and asked for Detective Puhl. I'd first seen her on TV a few days earlier, tall, sharp, and serious in her navy blazer. She was the first person I'd thought of after the break-in, but it had still taken me a full hour to muster up the courage to go in to see her.

As I sat in front of her and Detective Greg, I wished I'd rehearsed a little bit less; the words fell from my lips in a way that was too practiced, too perfect.

I'd started off by telling them about the grandparents.

"I was downtown because I'd just dropped off a lovely couple. New grandparents. I took them to Lurie Children's." I paused and let a wistful expression take over my face. "They were so happy. Their son-in-law ordered the DAC rideshare to the hospital for them, and I took them there to meet their new granddaughter, Elizabeth."

The detectives needed to know that I could remember details.

Names, dates, places.

I wasn't lying about those things. I had taken *that* couple to *that* hospital to see *that* baby.

I just hadn't found them very "lovely."

6

"This is our first Drive Away Car," the chatty woman had said proudly as she got in the car. I had a feeling she meant their first rideshare of any kind. It was a warm, muggy August night, and my windshield was covered in a light mist, an early sign of the rain that was expected overnight. The man who ambled in behind her took a moment to shake out his large umbrella before pulling it into the car and closing the door.

"Our son-in-law, Gregory, called it for us," the woman continued. "We would've been there at the hospital already, but we came home to get some rest, because you never know how long these things can take, you know? The female body is so fascinating, don't you think? No two are the same. The doctors have been giving us all sorts of estimates, but we had no idea when our grandbaby would actually come."

I didn't know how to respond, so I asked the only question I could come up with.

"Is it a boy or a girl?"

I looked up into the rearview for just a moment. Even though the back seat was dimly lit, I could see the woman staring at me earnestly. I quickly pulled my gaze back to the road. I've always had a thing with eye contact. It's like a game of Russian roulette, stickier and more personal than a touch, and I'm always the one to look away first. One of my biggest problems with being a DAC driver is the prolonged eye contact you often have with passengers.

"A girl," the woman said. "Just what I wanted. I would've been happy either way, of course. But I've been dreaming about little Lizzie ever since my daughter got married."

The woman's husband said something quietly to her, something I couldn't hear, and then she responded.

"I'm just talking," she hissed. She cleared her throat and then spoke louder, to me. "My husband said I'm talking too much, that

I'm being selfish and not asking enough about you. Because that's really the point of these things, right? Tell us, honey, how long have you been a driver?"

"About six months," I said.

"Do you like it?"

It was the most common question I got from riders. Some didn't talk at all, but of those who did, at least 75 percent asked it by the time the ride was over.

I bit my bottom lip.

What could I say?

No, I don't like the close quarters with strangers, the complaints about the temperature, the small talk with excited new grandmothers, or the drunk passengers who sway in the back seat.

No, I would very much rather be at home with Keith, even though he'd been in one of his moods when I left a few hours ago.

No, I don't enjoy driving people around, not after a long day waiting tables at the diner.

Driving DAC was a job, just like any job, and I'd be hard-pressed to say I liked it.

"I *love* it," I said with a smile and another quick glance in the mirror. Because, of course, there was nothing more "hard-pressing" than the possibility of a tip. The woman leaned forward as I continued. "I get to meet a lot of great people, so that's nice."

"Oh, I bet you do," she said. "You must meet the most inter-esting people! Much more interesting than us…"

"Not at all," I said, and then, without an ounce of shame, "You guys are such a joy, honestly…my best customers all day."

When she got out of the car, the woman placed her hand on my shoulder. I looked down to see a rolled-up bill in her hands. I hadn't been tipped outside the DAC app in a while, and it made me smile.

"You stay safe, dear," she said.

For a while after they left, I sat in the hospital parking lot. I cranked up the air conditioner; the thick, stale heat made me want to open the windows, but the rain was beginning to pick up. I toyed with the bill the woman had handed me. I'd been shy at first, unwilling to work too hard for the tip, proud, even in one of the most difficult times of my life. But once I started to understand the difference between a good tip night and a bad tip night—easily a difference of a hundred dollars or more—I'd gotten a lot bolder about it.

Part of me knew I should go home; I hadn't showered since I'd left that morning, and I needed to check on Keith. To be honest, he was both the reason I should go home and the reason I wanted to stay out. There's no rule that says you can't love someone deeply and still need time away from them.

I was still making up my mind when the app went off again, and I sighed.

One more, and then I'd call it a night.

Besides, "Lotti" was at the Renouvelle Hotel, just ten minutes or so away, in Chicago's South Loop. I pulled away from the hospital and headed in her direction. The rain was picking up, and I put on my wipers, somehow comforted by the slow and steady squeak of the blades against the glass. A few minutes later, I was turning onto her block, a narrow two-lane street with dark and shadowy boutique stores and restaurants on either side. The only activity was at the end of the block, where I saw the lights from the hotel and a handful of people standing around outside.

As I drove up, I spotted the man right away.

He was standing perfectly still in the street, right in front of the hotel, wearing a sweatshirt with the hood pulled up around his face. I knew instinctively that it was him—that *he* was Lotti—but I was still hopeful that another grandmother would emerge from the shadows and ask to be taken to meet a newborn.

I could handle chatty.

I could not handle serial killer.

I pulled over, and the man strode quickly to the car, his head down as the rain pelted his body. As he opened the back door, my body tensed the way it did every time someone got into my car. With my left hand, I gripped the can of bug spray I held between my thighs every night, and I swung around to look at him.

He spoke quickly as he got inside. "Rideshare for Lotti?"

His voice was warm and deep, smooth like suede brushed the good way. That was the very first thing I felt, followed quickly by relief. The fact that he'd called the DAC—or knew the person who had—didn't make him any less of a serial killer, but it certainly seemed like a start.

"Hey, yep," I said, not letting go of the can but turning back and using my other hand to scroll through the app for his destination. "You're going to 115 West Oak?" I asked, quickly dragging my finger across the map. Not on the way home, but not too much of a detour either. "Gold Coast?"

"Yes," he said simply.

I snuck a peek in the rearview. He wasn't looking at me. His head was turned to the side, and he stared out the window into the darkness.

"Cool," I said and meant it. I liked the silence. I reached out and turned on the radio. A pop song filled the car, something bouncy and melodic, and I turned it down to a palatable level for the time of night. I pressed the gas and settled in. I could drop him off and make it home within thirty minutes. Maybe Keith would still be awake.

I didn't notice that the first song had ended until the next one started, but suddenly, a man's voice filled the car. It was whispery and seductive, and more than slightly off-key. I cringed, a soft "yuck" escaping my lips, before changing the station to a couple of disc jockeys trading jabs with each other.

I heard a noise from the back seat, something like a cough or a chuckle, and my gaze darted to the mirror. I could barely make out his features, but I could see the man had turned to look at me. As he caught my eye, he leaned forward.

"What happened?" he asked. "You didn't like that song?"

"Ugh, no," I said without thinking. "Did you hear him? He sounded like a pervert."

The man laughed clearly this time. "I did hear him," he said. "He must not be so bad though, right? He has a song on the radio."

"Yeah, how hard is that these days? You don't exactly have to be Luther Vandross to make it. This guy is probably good-looking enough to have hordes of prepubescent fans who couldn't care less that he sounds like someone from the funny clips on *American Idol*."

He laughed again, and I snuck another peek in the mirror.

I'd just braked at an intersection, and he was leaning forward even more. His hoodie had slipped back from his face, and the streetlight filtered in, allowing me to see him more clearly than before. His face was a canvas of hard lines and angles. The only softness was in his eyes, which were dark, attentive, and warm like his voice. He was attractive, sure, but it wasn't just that. He stared at me inquisitively, as if he was waiting for me to say something. When I didn't, he smiled softly and sat back. We maintained eye contact for a few moments, and then he spoke softly.

"Light's green."

I whipped my gaze away and drove off, embarrassed, my heart beating a million miles a minute.

What the hell was that?

"You know, you're probably right," he said after a few moments, and I hazarded another quick glance up. "About the prepubescent fans."

I cleared my throat and looked back at the road. "Of course," I said. "The entertainment industry these days is a popularity contest, not a talent show. At least, that's what my husband likes to say."

There.

Husband bomb dropped.

Cleared to proceed.

"Seems like you've thought about this a bit," the man said, ignoring that last sentence. "So, what do you like to listen to?"

"Lots of stuff," I said. "I'm not that picky. Jazz, funk, soul, pop…"

"Just as long as the singer doesn't sound like a pervert."

"Exactly," I said. "I'm a simple girl."

"I doubt that, Paula."

I sucked in a breath and looked up into the mirror. He'd know my name from the DAC app, but it caught me off guard. He was still staring at me, this time with a small smile.

A small, flirtatious smile.

And maybe because I was tired and makeup-less, with my unwashed hair pulled into a messy ponytail on top of my head, or because I felt I'd done my part by telling him I was married, or because I'd spent the hour between my two jobs scrubbing vomit off the bathroom floor because Keith had missed again, or because I knew I would never, ever let it go an inch past this conversation in this car on this night—maybe for all those reasons, I held the eye contact for just a moment too long.

And then I smiled back.

"You don't even know me, Lotti."

Better people have done worse than that.

Much better people have done much worse than that.

◆ ❖ ◆

"You're telling us you didn't recognize him at all?"

Detective Puhl asked the question as we sat across from each other. She was staring at me the way an adult stares at a misbehaving child.

"No, I didn't," I said. I thought back to the man's expression as he'd leaned forward. "He seemed almost pleased when I didn't react. I think he was amused that I didn't know who he was."

"Okay," Detective Puhl said slowly. "So, when did you find out?"

"The next day while I was out at a bar." I waited for them to say something, but they didn't, so I kept going. "I'm an artist. I draw portraits for a living… Well, I used to, and—"

The detective held up her hand, and I paused before clearing my throat.

"Anyway, I never forget a face. I saw him on one of the TVs, and that's when I realized who he was. Funny thing is, one of his songs came on the radio while he was in my car. We actually talked about it—"

"And you still didn't know—"

"No."

"So, you've never heard of Ryan Hooks?" she asked.

Detective Greg snorted, the first noise he had made all day, and I could've kicked him for having nothing more to contribute than that.

"Of course I've *heard* of him," I said. "I just didn't make the connection that he was the man I picked up that night."

Puhl let out a long sigh and leaned forward, placing both elbows on the table. She used two fingers from each hand to rub her temples.

"Okay, so let me get this straight," she said. "You pick up one of the biggest pop stars in the country and drop him off at an address in the Gold Coast. That was on…"

"August 1," I said. "The Saturday before last."

"Then you just go home. You don't call anyone, don't snap any pictures. Nothing."

"Yes," I said, working hard to keep my composure. "Because I didn't know—"

"Right, right," she said. "We get it. So fast-forward to this *past* weekend. You see the news about the murder at 115 West Oak, and you think, for some reason, that since you dropped him off there last week, Ryan Hooks could've been involved."

I swallowed.

I'd known that this was where things would get dicey, since I couldn't tell them *everything*. I bit my lip and nodded. "It seemed like somebody should know that he'd been there just a week earlier, so—"

"Yeah, maybe *TMZ*," Detective Greg muttered.

"—*so*, I texted your tip line," I said, ignoring him.

Detective Puhl nodded. "Yes, we got that tip," she said, looking down at a sheet of paper in front of her. "We got a lot of leads about that case, but I have to say, yours was the most"—she raised an eyebrow and looked at the other detective—"entertaining?"

Detective Greg smiled but didn't respond.

"That should have been the end of it," Detective Puhl continued, and there was almost something like exhaustion in her tone. "But instead, you're saying that the same man—the same *pop star*—broke into your home earlier today and attacked you for no reason at all."

I squared my shoulders. "The police were at my house this morning. You can ask them—"

"No," she said. "I'm not doubting you had an intruder, Mrs.

Wilson, and I'm sure that was very scary. But I'm asking why you think it might have been Mr. Hooks."

I bit my lip.

Careful…

I'd drifted in and out of a wine-soaked sleep for hours after the police left, staring at our belongings tossed so carelessly around the living room and asking myself the very same question.

As I'd replayed the events of the past week over and over in my mind, I'd become more and more convinced: it had to be Hooks.

It simply had to be.

I'd finally jumped up, my entire body still shaking, and called a cab to the station.

The thing is, Detective Claire Puhl had looked a *lot* nicer on TV.

As the wine began to wear off, I realized I didn't have a good answer, at least not one I could tell them, so I fumbled to make something up.

"I don't know," I said, swallowing. "He must have figured out that I was the one who texted your tip line and told you that I'd dropped him off. Was he ever contacted by the police? That's the only thing I can think of."

Detective Puhl sighed. "We follow up on all leads as appropriate," she said dismissively. She wrote something down and then looked up. "The night you dropped him off… Did you see him with the deceased?"

She asked it so casually, and my stomach flipped over at the phrase. Since I'd arrived, she'd been tossing around phrases like *the body*, *the deceased*, and *the victim*, and I wanted to scream at her that she was talking about a real person.

"No," I said slowly. I took a deep breath. "But I did see him with someone."

"Did you?" she asked. "And how did you happen to see that?"

"Well, he got out of the car, and I was still there for a little bit, you know, wrapping up the ride."

"Okay…"

"He was walking across the street, and I saw a woman watching him out a window."

"You saw someone watching him?" Detective Puhl asked, raising an eyebrow. "Not *with* him?"

"Well, she was on the second floor of the apartment, and she was sort of…pressed against the window," I said. "I could tell that she wanted him to see her. You know what I mean?"

Both detectives stared at me, and I swallowed. The words felt silly on my lips, but I pushed on anyway.

"She wasn't…" I cleared my throat. "She wasn't wearing much."

It was an understatement, but it didn't seem like the time or place to go into detail. The woman had been framed clearly in the light of the window, her chin-length blond hair grazing her collarbone. She was wearing a red lace bra beneath a sheer, black nightdress, the windowsill cutting her off right at the top of her hip bone.

And she'd just stood there, peering down into the darkness. Even from the distance, I could see the smile that tugged at the corners of her lips.

"Okay, Mrs. Wilson," Detective Puhl said, jolting me from the memory. She tossed another glance at her partner and then stood up. "Is it all right if I call you Paula?"

"Yes," I said.

She nodded. "Is there anything else you want to tell us, Paula?"

I blinked before shaking my head and leaning down to pick up my purse from the floor.

"No, that's all," I said. "I just thought you should know that he

16

was there a week before the murder, *and* that I'm almost positive he's the one who broke into my apartment."

"Okay," Detective Puhl said again. "Thanks for coming in. We'll definitely look into it, and we'll be in touch if we have any more questions for you. You won't be hard to get ahold of, will you?"

I frowned. "No," I said. "Of course not."

I was turning toward the door when Detective Greg spoke up.

"I have a question for you," he said.

I stopped and turned back to face him.

"Did you ever go back?"

I froze, and we watched each other for a long moment before I could come up with a response. "Sorry?"

The detective shrugged and placed both hands on the desk in front of him. "It's been almost two weeks since you dropped him off, and now with the murder, 115 West Oak is all over the news," he said. "I'm just wondering, since August 1, have you had any reason to go back to that apartment?"

I blinked.

"Mrs. Wilson?"

They needed to know the critical facts.

"Mrs. Wilson?" he said. "Did you ever go back after that night?"

Not the tiny, unimportant things.

"No," I said, maintaining eye contact. "I never went back."

the week before
the night in
question

CHAPTER 1

Paula

Seven days before

KEITH WAS ASLEEP WHEN I got home after dropping off Lotti. He's always asleep, his body folded up in the sheets like piles of extra laundry. During bad weeks, he can sleep for ten, twelve, fourteen hours at a time. I never know when to wake him, so I don't.

There's always a brown-tinted glass on the nightstand. It wasn't there before, not for the first thirteen years of our life together, but now it's always there, whiskey-stained decor in our small, two-bedroom home on Chicago's northwest side. Empty except for the last amber drop of evidence. It's rare that I actually see Keith drinking it, though the smell of liquor is always there.

I lay on the bed beside him for about an hour every night, the scent tickling the back of my nose, making me just the slightest bit queasy. Those sixty minutes hurt like hell. My doctor, Marilyn Keyes, said it's normal, even though she seemed surprised when I told her how much it hurt.

"What does it feel like, Paula?" she had asked a few months back.

"An epidural," I had said, and her eyes widened. "Or at least what I imagine an epidural feels like. I've never had a baby. Is that normal?"

"That you've never had a baby?"

"No. That it hurts to stay in bed when I can't sleep."

"Well…" I could almost see her brain working. "It's a pretty strong emotional response. But there's plenty of evidence that links psychological state to physical symptoms. Caregivers have a wide range of emotional responses, so the insomnia is not unusual. I'd say what you're experiencing is normal…but we should monitor it for a few weeks."

I'd been seeing Dr. Keyes for a couple of years, and though she tended to speak in Google search results, I liked her. So I did what she said, and we monitored it. For months, not just weeks, since nothing had changed, and I wasn't ready to graduate from monitoring it to trying to fix it. On the night I dropped the man off in the Gold Coast, I went home and did what I always did: I lay in the bed next to my husband, hoping for sleep I knew would not come. After sixty minutes, I rolled over and let my feet drop to the floor, shifting my weight slowly so as not to shake the bed.

It wouldn't have mattered if I did.

Keith wouldn't be waking up until morning.

I walked around the bed and picked up the glass from the night-stand. Keith's wheelchair was propped up against the window ledge. The shadowy image of our bedroom danced in front of my eyes—the antique oak dresser we'd gotten from Keith's grand-mother, the silhouette of his body underneath the covers—and it occurred to me that if I could just edit out that chair, everything would go back to normal.

With the drag of a mouse, I'd blur out the wheelchair and replace it with something like an exercise bike or a nice indoor plant. Better yet, I'd back up and erase the car that had sped out of the alley on the west side of Ashland Avenue on that balmy Thursday afternoon eleven months ago. Or maybe I'd crop out the moment, just an hour or so before that, when I had asked Keith to go to Trader Joe's in the first place. I'd just made Ina Garten's beef short ribs, and we only had white wine, and that simply wouldn't do.

Keith had been tired and a little annoyed, but then I'd said something funny or cute, and the thing about Keith was that I could always get him with funny or cute, at least back then.

So he grabbed his keys and left.

Maybe instead of editing something out, I would have Photoshopped something *in*—for instance, the name of a different road on the street signs. We sometimes took Western Avenue instead of Ashland to avoid the traffic from Lake View High. If he'd gone that way, Keith would have avoided the speeding SUV altogether. In the grand scheme of things, the teen driving it hadn't been going that fast. I always thought major crashes, the ones that defined people's lives, happened on the highway at speeds at or above seventy miles an hour. The black SUV had barely broken thirty, but at the perfect angle, it was more than enough to spin Keith into the path of a bus that was in the middle of changing lanes.

Keith said it sounded like two explosions—one loud, the second *deafening*—and when the dust finally settled, he was on his back in a hospital bed, and his body—and his life—had changed forever.

If all else failed, I'd start to edit there, in room 213 at Presence Saint Joseph Hospital. I'd blur the face of the surgeon so it wouldn't haunt me for months to come, or maybe I'd lift the corners of her mouth as she broke the news, making her say Keith's chance of walking again was 30 percent, not *three*.

I could've taken thirty.

But three?

She could've just said zero.

With the whiskey glass in hand, I left the bedroom and walked into the kitchen to place it in the sink. Then I moved into the living room, making sure to leave the lights off so as not to wake Shelby, our three-year-old honey-blond boxer. She wasn't actually sleeping—I knew it, and I'd bet my tips from the night that *she knew* I knew it. But this had become our nightly dance: me restlessly navigating through our dark apartment while Shelby pretended not to notice. Some nights, I sat on the couch and read or sketched; other times, like tonight, I'd take a shower and head back out the door. I tiptoed past her quilted doggy bed toward the bathroom, bending down as I passed to look at her face. In the thin trail of moonlight that slipped through the window, I could see her eyes were closed, just barely, as she lay there sprawled on her stomach.

"Yeah, right," I muttered, loud enough for her to hear as I stood back up, because I am, for better or worse (but really just for worse), the kind of person who engages in passive-aggressive turf wars with her dog.

Getting a dog had seemed like a good idea before the accident. Keith and I had talked about kids and knew we'd be pretty good parents. But we also knew deep down that we'd be okay if it didn't happen. We had nieces and nephews who adored us as Uncle Keith and Aunt Paula, the artists from Chicago. He had the addictive, rumbling laugh; I let them eat brownies for dinner sometimes. Keith was a swim coach by day at nearby Morton College, and he made amazing ceramics by night; I painted portraits for private collectors, a job that made us feel wealthy in good months and practically destitute in bad. We ordered out constantly and drank a bit too much wine on weekdays, but we worked. We didn't know what children would do to that equation.

But a dog?

We could handle a dog.

It took me fewer than fifteen steps to cross the small room and make it to the bathroom. Moments later, I was in the shower, scrubbing the day away. I stayed in so long that when I stepped out, my skin was soft and wrinkled. With the palm of my hand, I cleared a circle in the steamy mirror and leaned close to it, inspecting the puffiness beneath my eyes—one blue and one brown—and my hairline, which seemed just a bit thinner and grayer than the day before. With two fingers from each hand, I pushed the skin beneath my jaw up and back, toward my ears. Not for the first time since I had driven away from the apartment at 115 West Oak, I thought about the woman with the heart-shaped face and chin-length blond bob who I'd seen in the second-floor window, peering down at Lotti.

She'd stood in the glow of apartment lights, the blinds pulled completely open. And the only word to describe her appearance was *powerful*. I could clearly see the outline of her body, svelte and toned, through the sheer nightdress she was wearing, and there didn't seem to be an ounce of loose skin to be pulled or tugged *anywhere*. She looked like the kind of woman who dared to take pictures head-on, not turned strategically to one side; like she'd never owned a piece of shapewear but said things like "I should try it sometime!" while pinching the invisible fat above her hip bone.

It wasn't just her appearance that struck me; it was her confidence. She looked powerful because of the *way* she peered out into the night, that smile tugging at the corners of her mouth. I knew I should look away from what was clearly a moment of exhibitionism meant for the man who'd just gotten out of my car, yet I'd remained frozen, arrested by the scene. She was either unconcerned or unaware of the fact that I was still parked across the street. The man had his back to me, and he had frozen too, his head angled up toward the window. I couldn't see his face, but I could feel the tension in his body as he stood there motionless in the rain, his gaze on the woman.

Then, as if embarrassed, he had turned back briefly to look at my car before putting his head down and rushing toward the apartment.

I had sat there, overwhelmed by something I couldn't quite define—embarrassment for watching them, jealousy, longing—and I had finally put the car in Drive, set the wipers in motion, and pulled away.

As I had headed home, I had imagined that the woman had texted "Lotti," and he'd called a car to go see her. He'd been staying at a hotel, so maybe he was an old flame from college, in town for business. Or a traveler she'd met in a bar earlier that night.

Whatever their relationship, that interaction—the expression on her face, the rigidness of his body as he stared up at her in the rain—had told me everything I needed to know about them. They were normal, and sexy, and infatuated with each other.

They were Keith and me—before the medications, the fear, the whiskey, the guilt, the sleepless nights.

They were us, before.

As I stood naked in the bathroom, I tried to get the couple out of my mind. I did that often, making up stories about my passengers as I dropped them off. It seemed to make the monotony of pickup, drop-off, pick-up, drop-off more bearable.

But there was something about this couple that I couldn't shake. Maybe it was Lotti's flirtatious smile before he got out of my car; maybe it was the expression on the woman's face.

Maybe I was just tired.

I dropped my hands away my face and stepped out into the living room, a towel wrapped around my body.

When Keith and I had first moved in three years ago, we'd been concerned about the size of the small home and the fact that there was only one bathroom.

What happens when we have visitors?

Maybe it's too much of an inconvenience.

Maybe we should hold out for a place with one and a half bathrooms.

Maybe Keith will get into a car accident exactly six days after our thirteenth wedding anniversary, and the pain medications will make him so sick that he'll need a bathroom close by at all times.

We never imagined that last one.

Aside from the size, Keith and I had grown to love the place. The house had been an investment of a lifetime—small, simple, and worth every single penny of the savings we'd put into it. We'd both dreamed of owning our own home our entire lives, a fact we learned about each other very early on in our relationship.

"My parents are both social workers," he'd told me on our second date as we ate dinner in a small restaurant in Chicago's Greektown neighborhood. "They found their calling in each other and in missionary work, which means I lived in nine apartments on three continents by the time I went to college. Don't get me wrong—my parents are the kindest people I've ever met and probably ever will meet, and I wouldn't change my childhood for anything. I just think I've always craved a little stability in terms of the place I call home."

I had nodded. We were in a U-shaped booth at the back of the restaurant. Throughout the course of the night, we'd each moved toward the center and were sitting side by side, our shoulders almost touching. I remember thinking that we'd gotten too close to each other, that it should be awkward by now, but it wasn't. I'd started falling in love with him that night—with the soft smile that came across his face when he talked about his family, the broadness of his shoulders, his nerdy sense of humor, and the gentle, polite way he asked the waiter for more water.

"I know what you mean," I'd said. "I can definitely relate to not feeling like you have a place to call home."

"Oh yeah?" he'd asked. "What was it for you? Let me guess: Military parents? No, high-powered execs who moved around all the time? Or was it missionaries too?"

I had smiled softly as I thought about all the times I'd watched my parents scream at each other until they lost their voices. "Nothing so noble," I had said, and when he raised an eyebrow inquisitively, I had shaken my head. "But that's for date number three…if you're that lucky."

Now, almost fourteen years later, I stepped into the bedroom, and the sound of Keith's breathing filled the air—he always snored when he drank too much before passing out. I opened the dresser next to the bed and quietly began to pull out clothes, sneaking a look back at him as I did. It was dark, but in the moonlight, I could make out the craggy lines of his face, his strong jaw, the curve of his lips. In my mind, I could see the graying hair around his temples and the laugh lines that had crept up in the last few years.

I know it's selfish: my sadness, my exhaustion, my inability to accept it all. They're thoughts I keep close, tears shed only in sudden fits in the back aisles of grocery stores or in the breakroom at work. Keith's right there beside me all the time, yet he's gone, so far gone, and I miss him. I can only admit that in tiny, shallow whispers to myself, because no good person could say something like that out loud. But it was the truth. I missed Keith, the carefree couple we once were, and the people we'd always planned to be.

Before, we would lie awake in bed for hours, talking about everything under the sun. That was one of my favorite parts about marriage—talking about mundane things like what kind of salad dressing we'd had for lunch or a friend's annoying Facebook status, content in the knowledge that someone cared enough about me to spend so much time discussing nothing at all.

Once, while lazing around in bed, we got into a long, fairly academic discussion on the topic of booty calls.

"That's not what it was!" I had exclaimed, whipping him with a pillow as he'd doubled over in laughter. "How dare you cheapen our relationship like that?"

"I'm not trying to cheapen it," he had said, flinging the pillow across the room and then pulling me close, his nose nestled against the back of my neck. "How do *you* define a booty call?"

"I don't, typically."

"Okay, but if you had to, what would you say?" he had asked, and I could feel him smiling against my skin. "Is it the actual encounter itself, or is it the intent behind it? Because even though I knew we had something special from day one—"

"Yeah, yeah…"

"—I did *call* you late at night sometimes, and those calls often resulted in *boo*—"

"Ugh!" I had cried, yanking the other pillow from beneath his head and smacking him with it. "You're disgusting," I had said, but my giggles had made it clear that I didn't find a single thing about my husband disgusting.

◆ ❖ ◆

I think that was why I couldn't get Lotti and the woman in the window out of my mind. I was jealous of their modern-day booty *text*. It was so incredibly silly, so pathetic, so disappointing, but that's how I felt. I could see the stiff brushstrokes that would illustrate the tension in Lotti's shoulders as he gazed up at the window, the whispery curves of the woman's body as she pressed herself against the glass.

And I was jealous as hell.

I finished getting dressed and looked back at the bed. There was a part of me that wanted to crawl back in beside Keith and pull him on top of me so I could feel his weight crushing down on me. But I knew he wouldn't wake up, or worse yet, he would and turn his back to me. So instead, I picked up my purse and left the bedroom.

I walked past Shelby, who was still sprawled on her stomach, unmoving. I grabbed my phone off the coffee table where I'd tossed it earlier. It was sitting on top of a pile of scratch-off lottery tickets I'd bought from a gas station on my way home. I scooped them up so I could throw them away later; if Keith found them in the trash, I'd hear about it for days.

"It's a waste of money," he'd said when he'd found one errant ticket a few weeks back. He had become better at moving around, the wheelchair sliding easily between his fingertips, and he'd rolled himself up to the coffee table. "Besides, you know how I feel about gambling."

I did know how he felt about it. He made a point to remind anyone who'd listen that he'd struggled with a "little gambling thing" in his early twenties, and even casual use of the term *bet* made him wag his finger.

"I only buy them once in a while," I'd said. "And it's not like I'm trying to become a multimillionaire. People win the smaller amounts all the time. We just need—"

"A hundred and eighty thousand dollars?" he'd asked, and he had let out a sigh of frustration when I averted my eyes. "Come on, Paula. How many times do we have to go over this? We can't afford it. You have to let it go."

As I stood there weeks later and stared at the tickets, I wondered, not nearly for the first time, if Keith was right.

Maybe I should just let it all go.

I stuffed the tickets in my purse and looped the strap over my shoulder before walking toward the door.

But I stopped abruptly in the middle of the living room.

The only excuse for what I did next is that I was angry, sad, and feeling sorry for myself. And that misery does, indeed, love company.

For no good reason at all, I spun around and darted back across the room, just four quick, quiet steps in the direction of the bedroom where Keith was fast asleep.

Shelby reacted immediately.

In an instant, she was up on all fours, just as I knew she would be.

The pretense of sleep long gone, she panted loudly, her gray eyes cutting through the moonlit room. I stared back smugly, prouder of myself than any decent person should be, and turned to leave the apartment.

"See ya, sleepyhead," I said as I turned and walked out the door.

CHAPTER 2

THE RAIN HAD LET up by the time I left the house, but the oppressive, muggy heat remained, wrapping itself around me as I walked the four blocks to Deluxe Diner, my part-time gig, oft-time home away from home. It wasn't the first time I'd shown up at the dusty, vinyl-covered restaurant at two in the morning with IKEA-sized shopping bags beneath my eyes.

My boss, David, was standing behind the counter as I walked in, and he tossed his head back dramatically when he saw me. "It hasn't even been twelve hours, Paula," he said, his shoulders slumping. "You know we've got labor laws around here. Can't have you burning customers with coffee or shaking bleach in the eggs instead of salt 'cause you're half-asleep."

He walked around the counter and stood in front of me. He was a tall teddy bear of a man with thinning but neatly combed hair that was so black, it had to have a name, like midnight ink or shimmering onyx. He stared at me, the concern evident on his face.

"Go back home and go to sleep."

"I would if I could," I said, sidestepping him and sitting down on a stool. "Don't worry. I didn't come here to try to convince you to let me work. I just came in for a cup of tea."

David sighed and walked back around the counter, grabbing a mug from the rack above his head.

Deluxe Diner is a diner, yes, but it's anything but deluxe. The black vinyl stools that surround the main counter had uniform rips down their centers, and the tables, though clean, had scratches in them from decades of use. Still, there was something about the fluorescent-lit forty-seat restaurant that made you want to come back, and it was the first place I'd gone to ask about a job after Keith's accident.

"Do you have any restaurant experience at all?" David had asked me a year ago as I sat on the same stool and pleaded with him to hire me. "Anything?"

"Does the fact that most of the meals I've eaten in the last ten years have been prepared in restaurants count as experience?" I'd asked.

He had glared at me. "Not at all."

"Well then, not really," I'd said. "But come on, David. How many times am I here a week? Four? Five? Who else can recite all of the ingredients in the Deluxious omelet?"

He hadn't said anything, but he had raised his eyebrows.

I had leaned forward across the counter. "Bell peppers, mushrooms, onions, chorizo, spinach, tomatoes, jalapeños, chives, and, of course, your Deluxious choice of cheese."

He still hadn't spoken, but one corner of his mouth had turned up slightly. I'd started working there three days later.

As he put the tea down in front of me, David frowned. "Tell me again why you continue to resist my insomnia home remedy of a slice of cheesecake and a bottle of wine?" he asked. "It puts me out in minutes. It's a Smith family not-so-secret. Sugar and alcohol. The quickest way to nighttime bliss…"

I smiled. I liked alcohol, but it didn't like me, and since Keith had started using it to fall asleep, I tried my best to stay away from it.

"I'll stick with chamomile tea," I said, lifting the mug. "Thanks a lot."

He nodded and turned to walk back into the kitchen.

Besides a tall, thin man eating eggs sitting next to me at the counter, there were only two tables filled in the diner—a group of teenage girls giggling and sharing french fries, and an elderly woman sitting alone by the front door, reading a book. It was a quiet night for Deluxe; usually, there was a steady stream of customers throughout the day and night, since the restaurant sat at a busy intersection in Chicago's Irving Park neighborhood.

I heard a noise and looked up as the reason I'd come in emerged from the back of the diner. My friend Vanessa Flowers stepped out, carrying a pitcher of water. She strode quickly toward the woman with the book but stopped in her tracks when she saw me.

"What are you doing here?" she asked from across the room, making both the woman and the man sitting beside me look up. "Couldn't sleep?"

I shook my head, strangely embarrassed, and took another sip of the tea.

Vanessa filled the woman's glass and then walked over and perched on the stool beside me, setting the pitcher down between us. "Did you try David's cheesecake and wine trick?"

"No," I said with a laugh. "We don't just keep cheesecake in the fridge, first of all—"

"Why not?" she asked.

"—and second," I said, ignoring her, "it's not really a trick, is it? It's just getting drunk and eating dessert before falling asleep."

"Best trick I've ever heard of," she said.

I'd met Vanessa three years ago when Keith and I first moved into our house. I'd started going to the diner on a regular basis, and we'd clicked instantly. She'd talked to me about her crazy ex, Terry; her hilarious family; and her borderline obsession with celebrities. I talked to her about Keith and the drama of our small circle of friends, who Vanessa called the "la-di-d'artists." At thirty-six, Vanessa was only a year younger than me, but people often thought she was in her mid- to late twenties, with her smooth, youthful skin and short, curly brown hair. But it was more than just her looks. She was a fireball of personality, bold, funny, and refreshingly honest, qualities that had helped me get through some of the roughest moments after Keith's accident.

"How was your night driving sixteen-year-olds to house parties?" she asked.

I smiled. "Fine. Uneventful. Which means it was a great night, actually."

"What time is your shift today?" she asked.

"I'll be back in at noon."

"And after that?"

I frowned. She already knew the answer to that—I was going to do what I did every day after I left the diner—which could only mean she had other plans for me. "I'll probably drive for a few hours…" I said slowly.

As I expected, she shook her head. "No," she said. "You need to take the night off."

I sighed. "I'm fine—" I started, ready to launch into a lie about how I'd gotten a little sleep when I went home and that I'd try to nap again before my shift.

But Vanessa shook her head again. "No, not for you," she said. "Look, I know anything I say about your health and how you're running yourself into the ground working here and driving DAC every night, though totally valid arguments, won't work. So I'm not going down that route. Forget that. You need to take the night off for me."

"For you."

"Yup. We're going to a party." She drew out the last word and leaned forward, shimmying a little as she said this.

I heard a chuckle and turned to see the guy eating eggs looking over at us. I reached over to grab the pitcher of cold water and poured some on top of the tea bag in my mug.

"A party?" I asked. "You mean like those sixteen-year-olds I spend my nights dropping off?"

"Yes," she said. "I'd ask somebody else, someone who won't take as much convincing as you're going to, but then I remember that my only other friend is my teenage daughter, and she doesn't need to see what I'm about to shell out tonight."

I almost choked on my water. "I'm not sure I need to either."

She grinned. "Oh, yes you do."

"I *don't*."

"I wouldn't mind," a voice behind me said, and we both turned to see Eggs staring at us with a smile on his face.

"Of course, you wouldn't," Vanessa said without missing a beat before turning her attention back to me. "Anyway, come on! Like I said, do it for me."

I sighed. "I don't know," I said. "We really need the money."

"I know you do, but one night off from driving DAC isn't going to make or break the bank," she said, leaning forward. "Come on, Paula. It's at that new restaurant, Agave. Tim—met him online, don't ask, don't judge—is hosting it. He said he could put us on 'the list.' Doesn't that sound sexy? I think a night out would be good for you."

"I thought you weren't going to pretend this is about me."

"I wasn't. Then I started feeling desperate," Vanessa said, and I smiled. She leaned in. "What's that? Does that smile mean you're thinking about it?"

I shook my head. "I don't—"

"Look, you need to go out. We both do. We're going."

"Ness—"

But she picked up the water pitcher and hopped off the stool. "Everyone," she said, turning to face the room. "Sorry to interrupt, but this here is my good friend Paula, and she's going through a pretty tough time right now. So we're going out. I'm going to meet cute guys, and she's going to get drunk. We haven't been out in over a *year*. Don't you think we deserve it?"

The group of young girls looked over and responded affirmatively, pounding the table with their hands.

"Hell yeah!" one of them said.

The older woman sitting by herself smiled slightly, and Eggs watched with a gleeful, albeit sketchy expression.

David had walked out of the back and was watching Vanessa with an amused smile on his face. He turned to me and raised one corner of his mouth.

"I don't think you're getting out of this one," he said. "Sounds to me like you're going out tonight."

As I walked home from the diner, I had to admit that I was just a little bit excited. Vanessa was right that it had been over a year since we'd done anything like that, and it would be good to take a night off.

It was exhausting—the long shifts at the diner, driving people all across the city, going home to take care of Keith, and getting up to do it all over again. But I didn't have a choice. My mother had been diagnosed with lung cancer when I was nine years old, and I'd witnessed firsthand what illness could do to a family. The anger, the depression, the ever-present sadness that hung in the air—those things took a toll on even the strongest of couples, and my parents were no exception. Whereas some people were able to come together during tough times, my mother and father had retreated to their own corners of the world through what, I've realized with age and time, was probably a little bit both their faults. Four years after her diagnosis, when my mother's cancer was in remission, the relationship ended, along with the family and structure I'd always assumed would be forever.

Still, all that being said, Vanessa was right.

One night off wasn't going to make that much of a difference.

Not for the bills.

Not for the back payments we owed on the house.

And not for...

The surgery.

Keith and I would be meeting with his doctor, Ruby Bryant, tomorrow. She would most likely say that he was doing okay in therapy, but his chances of regaining full mobility in his legs were still slim to none. Then she would ask us to take note of any changes and if we had any questions.

Somehow, before the conversation was over, she'd manage to mention the surgery.

At first, like Keith, I'd been angry at her for bringing it up when we couldn't have it, couldn't even come close to affording it. She'd gone to medical school with a man named Christian Reveno, now a surgeon in Paris. Dr. Reveno had developed a new technique that involved transplanting cells from other parts of the body into the spine, which was showing some signs of success, at least in the limited trials that had been conducted.

The cost of the trips back and forth to Paris and the treatment would run us close to $180,000.

It should've been a no-brainer. We could never afford that.

But somewhere along the way, as the months went by and the barrage of treatments and therapies we tried didn't help, I started to wonder, *what if?*

What if we could afford to fly to Paris and meet with Dr. Reveno?

What if the twelve case studies he'd published online were all true?

What if it worked for Keith?

What if we could have our lives back?

I think Dr. Bryant would've let it go if I hadn't started asking more and more questions about it. .

If it works, he'd be able to walk again?

Yes.

Run?

Maybe.

Swim?

That, I don't know.

But there would be more than a three percent chance.

Yes. Much more.

And just as soon as we'd start talking about it, Keith would get upset and demand to know why we were still discussing a treatment we couldn't afford. One that couldn't be "won through lottery tickets or pieced together from DAC fares," he'd told me once in a conversation-turned-argument.

"It's like it's all you can think about," he'd said. "Finding ways to scrape money out of couch cushions so that we can afford to make me better. Has it occurred to you that I don't want you doing that?"

"Why not?" I'd asked. "Dr. Bryant said—"

"I don't care what Dr. Bryant said!" he had said. "I am so damned tired of talking about this. We can't afford it. Please, Paula, just let it go."

We didn't talk about it much after that, but I hadn't let it go. In fact, it had become almost an obsession, a pipe dream I couldn't shake. Because if all that separated us from the life we once had—the one where we rolled around in bed on Saturday mornings and drank whiskey cocktails for fun, not straight from the bottle to go to sleep—was $180,000, then I would search every couch cushion and pick up every DAC I could find.

I would do whatever it took.

In fact, as I neared our apartment building after leaving the diner, I stopped next to my car where I'd parked it on the street a few hours earlier.

Unlocking it, I opened the back door and leaned inside, letting my hand brush the cushion of the back seat.

I did this once or twice a day, looking for loose change, jewelry, wallets, or anything else of value. People left the most ridiculous things in DACs, and it was surprising how few actually followed up for them.

The seat was empty, and I was about to slam the door when the streetlight bounced off something on the mat behind the passenger seat.

I leaned in to pick up the item and actually pumped my fist in the air when I saw what it was.

A phone.

A *nice* phone.

I had a two-week rule with phones. If nobody contacted me within that window, I put it up for sale online and acted like it had never happened. I'd done it twice already and made seventy-five bucks each time.

This was who I was now.

I sold things online that did not belong to me.

I walked around to my trunk and opened it, tossing the phone into the small bin I kept there for just that purpose. I hoped I wouldn't have to take it out again until it was time to sell it.

As I slammed it shut, I wondered if the phone belonged to Lotti.

I imagined him calling the phone and the sound of his warm, deep voice flowing through the line as he asked me where I found it and how he could get it back.

I quickly pushed the thought away. As nice as it was to think about hearing his voice again, I'd be much luckier if he *didn't* call.

I could probably get at least a hundred for it.

CHAPTER 3

Claire
The Night in Question

A FEW HOURS BEFORE SHE got the call about the body in the Gold Coast, Detective Claire Puhl was at a bar on a Tinder date.

She wouldn't admit it to anyone—not her meddling mother and certainly not her overly familiar coworkers—but that's where she was and what she was doing.

Later, she would walk into the scene of the crime as the formidable Detective Puhl, wearing the blazer and the lower, more sensible heels she kept in the back seat of her car. She would set the scene into motion, questioning the first responders and neighbors in her quiet, assertive way. She dealt with people who had the audacity to end another person's life; she didn't have time for anything short of scrappy, determined professionalism. She would walk in, and she would get answers, because that's what Detective Puhl did.

But at eight o'clock that evening, she was just Claire.

Forty-one years old, nervous, and on a date with an accountant named Bill. She'd stood in the mirror a long time before leaving the house, examining the completely out-of-character bright-pink blush on her toffee-colored skin and the plum lipstick that kept getting on her teeth. It had been raining all night, and she had considered using that as an excuse to cancel, but she'd decided against it. So she was pushing small pieces of asparagus around her plate with the tip of her fork while Bill talked ad nauseam about things she already knew from his dating profile.

He "liked sports" but could only name teams, not players.

He "read books sometimes" but could only tell her genres, not titles.

He "worked out when he had time," which was, quite simply, a damned lie.

All that aside, Bill seemed nice enough. He didn't look very much like his pictures on the app—he was skinnier and considerably less attractive—but then again, they never did. His profile had included the words *Chicago's Idris Elba*, and that should've been her first big hint of the disappointments to come.

Claire didn't understand the tendency to oversell. In fact, she tended to do the opposite. She chose to upload photos that were slightly *less* attractive than she was in real life. She could handle not being contacted in the first place, but she'd be damned if she had to deal with disappointment that she didn't measure up to the pictures she posted online.

Bill was on his third Jack and apple juice and telling a story about his ex-wife, a story he never should have started. Claire was trying hard to focus instead of plotting her escape.

"Mara was a real go-getter, and now she's a cop, just like you," Bill said. "I think that's one of the reasons why your profile caught my attention. I guess I'm just used to, you know, dealing with women in law enforcement."

Claire speared a piece of asparagus and looked up at the word *dealing*. She bit her lip. It was only the second red flag (the apple juice had been the first), and she tried to remain open-minded. She was working hard on not writing men off too soon, since *every single person* in her life seemed to think she wrote men off too soon.

"It's all those romantic comedies you watch," her mother, Elaine, had said more times than Claire could count, spitting out the words with her heavy Jamaican accent. "You want everything to be roses. That's what you expected from law school too."

It *always* came back to the lawyer thing. Always. There was no misfortune, no disappointment that Elaine Puhl couldn't tie back to the fact that Claire had graduated from University of Chicago Law and spent just three years practicing before deciding that it wasn't for her.

Claire had loved that her life's work centered around seeking justice in what often felt like an unbearably unjust world. But the law had tied her hands too much. So much was out of her control by the time the cases came her way.

Joining the Chicago Police Department had been the best decision of her life. Police work had given her a way to get closer to the crimes and the people who committed them. In the fourteen years since she had left law to become a detective, Claire had never once looked back.

Elaine Puhl, on the other hand, had made a career of looking back.

"I just don't understand how you could put that much time and effort into something and walk away from it so easily," she'd said once. Even though it had been more than a decade, she still found ways to weave it into conversations.

Lately, she'd switched gears to focus on why Claire hadn't found anyone to settle down with yet.

"It's because you're too picky," her mother had said. "You have to stop judging men so harshly. Like how you judged being a lawyer before you even had a chance to get settled in the field."

Two hours after she and Bill had sat down, Claire was down to the final bites of her asparagus, and she put her fork down. It was a little after ten o'clock. He'd ordered slowly and ate even slower, and the restaurant had started to clear out. She didn't want to finish first; she wouldn't know what to do with her hands. But Bill had been talking almost nonstop, and he'd barely made a dent in his brick chicken.

"Can I just say that you're really pretty, and I really like this whole 'natural' look you have going on?" he asked, leaning forward, rolling a tightly coiled tendril of hair near her temple between his fingers. Claire jerked back in her seat, but he didn't seem to notice. "I'll be honest, that's really how I prefer my women. Looks like you just rolled out of bed. It's kind of hot…"

Strike three.

If she were honest with herself, Claire had known from the minute he had walked in that he probably wasn't "the one." She had met a lot of men in her life, and she'd become fairly skilled at determining which ones had potential and which ones were more likely to have major life regrets.

Now, as she sat across from him, she was ready to go, tired of having to try *so hard*, and tired of feeling less confident than she was in almost every other part of her life. There was too much to prove on these dates.

She didn't have anything to prove at work.

In fact, she had solved every single case she'd taken on in the last ten years.

It wasn't something she bragged about, at least not often. It was worth noting, however, that there were very few detectives who held the same record on her team, and she was the only woman in that position. It took focus, dedication, and, above all, a complete commitment to seeing every case through from start to finish.

When Claire Puhl took aim, she didn't miss.

She wished the same were true for her dating life.

But right now, she just wished she could *go* home.

Thirty minutes later, she was behind the wheel of her car, doing just that. She was already regretting how she'd spent the first part of her night off, but there was no need to dwell on it. She would go home, climb into bed, turn on *Midsomer Murders*, and settle into a deep, deep sleep.

Five hours later, she wasn't settled into any sort of sleep, deep or otherwise.

Instead, she was standing under an umbrella in front of the three-flat apartment building at 115 West Oak. She was wearing the blazer and comfy heels from her car on top of the black slacks she'd pulled over the shorts she'd been relaxing in. When she'd heard her phone ring and saw Detective Greg Kuchi's name on the screen, she'd groaned out loud, since it had to be something huge for him to interrupt her on one of her very few nights off.

"Kuchi," she had said.

He had sighed loudly into the phone. Greg was adamantly opposed to the use of his last name—which, in his own words, was pronounced "like 'cookie,' but in the way Cookie Monster says it." He insisted that everyone call him Detective Greg, a rule by which Claire *typically* abided, except in rare circumstances when she was annoyed with him.

"All I wanted was one night. Just one."

"I know," he said. "Tell people to stop being assholes and quit killing people."

"Where am I going?"

"Gold Coast."

It had taken her about twenty-five minutes to get to the apartment, and when she arrived, there was a crowd gathering. She walked toward the building with her shoulders squared, her eyes shrewd, her jaw determined. Around her, a few cops looked up and then whispered to one another.

She saw them and held back a smile.

The apartment sat in a long line of mansions and row houses at the northeast end of the Gold Coast. They were just a few blocks away from Lake Michigan and the typically bustling shops of Michigan Avenue. It was almost 3:30 a.m., and cars still whizzed by on Lake Shore Drive as the warm Chicago night came to an end.

The building looked like something out of a historic painting. It was a warm-brown brick three-flat with ornate black-iron trimming around the windows and Juliet balconies that added little beyond a bit of added charm. The hedges out front were immaculately trimmed, so perfect, they looked like they'd been clipped one leaf at a time. The concrete steps led up to a beautiful, chocolate-stained door, and there was an orange-cushioned swing on one side of the small porch. It was a stately and beautiful building, at least from the outside.

Claire had a feeling that what she would find inside would be a sharp contrast.

"I've heard there's a vacant unit now if you love it so much." The voice came from behind her, and Claire turned to see Greg walking toward her. He looked at her and raised an eyebrow. "You look nice."

There was a question in there—something like *"why* do you look so nice?"—and Claire felt heat rise to her cheeks, remembering that she hadn't actually taken the time to remove her makeup from earlier that night.

"Thanks," she said and then turned toward the building to signal that the conversation was over. As they walked up the steps side by side, Claire tried to prepare herself for what she was going to see inside. She had a strong stomach—she had to in this line of work—but it didn't mean that it was easy for her to be the person who had to walk into a crime scene when everyone else was running away from it. One of the doors had been propped open, and she passed through the threshold, Greg a couple of steps behind her.

The inside of the building was not as impressive as the outside. It was obviously well-kept, but there was no hiding the fact that it was an old building, and old buildings had old-building problems. Beneath the beautiful rug in the foyer, the floorboard gave, just slightly, under their feet as they walked in, and there were noticeable chips in the paint on the walls near the baseboards.

On their left, there was a door to the first-floor apartment, which was slightly ajar. Across from it was a small table that contained a scattering of postcards and mailers, left there to collect dust. Claire moved past them, Greg close on her heels. Just past the small table, on the right-hand side of the hallway, was the start of a flight of stairs that led up to the second floor.

"There are three units, but the main action is on the third floor," Greg said, pointing his chin up the stairs.

Claire nodded. She followed his lead and walked toward the staircase before climbing up, her shoes sinking into the plush floor runner as she did. As she walked, she noticed smudges on the wall and the carpet, along with a noticeable chip in the paint the size of a quarter.

"Is that blood?" she asked, eyeing the smudges.

"Looks like it," Greg said. "There's more."

Indeed, Claire saw another few spots of the same, reddish-brown substance on the wall leading up to the second floor. When they reached the landing, there was a woman there holding a box with latex gloves, and they both took a pair. Slipping them on, they turned the corner to see the door to the second-floor apartment open.

"Guess everybody's up, huh?" Claire said, looking back at Greg, and he nodded.

Dr. Claribel Ortiz was walking out of the unit with a tape recorder in her hand, and she nodded hello to the two detectives as they approached.

"Dr. Ortiz," Claire said as she walked up. "I thought you were still out on maternity leave."

"Second week back on the job," she said. "Never a dull moment."

"What happened here?"

"Victim's up on the third floor," she said. "That's the primary site. No one has been up there except the responding officer and me. Her name is Beverly Brighton. She and her husband live in apartment 3. Time of death is about 2:00 a.m. Apparently, there was a dinner party going on down here, and Beverly and her husband attended. Not sure when it ended, but the host agreed to let us swab for prints in there too." She paused and then nodded her head upstairs. "It's not pretty."

Claire turned to head up with Greg and the medical examiner following close behind her.

She saw the hand before she was halfway up the stairs.

"Wow," she heard Greg mutter as they reached the top. The landing on the third floor of the building was a small, rectangular space that couldn't have been more than eight feet across and five feet wide. Against the far wall was the door to the third-floor apartment, which was propped open. The only furniture in the space was a hip-height glass table next to the door.

The woman was sprawled on her side, one arm flung over the top of the staircase. She was in her mid- to late thirties, with shoulder-length brown hair, olive skin, and bright-green eyes that stared lifelessly in front of her. She wore a pair of red pajama bottoms and a black spaghetti-strap tank top, and her feet were bare. There was a large gash near her temple and a bloodstain beneath her head that feathered out from under her hair and seeped into the carpet. Next to her lay a large, shiny, black-and-white statue of a zebra.

The three people on the stairs stood there silently for a few moments, the unimaginable sadness of the scene not lost on them, even though they'd each seen many bodies before.

"Cause of death was two blows to the head," Dr. Ortiz finally said softly. "One right in the center of the back of the skull, most likely from being struck, hard, by that statue. The second is near the left temple. That's the one responsible for most of the blood, and it was made by impact with something very hard and equally sharp."

"So, in other words..." Claire said.

"In other words, I think she was hit with the statue and then fell to the side and struck the corner of the table as she went down."

Claire nodded, taking a step forward, moving carefully around the body. "Where's the husband?" she asked, turning to Greg.

He nodded his head toward the door of the apartment. "He's inside. The officer on the scene woke him up when he got here. He was inside, in bed. I think you're going to have to wait a little bit to talk to him. I heard he's been retching for the last hour."

Claire nodded. She, Greg, and Dr. Ortiz turned and walked back down the steps. When they reached the ground floor, Greg indicated that they should move toward the back of the building. Claire followed down a narrow but still-bright corridor that led to a short of flight of steps down to the building's back door.

It was a simple wooden door with a dead bolt and lock on the doorknob. Claire saw immediately that one of the glass panels in the window next to the door had been busted open, and there was glass on the floor covering the large mat. She took a look around, examining the broken shards of glass all over the mat and concrete floor.

"We think this is how the perp got in," Greg said. "Busted the window, opened the lock, and then, for some reason, made it up to the third floor and encountered Brighton."

Claire peered at the floor for another moment and then finally looked up. "Do we know what Beverly was doing out of her apartment?"

"Nope," Greg said. "That's the million-dollar question. Or at least one of them."

They both looked up as a tall, wiry officer walked toward them from the front of the building. He couldn't have been more than twenty-five or twenty-six years old, and his hands were clenched into fists at his sides.

"That's the responding officer," Greg said. "If you want to talk to him."

Claire nodded and walked over to the man, who looked as if he'd seen a ghost.

"You were on the scene first?" she asked.

The officer looked at her nervously and nodded without saying anything before dropping his eyes to the floor.

Claire lowered her voice. "First body you've seen?"

The officer looked up for a moment and then nodded before averting his eyes again.

"If it's any consolation, it doesn't get easier for anyone, not the first time or the hundredth."

He looked at her and nodded, letting his shoulders slump.

"I know it's in your report, but can you tell me about what happened when you got here?"

The officer took a deep breath. "The couple that called it in, apartment 1—they're the ones who let me in. I walked up to the third floor with them and saw the body," he said. He swallowed and then continued. "I called it in and then pushed the door open and went inside."

"It was unlocked?"

"It wasn't even fully closed. When I got inside, I went into the bedroom and found the husband asleep. I thought something was wrong with him. I had to shake him to wake him up. Turns out he was pretty messed up from whatever they were taking at that party."

Claire nodded. "Security cameras on the property?"

"I don't know, ma'am."

"Landlord on premises?"

"No, ma'am."

"Where are all the tenants now?"

"They've all gone back to their apartments," he said.

"Okay, thanks," she said before turning to walk away. She took two steps and then paused, looking back over her shoulder. "And nice job, by the way."

The cop blinked and then nodded slightly. "Thanks."

Claire walked back over to Greg, who was standing by the bottom of the staircase. "All right, let's go see who's awake," she said.

Greg frowned, looking at his watch. "Really?" he asked. "At this time of night? You're not going to let the dust settle a bit?"

Claire shook her head. "Nah. Let it settle, and people tend to find their footing. That's exactly what we don't want." She turned and looked at the back door. "At least we know one thing for sure."

"What's that?"

Claire jogged down the short flight of steps that led to the back door and crouched on the concrete where the busted glass was scattered all around. With a gloved hand, she picked up one of the largest pieces and held it between her fingertips, her thumb pressed gently against one of the sharp edges. As she examined it, she spoke softly, more to herself than to anyone around her.

"We know this is complete and utter bullshit."

Greg had reached the top of the short staircase, and he stared down at Claire's crouched frame, a frown on his face. "What are you talking about?"

Claire didn't say anything for a moment, just continued to press her finger against the glass as Greg slowly made his way down the steps to join her. She finally dropped it and stood up, turning to face him.

"This so-called break-in. Careless, sloppy, and almost insulting, to be honest."

"What are you talking about?" Greg asked again, looking at the busted window and glass shards that surrounded their feet.

"It's completely dry," Claire said. "The floor, these stairs, not a drop of water. It's been raining all night, and you mean to tell me that somebody managed to break that window, open the door, come inside, and walk to the front of the building without leaving a drop of water on this concrete floor?"

Greg followed her gaze and cursed softly.

"Somebody staged it," he said.

Claire nodded. "And the only reason you'd do that is if—"

"You're trying to hide the fact that the killer was already inside the building."

Claire raised an eyebrow. "Still want to let that dust settle?"

CHAPTER 4

Paula

Six days before

V ANESSA AND I HAD been at the party for all of twenty
minutes, and I was already giving her the look.

Me: You regretting this yet?

Her: No.

Me:

Her: Well...maybe a little.

Me: How much longer do we have to stay?

Her: Just until I find Tim and say hi.

Me: Then we can go?

Her: Then you *can go.*

We were standing at an impossibly small table in the middle of
Agave Restaurant and Bar, a beautiful, modern restaurant in Chicago's
River North neighborhood. To be fair, the high ceilings; deep, red-
and-gold booths; and inherent sense of celebration were infectious,
and there was a small part of me that was happy we'd come.

But the rest of me was uncomfortable, awkward, and, more
than anything, tired.

All I could think about was how much money I could make if,

instead of partying with them, I was spending the night taking all these people home.

The large-screen televisions around the room were showing pop music videos, the sounds of which had several people bopping back and forth while they sipped their cocktails and pretended to be disinterested in everyone else around them.

"I know what we need," Vanessa said suddenly. "Shots."

"No," I said. "That is precisely what we don't need."

"Yes!" she said, launching both fists into the air, as if I'd agreed with her. She spun around toward the bar. "I'll be right back."

I sighed and finished the cocktail I'd bought when we first arrived, the one that I'd promised would be my first and last. It was sort of an unspoken rule: the more Keith drank, the less I did, since it seemed that one of us should be sober, at least most of the time.

Besides, I'd never done well with alcohol. I treated alcohol the way some people treated sweets. I never had to have it, but one taste, and I craved more, and more, and more. Whereas Keith could drink just the right amount to knock him out and allow him to wake up refreshed in the morning, I tended to be either completely sober or completely horizontal—there was rarely much in between.

As I stood there, I felt a tap on my shoulder. I turned, expecting to tell Vanessa that she was on her own with the shots, but instead found myself face-to-face with a man who was about my height and wearing a leather vest with no shirt beneath it.

"Hey," he said, stepping close and talking loudly near my ear. "What kind of guys…"

"Sorry?" I asked as the end of his sentence got lost in the noise around us.

"Oh, I just said what kind of guys do you like?"

I held up my left hand. "Oh, I'm married," I said. "Thanks, though."

He frowned. He started to walk away and then turned back. "Thanks for what?"

I blinked. "Huh?"

"You said 'thanks.' Was that 'Thanks for coming to talk to me, now go away'?"

"I didn't—"

"'Thanks for putting yourself out there so I can make you feel like an idiot'?"

"No—"

"'Thanks for making me feel attractive because my husband sure doesn't, and that's the only reason I came out tonight'?"

Before I could respond, Vanessa walked up with two shot glasses in her hands, and she looked back and forth between the two of us before stepping closer to him.

"How about 'Thanks for understanding that sweat, armpits, and cheap leather do not go well together and for moving on to stink up some other area of the club'?" she said.

The man grumbled something, shook his head, and walked away.

Vanessa turned back to me, holding out one of the glasses. "I think you ordered this?"

I stared at the retreating leather and then the shot glass, all my planned protests flying out the window.

"What the hell," I said, taking it and lifting it up.

She smiled and lifted her glass as well before we tossed them back. The thick liquid burned, like it was supposed to, and I coughed loudly as I put the glass down on the small table.

"What the hell!" I exclaimed again, wiping my mouth, those famous last words some of the last ones I remembered of the night.

◆ ❖ ◆

Two hours later, I was in the fiery pit of hell but too drunk to know it.

There were karaoke singers wailing everything from "My Heart Will Go On" to "Shoop." Nearby, Vanessa was making out with a man who she said was Tim, but I had a good feeling he wasn't. And my hand was sweaty and sticky from the number of times it had been grabbed by a faceless stranger before I could react and yank it away.

Still, I put my name on the list for karaoke and gave in to the night. When my name was called out, Vanessa pulled away from her date and yelled something as I navigated the crowd to get to the front of the room. There was no stage, just a cleared-out space near the DJ, and I took the microphone and got into place.

I heard the opening chords to "You Oughta Know" by Alanis Morissette—my go-to karaoke song—and I began to sway. I was walking the fine, liquored line between complete happiness and total breakdown. I swallowed and pushed on, letting the familiar lyrics drip off my tongue.

The words were scrolling across the monitor too slowly, but it didn't matter; I knew them by heart. As I sang, I let my gaze scan the crowd of people dancing, some watching me, some singing along. This was *fun*. Keith and I used to do things like this every weekend, laughing and drinking until we forgot our last name. I didn't want to give in, didn't want to be *that person*, yet I wondered what our lives would be like if I hadn't asked him to pick up that bottle of Merlot.

If he *hadn't* chosen to head south down Ashland Avenue that day at the exact same time that the kid in the black SUV decided to look down at a text message.

Where would we be?

Behind the karaoke screens, the pop videos still played on the television screens in the background, even though they'd been muted for the amateur singers.

As I sang, a motion on one of the television screens caught my eye.

It was the group of people dancing that made me look in the first place, but then I was focused on the man in the center as the camera zoomed in close to his face.

I kept singing as the shot zoomed out again, the connection brewing in my mind but still fuzzy.

When the camera zoomed in again, the man's face was clear, right in the middle of the screen. I stumbled over the lyrics that I knew so well before stopping completely, the cool head of the microphone pressed against my lips.

I stared at his face, but I wasn't seeing him there, on the TV. I saw him in the back seat of my car, his body leaned forward, his gaze locked on mine in the rearview mirror.

Lotti.

He was right there, dancing on the television in the middle of a group of gyrating, scantily clad women, as if it were the only place in the world he belonged.

At some point, the microphone slipped from my fingers and crashed to the floor.

"What do you mean, he flirted with you?"

There was a voice asking me that question, but I couldn't place it. There was an entire room full of people watching me, and I swayed a little.

"Who liked your unwashed hair?"

I blinked and finally looked up to see the DJ looking at me, a smile on his face. He was watching me, waiting for me to respond as Alanis carried on in the background.

Surely, I had not said that out loud.

Surely. I had not. Said that. Out loud.

But the moments before I'd dropped the microphone were a blur, and the expressions on the faces of the people standing in front of me suggested otherwise.

I opened my mouth, and a squeak came out. Closing it, I scanned the group until I landed on Vanessa. She was watching me, her eyebrows raised, but the moment we locked eyes, she sprang into action.

Bathroom, she mouthed, bolting toward me. She reached down and scooped up the microphone before handing it to the DJ. Then she took my arm and dragged me away. As we navigated through the crowd, Alanis was turned off, and as if to further test the limits of my sobriety and sanity, the song from the video screen was turned up.

I gasped as the sounds floated through the room.

It was the song from the car.

The one I'd talked about with Lotti.

The man on the television was singing the same song I'd talked about last night *with the man on the freaking television.*

What the hell?

As we stepped into the bathroom, Vanessa let go of my arm and walked quickly past the stalls, stooping to look beneath each one in a clean and easy motion—she'd obviously done this before. When she was done, she whipped around and placed both hands on her hips and tilted her head to the side.

"What happened out there?"

I swallowed, swaying, and Vanessa shook her head. "Somebody's tolerance has gone *way* down," she said. "You've had, what, a drink and a half?"

"I…" I stared at the bathroom door, where I could still hear the faint sounds of Lotti's music video.

"What happened out there?" Vanessa asked again. "You said he flirted with you?"

"I did?" I asked.

"Yes," she said with a laugh. "And that he even likes your unwashed hair, which, for the record, is disgusting."

I took a deep breath but didn't respond.

Vanessa had very quickly become one of my closest friends, and even so, I wasn't sure I should tell her the truth.

I barely believed myself. Why should she?

"Paula?" she asked, watching my expression. "Who were you talking about?"

I winced, lifting my finger to point in the air.

"Him."

Vanessa followed my finger up to the ceiling and then looked back at me. "What?"

I sighed and walked over to the door. Yanking it open, I let the music stream in. I pointed out across the room at one of the television screens and spoke again.

"Him."

She looked out into the crowd and then back at me. "Who?" she asked, clearly losing patience.

"*Him*," I said a third time, this one a whisper. "On the TV."

Vanessa looked up at the screen, turned back to me, and then looked back out at the TV. She blinked a few times, her mouth open, and then her expression quickly turned to worry.

"Okay, maybe I shouldn't have forced this night out," she said with a chuckle. "Come on. We should go home—"

"No," I said. "I'm serious. I picked that guy up. In my DAC. Last night."

Vanessa blinked and stared out at the televisions.

"Lotti" was on screen, still standing in the middle of the group of women. He pumped his hips back and forth while the women executed sexily choreographed dance moves around him with remarkable precision.

Vanessa finally spoke. "You mean…Ryan Hooks?" She said it as if she'd said "Santa Claus" and my sanity was at question. "You picked up Ryan Hooks in your DAC last night?"

I blinked. "*That's* Ryan Hooks?" I asked. "Ryan Hooks, Ryan Hooks?"

"Yes…" she said slowly. "You do know who Ryan Hooks is?"

"Of course," I said. "I guess I didn't know what he looked like." I'd heard of the Grammy-winning singer and could even sing a few of his songs, but I'd always imagined that he'd be a bit younger and more baby-faced than the sultry man I'd met the night before.

But it was definitely him.

I knew faces; I *drew* faces.

"Ness, that's the man I picked up, I promise."

Vanessa knew me well enough to know that it wasn't the kind of thing I'd make up. Her expression slowly began to shift from confusion to concern to excitement.

"How? Where?" she asked.

"I picked him up at the Renouvelle. In South Loop. And took him to an apartment building in the Gold Coast."

"No way," she said breathlessly. "Not possible. It had to be a look-alike."

"No," I said, looking back at the screen as he spun around in a circle and then stared seductively at the camera. I thought about the man's face as he leaned forward in the back seat of my car. "It was him."

Vanessa seemed to be processing, and then her eyes lit up. "What did you mean he flirted with you?"

I blushed. "That might've been a stretch," I said. "But he was very nice."

Vanessa shook her head. "There still a good chance it was a look-alike," she said. "But if it wasn't, hot *damn*. That's amazing. He is so hot. You should've flirted back."

I laughed. "Well, he forgot all about me once he saw his date."

I didn't think Vanessa could look any more shocked than she had, but her eyes got even wider, and she took a step backward.

"You saw Tiffane!" she asked. "No, no, no. Paula, do not tell me you saw Tiffane and did not get an autograph for me."

"The actress?" I asked, frowning. "No…"

We stared at each other for a few moments, and then realization set in. Vanessa put both hands to her mouth.

"*You saw him with someone else.*"

It was a scream and a whisper at the same time, and I don't think I've ever seen anyone look so sad. I resisted the urge to remind her that she was a grown woman with a teenage daughter, since I knew how important celebrity gossip was to her.

She took a step closer to me. "Do not tell me you saw him with someone else. I wouldn't be able to handle it."

"Let me guess. He's dating Tiffane?" I asked.

"They're *married*, Paula. Where the hell have you been the last five years?"

"Living a life that has nothing to do with either of them."

Vanessa rolled her eyes. "Yeah, yeah, we get it. You're too cool for celebrity news," she said. "Ryan and Tiffane are my third favorite celebrity couple." She sighed loudly. "This is the best and worst news I've heard all year," she said.

"Your daughter graduated from eighth grade last month—"

"I just wish there was a way for you to *really* know it was him," she said, ignoring me. "For sure."

"How many times do I have to tell you?" I asked. "I draw faces for a living… Well, I used to. It was him."

"Yeah, but you can't prove it."

I froze, a thought crossing my mind.

"Actually, I might be able to."

"What?" she asked.

But I'd already spun around and walked out of the bathroom. I heard Vanessa call out after me, and then she was on my heels as we walked back through the restaurant. The song had changed, and the volume had been turned up, which seemed to be enough for people to forget my marvelous performance a few moments earlier.

"Where are you going?" she asked.

I stopped and turned to her. "I found a phone in my car last night, after I got back home from the diner. I don't know when it was dropped, but—"

"You think it might be his?"

"I don't know," I said. "I need to call it a night anyway. I'll check when I get home."

"So will I," she said with a determined look on her face. "I'm coming with you."

It took us twenty-five minutes to get back to my house. When we arrived, we both opened the doors of our DAC and stumbled down the street toward my car. I was sobering up enough to know how ridiculous we were behaving but still drunk enough not to stop. I popped the trunk when we were about two cars away.

"Wait," Vanessa said, putting out a hand to stop me.

"What is it?" I asked. I stopped in the middle of the street, and we stood there for a moment. She was smiling, a drunken, wistful smile, and I laughed out loud when she didn't speak. "*What?*"

"What will you do if it's his?"

I frowned. "What do you mean?"

"Assuming we find out it really is his phone, what will you do with it?"

"Besides letting you lick it?" I said, but she didn't laugh. She continued to stare at me, and I shrugged. "I don't know. Maybe try to find his number one fan and sell it for a grand? Problem is, you don't have that kind of money."

She laughed, and we walked on, crossing the few feet until we were standing behind my car.

I lifted the trunk and leaned in, rummaging through my lost-and-found bin.

"I know what I would do," she said. "As much as I love him, if Ryan is cheating on Tiffane, I would call up *Star* or *People* and sell it to the highest bidder. You know there are pics of other women on there."

"He'd deserve it," I agreed as I rifled through the box. I found the phone and pulled it out, holding it up to show Vanessa.

"This one," I said. "This is the one I found last night."

She grabbed it from me and held it up to her face, pushing a button. On the dark street, the screen lit up her features, and I could see every emotion that crossed it as she stared at whatever was on the lock screen.

The dubious excitement.

The moment of recognition.

The shock.

I think until that moment, I'd thought it wouldn't be his. That this little escapade, as fun as it had been tonight, would be over as quickly as it had started. But I knew immediately that it wasn't true when I saw Vanessa's face.

And that was *before* she squeezed her eyes shut, tossed her head back, and screamed into the night.

CHAPTER 5

I T WAS A PICTURE of Ryan and his wife, Tiffane.

But not just *any* picture.

It was unlike any photo of a celebrity couple I'd ever seen before. The starlet was makeup-less, and there were bags under both her eyes, none of which detracted from her beauty. Still, the intimate photo led me to believe that they'd woken up shortly before the selfie was snapped. Their faces were pressed close together, and they stared into the screen with matching grins. There was something so personal—so *ordinary*—about it, which let me know right away that I hadn't been mistaken.

I hadn't made it all up.

I wasn't delusional.

Ryan Hooks had been in my car.

"I can't believe it," Vanessa hissed as she seemingly came to the same conclusion. "It really was him! And you saw him *cheating* on Tiffane." She paused for a moment and then raised her eyebrows. "What are you going to do?"

"Do?" I asked, holding the phone in my hands and looking up at her. "What do you mean?"

"I don't know. You can't just go stick it in a drawer and forget about it," she said. "Let's see…you could tweet him and offer to return it in exchange for free concert tics. And a chance to meet Tiffane."

I laughed. "That is an option."

"*Or* you could hack into it and read all his texts. Or actually sell it to a news site, like I said! I bet they'd pay a ton for Ryan Hooks's cell phone."

I blinked a few times and then shook my head to clear it. "Ness, the only thing I'm going to *do* right now is go inside and get some sleep. You want to crash?"

"No, I need to get home," she said with a sigh, pulling out her own phone to call a car.

After she left, I stood outside for a while, staring at the image on the phone. When I finally walked into the house, most of the lights were off. Keith had gotten into the habit of leaving one on in the living room before he went to sleep, and I was grateful for it tonight; I needed all the help I could get. I stumbled to the couch and plopped down, turning to look at Shelby as I did. She was lying in her usual spot with her eyes closed, but I had the sense she'd just laid down as I opened the door. I pulled myself back up and walked over to her, kneeling, the alcohol encouraging me to make amends, even at this ungodly hour.

"Hey, girl," I said quietly, running my fingers through her soft fur. She opened her eyes and stared at me but didn't move an inch. "Let's bury the hatchet, okay? Truce?"

She stared at me with something that, in my current state, felt like a look of disgust, and I straightened up, walked back to the couch, and sat down. She watched me for a few moments more, but then she let her eyelids drop again.

"Fine," I said out loud. "Don't say I never tried."

I could hear the breath coming out of my body, and I opened my mouth to try to inhale and exhale normally. *Why was it so hard to breathe like a normal person?* I hadn't had that much to drink in a long time, and I knew I would feel it in the morning. My own eyes drooped, and I knew I should go to bed and take advantage of what would, at the least, be a solid night of rest.

But who could sleep after that?

I pulled my phone out of my purse and, with clumsy fingers, opened up a Google search. I took a peek at Shelby, who was still lying there with her eyes closed, and then punched in a quick search: *Ryan Hooks.*

I let out a long, slow breath as his picture came up, and there he was, just like that. It had been twenty-four hours since I'd met him, but I felt the same rush of attraction that I had as I drove him to the Gold Coast. Only this time, I didn't feel so bad. He was a *celebrity*, not just a random guy I'd picked up in the middle of the night. Keith and I spoke frequently about our celebrity crushes (more often, I told him about mine and grilled him on which ones he found attractive).

This was okay.

This was allowed.

Ryan Allen Hooks.

Born December 7, 1979, in Los Angeles. He was the son of a movie producer and an actress, which seemed fitting. As I scrolled through his Wikipedia page and a handful of news articles, he stared at me with the piercing eyes and jawline that could cut glass.

I navigated to his official webpage next, and that's when the pieces of the puzzle started coming together. He was in town for his "Love or Lust" concert tour, performing at the Chicago Theatre, only ten minutes or so from where I'd dropped him off. He was also doing a show down at a stadium in a town twenty miles outside the city. He only had two shows left, and then he'd be in Dallas a week after that. I wondered if he was staying in Chicago until then or if he was going somewhere in between.

Then I wondered why I wondered that.

I also wondered if I was losing my mind.

Go to bed, Paula.

Instead, I hit the blogs.

Very quickly, I learned two things. One, his fans called them-selves Hookers, which was horrible and hilarious at the same time, and two, people would say almost *anything* under the shroud of anonymity. The comments on the blogs were, at best, amazingly supportive; at worst, they were downright creepy. I wondered if I'd had access to sites like these when I was a teenager if I'd be as open about my unabashed obsession with my favorite artists.

> I met Ryan Hooks tonight, y'all, and now I can die.
> Srsly, that's it for me.

> I would leave my husband, my job, my kids, and my
> dignity behind for just one night. Just one night.

On one blog, I found a thread called "Chicago-August," and I clicked on it. It was filled with accounts from fans who'd seen him in different locations around town. The last one was posted at 3:30 p.m., two days ago.

> Saw RyHo at the W Hotel in downtown. Pretty sure
> that's where he's staying during his time here. I'll be
> camping outside in my car to catch a picture. Wish
> me luck, Hookers!

A very small, smug part of me wanted to post that she had it wrong—he was at the Renouvelle Hotel, not the W—but I closed the screen and moved on.

Next search: *Ryan Hooks and Tiffane.*

She only had one name, a popular one at that, but the auto search filled it in by the time I started Ryan's last name. They'd met at the MTV Music Awards a few years back, which again seemed fitting, and the rest was history.

Couple name, Tyan.

Together three years before getting married in a small ceremony with friends and family in Palm Springs. Their wedding cake was vanilla with fresh strawberries and a dark-chocolate shell.

The things you can learn on the internet...

I scrolled through countless pictures of them: him dark, brooding, and unbearably sexy; her small, curvy, and gorgeous. The last year, though, had been rocky. A *TMZ* segment of Ryan being chased down by cameras and accused of cheating. Tiffane quoted as saying she'd leave him if she heard any more rumors about him messing around. Another article stated there was "trouble in paradise" and even threats of a divorce, but nothing had materialized from it.

In the back of my mind, there was a question brewing, one that, even then, I knew would cause me a lot of pain, but I let it simmer there anyway.

What would Tiffane do if she knew about the woman in the Gold Coast?

It was such a ridiculous thought, but it lingered while I scrolled through article after article and watched video after video. By the time I realized that the sun was coming up, I'd watched Ryan Hooks singing at concerts, in music videos, at award shows, and even for fans at the airport. Every single one of his songs was about how much he loved someone, missed someone, or wanted to be a better man for someone.

And even though I'd watched him do something that looked a lot like cheating, I couldn't help but get drawn under his spell. Every interview was funnier than the last, every sultry pose sexier than the one before it. In the span of two hours, I all but fell in love, as much as the unending swamp of the internet would allow, and I couldn't keep myself from being dragged away.

It had to be the alcohol.

It had to be.

I dropped my phone on the living room table and then reached into my purse and pulled out Ryan's. I pressed the home button to illuminate it, and there he was again, smiling up at me with his face pressed against his wife's. I pushed the button again, causing the keypad to appear on top of their faces, and thought about Vanessa's words:

You could hack into it and read all his texts.

I swallowed and let my thumb hover over the screen.

It couldn't hurt to try, right?

Ryan's birthday was December 7, so I quickly keyed in 1-2-0-7 and held my breath.

Immediately, the entire screen shook.

Nice try, it seemed to say.

I grabbed my own phone and looked up Tiffane's birthday.
0-2-1-5.

Again, the screen shuddered.

Nope.

I decided to give it one more try. I typed in 7-9-2-6—for R-y-a-n—and this time, the phone actually did respond.

YOU HAVE ENTERED AN INCORRECT PASSCODE 3 TIMES. THE PHONE WILL AUTOMATICALLY LOCK AFTER 7 MORE ATTEMPTS.

I clicked the button at the top of the phone to turn off the screen and dropped it back into my purse before standing up. Shelby didn't move an inch as I walked past her and into the bedroom.

Keith was rolled over on his side, snoring, the whiskey-stained glass in its usual spot. If he'd known what I'd spent the last three hours doing, he would've thought I was crazy.

He probably would've been right.

I crawled into bed beside him and finally let the sleep take over.

"Hey."

Keith was sitting in his wheelchair at the side of the bed, peering down at me. I blinked at him through last night's mascara and wondered why he was talking so loudly.

"We have to be at Dr. Bryant's in an hour." He pushed himself back and rolled out of the room.

I was still in the clothes I'd worn the night before, my body sprawled awkwardly across the bed. I winced as I sat up, the sunlight hurting my eyes. Pushing myself out of bed, I went to the bathroom to get ready.

During our early trips to the doctor's office, Keith and I had been chatty—with each other, with the doctors and medical staff, and with anyone who'd listen. We thought talking a lot would make things a little less terrible. We simply couldn't give in to the paralyzing abnormality of it all. We talked loudly to drown out the sobs in our hearts. We held hands, and we laughed. We pretended.

These days, our visits were quiet, almost silent. We were too tired, and the doctor's office seemed to shrink with each visit. Too tight for any small talk to fit.

We were quiet on the trip there too, sitting silently beside each other while I drove the twenty minutes to her office. When we arrived, we sat wordlessly in her waiting room, our eyes trained on the silent television mounted in one corner. When she was ready, I pushed Keith into her office and took a seat beside him.

"When's the big day?" Dr. Bryant asked from behind her desk. "Heading back to work."

Keith cleared his throat and looked at me. "Tomorrow," he said. "And I'm not exactly going back. I'm just going to watch one of the swim meets."

It had been a year since he'd been to a Morton College swim meet, and I hadn't seen him so excited in a long time.

"I'm excited for you," Dr. Bryant said. She sat up straighter in her seat. "So, I've got good news and bad."

One of the things I appreciated most about her was her ability to quickly cut to the chase.

"Which one do you want first?" she asked.

"The bad," Keith and I said at the same time, and we turned to look at each other.

Dr. Bryant leaned forward, folding her hands on the desk in front of her. "Your range of motion hasn't improved since last time," she said. "And unfortunately, that's bad news. None of the treatments we've tried so far are helping."

"But it's not getting worse," Keith said. "That's got to be a good thing?"

"Sure, good in that it could be worse," she said. "But you're not improving as much as we'd hoped."

"What's the good news?" Keith asked quietly.

Dr. Bryant looked at me first, and from the expression on her face, I knew what she was going to say.

"That treatment I told you about—"

She stopped as Keith let out a long, loud sigh.

"*That's* the good news?" he asked.

Dr. Bryant stood up and walked around her desk. "I wouldn't keep bringing it up if I didn't think it could help you," she said.

"But we still can't afford it," Keith said. "Like we couldn't the last time we came in and like we won't be able to the next."

"But you're an *excellent* candidate for it," she said. "This treatment could radically change your quality of life. I don't recommend it to everyone, because Dr. Reveno's treatment requires a very specific patient, and you are really the perfect example of it. You're the right age, the right height, and everything else lines up. I don't want to oversell it, but I think it's something you should consider."

Keith sucked in a breath. "Thanks for the update, Doc," he said. He looked down at me. "I'll wait for you outside."

As he left, I stood and faced Dr. Bryant.

"Do you think it will actually work?" I asked.

She nodded. "I do," she said. "I wouldn't keep mentioning it if I didn't."

The ride home was tense.

"I can ask David for some extra shifts," I said after we'd been driving for nearly ten minutes in silence.

"When, at two o'clock in the morning?" Keith asked. He looked over at me for a moment and then back out the window. "I know you're not sleeping, Paula. You're never there when I wake up."

"You mean I'm never there to make sure you wake up?" I said, and I cursed as the words came out of my mouth. He let out a long, slow breath. "Sorry."

I peeked over at him, but he was staring stonily out the window. I remembered sitting in the back seat of the car as my parents drove along, just like that, the silence riding in the car with us like a fourth passenger. I used to try to make conversation at first, asking how long it would take to get to the restaurant or wherever it was we were going, what they were going to eat, anything to get them talking. I soon learned that it was better for me to retreat into silence too.

Now, I wished Keith and I had someone in the back seat, an eager little kid to help us break the tension and just *talk*.

When we got home, I pulled over and jumped out of the car.

I opened the trunk and pulled out his chair before carrying it over to the passenger door.

He frowned when he saw that I'd left the hazards on.

"You're going back out?" he asked.

I nodded. "I'm going to drive for a little bit." We were both silent as I helped him into the chair. I moved around to push him toward the front door, but he held up a hand.

"It's okay, thanks," he said before wheeling himself away from me.

I stood there watching him for a moment before walking back around to the driver's side, climbing inside, and pulling away.

At first, I wasn't really going anywhere in particular.

I didn't actually feel like picking up any rides, not yet, so I just drove, turning onto street after street, until the buildings around me got less and less familiar. As I drove, I couldn't help but think of the conversation I'd had with Vanessa the night before as we stood outside staring at Ryan Hooks's phone.

You could sell it to a news site! I bet they'd pay a ton for Ryan Hooks's cell phone.

It was a ridiculous idea that didn't deserve even a second thought, yet here I was, giving it a second and a third and a fourth. I shook my head and let my mind wander to the image of Hooks and the woman on Saturday night. It wasn't the best distraction, but it would do, and I let myself zone out as I drove along, my brain bouncing from the image of the two of them staring at each other in the night, to Hooks's smiling face on his Wikipedia page, and back again.

I'd been driving along aimlessly like that for ten minutes when I blinked, realizing where I was.

I hadn't done it on purpose—at least, I didn't *think* I had—but here I was, just five blocks away from the apartment on Oak.

I knew I should stop myself, knew I should turn around and go home, but I wasn't ready to face Keith again, and I certainly didn't feel like picking up any strangers.

With my fingers drumming lightly against the steering wheel, I accepted what I was doing, headed toward Oak Street, and began to sing a little song, just under my breath, a soft, rhythmic, self-deprecating chant.

You're losing your mind. You're actually crazy. This is not a normal thing to do!

Tap.

You're losing your mind. You're actually crazy. This is not a normal thing to do!

Tap.

I kept humming and tapping as I drove down the street toward the apartment. When I got there, I slowed down and pulled over, pressing tightly against the parked cars so the traffic behind me could get by, before shifting into park. Then I leaned across the passenger seat and peered at the building.

115 West Oak.

The building had seemed taller, statelier, and more manicured than it did now, like something out of a storybook. Today, I could see that it was an average though attractive building sandwiched in between two equally attractive three-flats on either side of it. As I sat there, my mind flashed back to Saturday night, when Hooks had stood there, riveted by the sight of the woman in the window.

I leaned even farther across the seat and angled my head to look up at the second-floor window—

And jolted back when I saw a tall, slender figure near the same spot where I'd seen the woman on Saturday night.

Shit!

I breathed heavily for a few moments and then dared to lean

over again, wondering if she was still there. I strained my neck toward the passenger window and craned up, letting out a breath when I saw who was in the window.

Or, rather, *what* was there.

A lamp.

Curvy base, with a short, white lampshade.

Not a person at all.

A giggle burst out of me, and I leaned back against the headrest. I deserved this, to be cowering in my front seat, hiding from an inanimate object. I put the car in Drive, waited for traffic to clear, and pulled away.

Of course the woman with the sleek blond bob was not *still* standing in the window since Saturday night. That would be both weird and insane.

No, she was probably in her second Pilates class of the day.

Or at the spa.

Or maybe she was—

Standing right there on the street.

I put on a hard brake and stared out at a woman fifteen feet away from my car at the entrance to a small park, a half block or so away from the apartment I'd just left.

I glanced up into the rearview mirror; luckily, there was no one behind me. I started driving again slowly.

The woman didn't notice me as I crept by because she was looking down at her phone, her forehead scrunched in a frown. I leaned forward and felt my breath catch.

It was her.

It wasn't just the sharpness of her blond bob or her small, delicate features. It was the way she held herself, the power in her frame.

It was definitely her.

I could've kept going.

I *should've* kept going.

But there was something empowering, something dangerous, something absolutely irresistible about the fact that I knew something about her and Ryan Hooks that I wasn't supposed to know.

And I had a feeling that nobody else knew.

At the end of the block, I made a U-turn and circled back to find parking.

You're losing your mind. You're actually crazy. This is not a normal thing to do.

CHAPTER 6

S TAY IN THE CAR, *Paula!*
The voice of reason was screaming at me, shrill, high-pitched, and desperate, but I ignored her. I opened my car door and stepped out onto the gravel surface, shutting it behind me. I had seen the tall, blond woman for only a few seconds on the night that I dropped off Hooks.

But I know faces. I knew the brushstrokes that would make up her face—short, curved flicks for her high cheekbones, light, feathery strokes for her skin. The moment I'd seen her standing outside the entrance to the small park, I'd known for sure—it was her.

It was a hot day, and I pulled my T-shirt away from my body as I walked from my car to the edge of the park. As I crossed the street, I knew I had a problem—I did not have an endgame for this little excursion. Some part of me just wanted to get closer, to see her face more clearly, to remove any last, miniscule shred of doubt.

Still, I couldn't exactly walk up and ask her.

Was that you I saw in the window staring down at Ryan Hooks two nights ago?

Yeah?

Cool.

Well, thanks.

My feet moved me forward anyway, and suddenly I was approaching the entrance to the park where she was still standing, talking to someone on her phone. When I was about five feet away from her, she looked up and smiled, the slight, unassuming, and uninterested smile reserved for strangers.

"Yeah, we're going to be at Klein's Boutique on Halsted," she said into the phone. "Their stuff is gorgeous and really well made."

This close, I could see that she was in her late twenties and pretty in a simple, put-together way. She was wearing a pale-green silk jumper that toed the line between pajamas and high fashion but skewed solidly enough toward the latter. She'd paired it with flat gladiator sandals and a small rectangular purse that was slung across her body. Her nails were painted a bright, vibrant red, and I didn't have to look closely to know that there wasn't a single chip there. And then there was the bob, cut into wispy layers that made her hair seem to bounce around her face, even though she was standing still.

I smiled back and averted my eyes quickly, moving past her to push back the gate and walk into the park. My feet sunk into the grass, and I looked around at what was an average, tiny park fashioned out of a sliver of empty space on Chicago's Gold Coast. I drove by the small spaces frequently, wondering what it must be like to grow up playing in something so small, so manufactured. When I was a kid, I played in our large suburban backyard, or my parents took me out to a forest preserve about ten miles away where I could run around to my heart's content.

The park was quaint and well-manicured, with a large play area in the middle and four benches surrounding it. Everything was tiny but pretty and well-kept, and it occurred to me that on another day, this would be a nice place to come to read a book.

The small park was relatively crowded for the time of day. There were two women with Starbucks cups in their hands, watching a pair of dogs that were chasing each other. On the other side of the park, a man and woman sat side by side on a bench with three dogs scurrying around their feet. It was at that moment that the absurdity of my excursion went to a whole new level.

I wasn't just in a park.

I was in a dog park.

And it must have been obvious to all four people who looked up as I walked into the small space—I did not have a dog.

I smiled and kept walking, feeling unbearably suspicious, because the reality of the matter was, I *was* unbearably suspicious. I paused for a minute, a few feet in, unsure what to do next. I could go and sit down on one of the benches, but then I'd be that woman—dogless, bookless, and friendless—who'd just come to watch the dogs play. I'd left everything besides my phone and my keys in the car. It didn't help that none of the small benches were empty, so I'd have to sit down next to one of the two groups.

I took a deep breath.

There's no crime in going to the park, Paula.

I knew what had made me stop in. They didn't.

Right?

As I approached the benches, I chickened out, which was a big mistake. With my pleasant, I'm-not-here-because-I'm-stalking-the-woman-at-the-gate-because-I-think-she's-the-secret-lover-of-a-major-celebrity expression, I forged past the benches with purpose toward the far end of the park. I was on a path, and I could not stop.

Except the path had no logical end.

I moved fully past the benches, and then it was too late to turn back. The park ended in a closed gate that separated it from an alley. In a few moments, I'd reach it, and then I would only have two options—turn around or climb it and run away as fast as my feet would allow. Since I hadn't climbed anything since I was a child, I knew the second option was out.

I kept walking, the heat beating down on me. When I reached the gate, I stopped, because there was nothing else to do, and stared out across the alley for a few minutes.

This is your life now.

I spun around, resigned to complete my walk of shame back out of the small park. Instead, I found myself face-to-face with the man from the park bench.

"It's nice, isn't it?" he said.

I blinked. "Sorry?"

"The park. It's only been here a few months, and so many people have stopped by to see it." He smiled. "You checking it out for your little one?"

"I—"

"What is she?" he asked. "Or he."

I blinked again, understanding suddenly dawning. "She," I said. "Boxer. Three years old."

"Nice," he said. "Well, this is a great park. Like I said, it's really new, and you can already see it's become quite the hot spot. And I'm just like you. I scouted out a few parks before I brought Crispy here because it's all about culture. Some people let their dogs do anything and everything, when we really just want a safe place where they can come and play, you know."

"Oh, definitely," I said.

We'd started walking slowly as we talked, and by then, we'd made it back to the benches. I almost gasped out loud when I saw that the woman with the short blond bob had come into the park and was now sitting in the spot where the man had been before. She was holding one of the dogs in her lap, and she looked up at both of us as we returned.

The man looked over at me. "This is…"

"Um, Christine," I said, clearing my throat, my middle name the first thing that came to my mind. "But you can call me Chris."

He nodded. "This is Chris," the man said. "Chris, this is Emma and Kayla. Neighbors of mine. See, we kind of get to know each other here. It's better for making sure our pups get along too, you know," he said. "Oh, and I'm Andrew."

"Nice to meet you all."

Emma was sitting with perfect posture, her upper body pulled just slightly away from the back of the bench. She smiled and shook my hand. It wasn't the same smile she'd given me when I walked past her earlier; this one was more aware, more interested, even curious.

"Nice to meet you," she said.

Andrew gestured for me to sit down, but I shook my head.

"Thanks," I said. "I was just stopping in. I've walked by this place a few times and wanted to see inside."

Andrew hadn't had a problem with the idea of me "shopping" for dog parks; I hoped his friends wouldn't either. They both nodded quickly. Emma's puppy squirmed in her lap and then jumped down to play. She stared after him fondly, and I thought about what Shelby would do if I ever tried to put her in my lap.

"Do you live in the area?"

I should've expected the question, but it caught me off guard, and I froze as they all watched me, waiting for an answer.

I couldn't tell the truth. What reason would I have to drive thirty minutes to a dog park in the Gold Coast of all places? I nodded without really giving it much thought.

"Yes," I said, racking my brain to think of some of the nearby cross streets. Driving DAC had given me an intimate familiarity with the city, yet I was pulling a blank. "I live a few blocks away, over on Elm Street."

It was the first street I could think of, and I knew that it was a popular street among the Northwestern medical students, which made me hope it had apartments that I could reasonably afford.

"Well, we did the same thing you're doing," Andrew said. "My wife and I. We moved here from Boston about ten years ago, and we used to look for nice dog parks out there too. Now we live just a couple buildings down from here." He pointed in the direction of the apartment where I'd dropped off Hooks, and I had to stop myself from gasping.

Were they neighbors neighbors? As in same building neighbors?

"I heard about one dog that got bitten at the new dog park on Elm Street," the woman named Kayla said. "Have you been there?"

"No, I haven't."

"Well, the culture here is great," Andrew said. "Really a lot of people who care about animals coming together to let their pups play in a safe environment. What more could you ask for?"

"Absolutely," I said, and I wondered what Shelby would think if she could see me right now. She'd probably roll her eyes and bark to call bullshit. My phone rang, and I fished it out of my pocket, thankful for the interruption. "Sorry," I said with a small smile and then turned away from the small group and looked at the screen. I answered when I saw it was Vanessa.

"Hey," I said, and I cleared my throat. "How are you feeling?"

"Like I'm too old for this shit," she said. "But I'll survive. How about you?"

"I almost fell asleep on my living room couch," I said with a laugh. "But I'm okay."

"You at home?"

"Um…" I looked out at the dogs playing around me, and I chose my words carefully. "No, I was out driving. I'm going to head to the diner soon." I said this quietly, taking a look back at the trio on the bench, but they were engrossed in conversation.

"Well, I might've done something that I shouldn't have," she said.

"What's that?"

"Last night when I got home, I did some Google stalking and found out why Ryan Hooks is in town."

I laughed. "Way ahead of you," I said. "He's performing at the Chicago Theatre and out at Greenway Field."

"Guess who's going to see him?"

"What?" I hissed and then turned to take a quick peek back at Emma and her friends. "What do you mean?"

"I got three tickets, for you, me, and Jen. For tomorrow's show in Prairie Hills. It involved putting my credit card into a site that I really don't feel good about, but it happened. I told Jen this morning, and she all but handed me the 'best mom' award. So feeling pretty good about myself right now."

"You're nuts," I said, but I couldn't deny the feeling of excitement that coursed through my body. "But thanks, Ness."

"No problem," she said. She dropped her voice. "Maybe you can talk to him about the you know what you found in the back of your car."

We disconnected, and I walked back over to the group on the bench. Andrew looked up as I approached. He was standing next to an elderly man in animal-print glasses who was holding a black pit bull with an incredibly shiny coat of hair in his arms.

"Who are you?" the man asked.

I blinked and looked at Andrew, who smiled awkwardly and laughed.

"Uh, this is Chris, Reg, and she lives in the neighborhood. Chris, this is Reg Bolton. He lives next door."

"Never seen you before," the man said. "And I know everyone around here."

"My husband and I moved in pretty recently," I stuttered, and I wondered if I sounded like I was lying.

He was eyeing me carefully, and he shifted his dog in his arms. "What do you do?"

"I'm an artist," I said hesitantly. "I draw portraits."

"Oh really?" Emma piped up, and I looked down at her. "I'm actually looking for some art. We need to talk."

I smiled, but the older man jumped in. "You're here for what?" he asked.

"Chris was just coming here to check out the park for her puppy," Andrew cut in with a patient smile. He looked at me. "What's his name again?"

"Her," I said. "Shelby."

"Mm-hmm," Reg said, eyeing me. "Well, just make sure you pick up after your dog. We've got somebody out here who's leaving their dog crap everywhere. Someone who comes in late at night. I've been watching to see who it is. I'm going to find them," he said. "It's illegal and unsanitary."

"I would never…"

"Mm-hmm," he said before turning and walking away.

Andrew smiled. "Reg is a little particular, but don't let him scare you away," he said as he sat down on the bench next to Emma. "So, will we be seeing you again with…?"

I blinked. It was a little too Stepford dog owners for me, but I smiled and nodded. "Oh, Shelby," I said, and it occurred to me that he wasn't really listening, since he'd asked for her name three times. "Yeah, I think so. Thanks for the warm welcome."

"Anytime," Andrew said.

I raised my hand and turned to walk away. I'd taken three steps when I heard him speak up again.

"Oh, we meet here most afternoons around this time," he said. "Just so you know. We'll be here tomorrow!"

I paused, my back to them, as a thought crossed my mind.

I shouldn't.

There was no reason for it.

"I wish I could," I said, turning back. "But my friend who just called me…crazy as it sounds…just bought tickets for me to go to a concert with her and her daughter tomorrow night, and we'll need to head out early. That's what she was calling to tell me. As if *I* should be going to a Ryan Hooks concert," I said with a small laugh.

They all chuckled, and a few comments were tossed around about his songs, a recent appearance on *E!*, and hopes that I would see the other half of his celeb power couple.

"Bevvy loves Tiffane. She's always going on about how beautiful she is," Andrew said, and then he looked up at me. "Oh, sorry, that's my wife."

I smiled and nodded and then turned to leave, but not before letting my gaze settle on Emma, just for a moment.

She did a pretty good job of keeping her face neutral and matching her friends' expressions of polite interest. The corners of her mouth were turned upward slightly, and she nodded and muttered along with the rest of them. She still maintained her perfect posture, her shoulders pulled back and square, her chin slightly raised.

An outside observer would think she cared not a bit more and not a bit less than anyone else in the group.

But an outside observer doesn't know faces.

Not like I do.

Behind the coolness of her steady gaze and unaffected smile, I could see something else.

Emma, with the perfectly styled hair, perfect manicure, and perfect style, was uncomfortable.

Really uncomfortable.

And I was the only one who knew why.

CHAPTER 7

Claire
The Night in Question

MS. EMMA BENTLEY?"

Claire watched the woman with the short blond bob as she swayed back and forth in her kitchen. Emma's arms were crossed in front of her chest, and her gaze was trained on the floor.

"Ms. Bentley?" she said again. "I'm Detective Claire Puhl. I need to ask you a few questions."

Emma blinked a couple of times and then looked up at the detective standing in the entryway.

"Yes," she finally said, her voice breathy and low. "Yes, of course."

Her shoulders were slumped forward, her eyes red and puffy, and she clutched a piece of tissue in her hand. She raised it, wiping at her nose in a small, delicate motion that for some reason felt more symbolic than functional. Claire had a sense that Emma Bentley wasn't the kind of woman who wiped away snot in public, no matter how tragic the circumstances. As if to support that suspicion, Emma sniffled politely and then turned and walked to the kitchen table, where she pulled out a chair and sat down. She reached out a hand and gestured toward one of the other seats.

"Thank you," Claire said, walking over to join her and pulling out a chair. "Am I right that you own this building?"

"Yes," Emma said. "My father left it to me when he passed away three years ago. My younger sister lives downstairs."

Claire nodded and wrote a note. "Her name?"

"Meggie. Megan Bentley, but everyone calls her Meggie."

"She was at your party tonight as well?"

"Yes," Emma said. As she spoke, she began to tap her finger against the kitchen table, a quick, nervous motion.

"You told the responding officer that Beverly Brighton was also here at some point this evening."

"Yes," Emma said again. "She was."

"How well did you know her?"

Emma frowned as if the question surprised her. "How well did I know her? Bev was one of my closest friends."

Claire nodded. "So you were just having a little get-together for your sister and friend?"

"No, Meggie's boyfriend, Patrick, was here too, and so was Andrew, Bev's husband…" She paused. "How is he? I should go up and see him."

"I don't think right now is a good time. He's getting some medical help at the moment."

Emma leaned forward, and suddenly, a sob racked her body, her entire frame shaking as she rested her forearms on the table in front of her. "I just can't believe it."

"I'm sorry," Claire said, leaning back in her chair and waiting a few moments for Emma to compose herself. "Were you celebrating something special?"

When the sobs subsided, Emma spoke again. "Well, no… I mean, yes… Well, sort of. We have a family clothing line, and we're going to be launching our spring collection at Klein's in July.

The owner, Joshua Burlap—he was here as well. The dinner was sort of last-minute. I just wanted to have a few people over to celebrate. I like to host and... I don't know, it wasn't anything huge."

Claire took a note. "When did Beverly and her husband move in upstairs?"

"Two years ago," Emma replied. "They're perfect tenants. Quiet and respectful. Bev and I started having each other over for dinner and drinks and became really fast friends. She's a lawyer, and when I needed some legal advice for the company, she was the obvious choice."

"What time did Beverly arrive at your party tonight?"

Emma used her palm to dab at her eyes and then sat up straighter. "Um, I can't really remember. Maybe around seven thirty? We ate dinner around eight, and she wasn't here that long before that. She had been at the office earlier today."

"On a Saturday?"

"Bev worked all the time," she said. "The firm was her life."

"What time did she leave?"

"Oh, wow, I don't know," Emma said, looking down at her hands for a moment. "Maybe around twelve? She was one of the first people to leave. Said she was feeling tired."

"And the last guest?"

"My sister and Patrick were the last ones here. They left at about twelve forty-five."

"What did you do after that?"

"I cleaned up a little and then went to bed. I'll be honest, I had a bit of wine," she said. "I didn't wake up again until I heard all the commotion out in the hallway."

"Did anything seem out of the ordinary to you tonight? With Beverly or anyone else at the party?"

Emma frowned, and her eyes narrowed as she jerked back in her chair. "What do you mean out of the ordinary? Wait, you don't think that someone who was here tonight did this, do you?"

Claire put her pen down. "I'm just trying to get a sense of every-thing that happened tonight," she said. Emma didn't say anything else for a few moments, and Claire spoke again. "Ms. Bentley?"

"Oh, no," she said. "No, nothing stood out. We ate, we had a nice time, and everyone went home."

"Okay, I think that's enough for now," Claire said, pushing back her chair and standing up. She took a look around the kitchen, sur-veying the room. It was tidy, with very little evidence that there had been a dinner party there that night aside from a few large foil pans stacked on top of the trash can. Claire walked over to the door to the back porch and looked at it. Pulling a cloth from her pocket, she tried the doorknob and saw that it was locked, then checked the dead bolt.

"Did you leave your apartment at any time tonight?" she asked.

"Sorry?"

"I know you had guests coming and going. But did you leave your apartment? Either through this back door or the front?"

Emma frowned, standing up and walking closer to the back door where Claire was standing. "No," she said. "Why do you ask?"

"I don't want you to be alarmed, but I'm just trying to figure out how someone might have gotten into the building and attacked Mrs. Brighton."

"I thought they said the back door was broken into."

"It was," Claire said. "But I've been doing this long enough to know that the first and most obvious answer is not always the right one. I just want to make sure there's no other way the person who did this could've gotten in."

"Wait," Emma said, the frown on her face deepening. "Are you saying...you think someone came in through the back porch, walked through my apartment while I was *sleeping*, and..." She trailed off, her voice catching, and she put a hand on her stomach. "I think I'm going to be sick."

"I'm not saying that happened," Claire said. "I'm just trying to rule out all possibilities."

Emma swallowed and then shook her head. "I don't think so," she said. "A few people went out to smoke after dinner. When they came back in, I locked the door from the inside. I remember it."

"One more question," Claire said. "What was Beverly's relationship with her husband like? Any problems you know of?"

"With Andrew?" Emma asked incredulously. "No, absolutely not. He adores her. He would never…" She shook her head.

"Is there anyone else you know who might have had a problem with Beverly?"

Emma hesitated, and Claire took a step forward.

"Any information you have is helpful, Ms. Bentley."

"Well, she did have a little…" She shook her head and looked down at her hands. "I shouldn't."

"Please, Mrs. Bentley."

She sighed and looked up. "Look, I don't think it means anything, so I probably shouldn't even bring it up, but she did have a little issue with Patrick a couple of months ago."

"Patrick?"

"My sister's boyfriend."

"Oh yes," Claire said, nodding. "What do you mean, 'an issue'?"

Emma's shoulders slumped. "Patrick does some work in the building. He does odd jobs here and there. In April, Bev said that she had some stuff that went missing one afternoon when he was in her apartment working on her ceiling fan."

"What kind of stuff?"

"A necklace she got from her grandmother and a pair of earrings."

"He denied it?"

"Yeah, of course," she said. "But Patrick has a bit of a temper. He blew up at her once at another get-together. I don't think he's ever gotten over it."

"Did you see them interact tonight?"

Emma stared at Claire and bit her bottom lip. "No," she said. "Look, there are a lot of things I could tell you about my sister's boyfriend that aren't really relevant to what happened to tonight. I wouldn't go so far as to say he could've done that to Beverly," she said. "But I will say that he has a temper, especially when it comes to issues having to do with money. I've seen it with my sister. He's a bad influence on her."

"Okay," Claire said. "Thanks for being so candid. I think your sister is still out in the living room. I'm going to go grab a few moments with her."

Emma nodded and followed her out of the kitchen. The apartment looked exactly the way a Gold Coast apartment should look: soft, tan furniture with black accents and well-placed, minimalist art that gave the room a museum-like feel. The room was slightly perfumed, with the smell of lavender or jasmine that didn't seem to have come out of a can or candle. The *air* in the room felt expensive.

As they walked into the living room, they both looked up as an investigator near the couch bent over to pick something up, a frown on her face.

"What is it?" Claire asked.

The woman stood up and lifted a woman's shoe in the air. It was a red high-heeled pump with a delicate gold buckle at the heel.

Claire walked over to the couch and leaned closer, examining the shoe. From a distance, it had looked well-made and expensive, but from here, she could see that the sole was made of cheap fake leather, and the shoe was fraying near the heel. She was no expert, but she would bet that the pair hadn't cost more than thirty bucks.

"Does this belong to you?" Claire asked, turning back to look at Emma Bentley.

Emma scrunched her face and shook her head. A moment later, her eyes widened. "Oh, that's Chris's shoe!" she said with a slight grimace. "Sorry. I really don't know what's wrong with me. There was one more guest tonight, a friend of mine named Chris. She's an artist."

Claire frowned. "Okay," she said slowly. "And what time did she leave?"

Emma scrunched up her face. "It had to be around twelve thirty. It was before you left, right, Meggie?"

Claire looked over to see a petite woman with bright-pink hair sitting on the couch, her hands folded in her lap.

Meggie nodded. "Yeah, me and Patrick were the last ones here."

Claire tried not to show her impatience. "Anyone else you're missing? Anyone else here tonight?"

"Besides the catering crew, no."

"There was a catering team?"

"Just two people," she said. "From Daphne's in Lincolnwood. I can give you their number if you'd like. But they left right after dinner ended, so I don't think they'll be of much help." She paused and looked at the shoe, which was being placed in an evidence bag. "I can't imagine how Chris could've left her shoe here."

Meggie laughed, a rough, humorless sound that seemed odd for someone with bright-pink hair. "I can," she said. "Did you *see* that woman? I don't know if I've ever seen someone drink so much in my entire life. I'm surprised she managed to take her head home with her, let alone her shoes. Maybe that'll teach you about hiring random strangers you meet on the street."

"Random strangers?" Claire asked, looking back and forth between the two women. "On the street? What are you talking about?"

"She is *not* a random stranger," Emma said with a sigh. "She's an artist who's hopefully going to be doing some work for us for the fashion show."

"Who you literally met five days ago," Meggie said.

Claire walked over to the couch and sat down next to Meggie. "I'll need her information too. Did she interact with Mrs. Brighton very much tonight?"

"Not that I noticed," Emma said. "Oh, and I don't actually have her info."

Claire and Meggie responded at the same time.

"What?"

"Why not?"

Emma shrugged. "I gave her my number at the park the other day, and she was supposed to text me so that I had hers, but she never did. And she already knew where I lived, so it wasn't that big of a deal."

Claire frowned. "Okay," she said. "Before I leave tonight, I need you to tell me absolutely everything you can remember about this artist named Chris."

CHAPTER 8

Paula

Four days before

G REENWAY FIELD IS A massive, modern concert-and-event venue twenty-three miles south of Chicago in an otherwise dusty town called Prairie Hills. I'd been there once before when I had won tickets on the radio to the station's annual Summer Soul Fest, and I'd dragged Vanessa along with me.

This was different. As we pulled into the congested parking lot, Vanessa cursed out loud and leaned forward, peering at the woman in bright yellow who was directing the carloads of eager fans.

"Where the hell does she want me to go?" she asked, squinting at the woman. "She is literally pointing in both directions!"

"That's the universal sign for it's up to you, Mom," Vanessa's thirteen-year-old daughter, Jen, said from the back seat.

I turned my head to look at her and smiled as she rolled her eyes.

For a woman with very few filters, Vanessa tended to drive like a student driver, something Jen constantly gave her grief about.

Releasing her grip from the ten and two positions, Vanessa chose the aisle on the right and turned in to find a space. We parked and began the trek across the parking lot, which was really just a big, open field with some ropes that added little order to the chaos. Around us, hordes of people shuffled along toward the structure that loomed in front of us with the promise of one thing only— hours of pure pop fun/torture, depending on why you were there. Groups of teenage girls squealed in delight as parents walked along behind them like zombies. Not for the first time, I wondered what I was doing there.

I'd been toying around with the idea of asking for a reward ever since Vanessa had told me about the concert tickets. It seemed ridiculous, yet there was a part of me that couldn't shake it, couldn't help but wonder what he'd say if I just *asked*.

I'd seen them that night.

I knew what he'd done, and how much he didn't want his wife to know.

And the phone was my evidence.

As we walked through security, I was surprised to see that the excitement on Vanessa's face seemed to rival that of her daughter. I shouldn't have been so surprised after her reaction in the bathroom when I told her about Ryan Hooks or when we found his phone in the trunk of my car. I had been shocked when she told me about the tickets, but I was a little excited too. I knew I shouldn't be. He was a celebrity who was cheating on his wife. *Of course*, he'd flirted with me. He'd probably flirt with a spoon, if the circumstances were right.

Still, I wanted to see him again, wanted to be in the same room with him, and, for some strange reason I couldn't explain, wanted him to know that I *knew*.

I knew something no one else in the entire auditorium knew except him.

We had a secret.

Twenty minutes later, we were settled in our seats in the second balcony. They weren't quite nosebleeds, but we'd be doing most of our watching on the jumbo screens. The opening acts were a blur—a group of four girls shaking what their mamas hadn't quite given them yet, and then a young boy who couldn't have been more than fourteen years old, crooning about the one who got away. I turned to Vanessa.

"What got away, his video game remote?"

She laughed, and Jen shot us a look, one that said we didn't deserve to be there if we didn't take it more seriously.

There was an intermission of about twenty minutes after the second opening act. The dim lights came up, and groups of teenage girls linked arms in search of the bathroom or snacks.

Jen was on social media with her friends.

Vanessa leaned over and smiled. "What do you think these girls would do if they found out you had Ryan Hooks's cell phone in your purse right now?" she asked. "Think they'd mob you?"

"Probably," I said, looking around nervously. "And don't say that so loud."

She shrugged. "It's not like they'd be able to get into it, since it's locked."

"You think that would stop me from getting mobbed?"

"No, you're probably right." She smiled. "I'm sure he'll be happy to have it back, though. Who knows what's on it?"

I frowned. "Have it back?"

She turned to me. "Well, yeah, isn't that why you brought it? I thought you were going to give it back and maybe even see about that big ole reward," she said.

I laughed nervously. "That was just a joke," I said. "Besides, what are we going to do, wait outside his tour bus?"

"Nah, we'll get backstage."

She said it so simply and so confidently that I laughed. I was about to respond when there was a loud crashing sound, and then the lights in the arena began to shut off, one area at a time, in perfect rhythm with a slow and steady drumbeat. Immediately, the crowd erupted in screams. I looked over at Vanessa, but she'd turned back to the stage in excitement, her face a mirror image of her daughter's.

Here we go.

Lights appeared on the stage, and there were silhouettes of four band members. The crowd went even wilder. The band started to play, and the lights came on slowly. The melody was familiar, something I'd heard on the radio while driving at night. Not the song I'd heard with Lotti but something else. I couldn't help but sway with the crowd. It went on for a few minutes, and then a few more, and just as the crowd began to get weary, there was another cymbal crash, and I heard a voice.

"Chicago, are y'all ready?"

Deep, buttery, and warm.

Lotti.

The entire room exploded, but apparently, it wasn't enough.

"I don't think you are, so let me ask again. Chicago, are you ready?"

The screams were so loud that I actually had to put my hands over my ears for a moment to block out the noise. My breath caught in my chest as we all waited, the anticipation of simply *seeing* another human being much higher than it should be.

And then, Ryan Hooks *wiggled* out onto the stage.

It was the best way to describe the gyrating motion as he slithered out in front of the crowd of screaming, mostly teenage fans. Vanessa and Jen actually clutched each other, and I wondered what could make it okay for a thirty-six-year-old woman and her thirteen-year-old daughter to be losing their minds over the same man.

He danced to the center of the stage, lifted his hands high over his head, and clapped them twice.

"One, two, three, four!"

The song that started was another one I'd heard before. I didn't know the name, but I'd heard it enough times to know most of the words, and as he started, I joined the chorus of people singing along with him.

When it finished, Ryan stared out at the crowd for a few moments, soaking in the screams. Adjusting his earpiece, he yelled out, "What's up, Chicago?"

The crowd exploded again.

"I want to let you know—and believe me, I don't say this everywhere I go—I am so excited to be here in Chicago. It's one of my favorite cities in the world, and not just because the audience is always so good-looking!"

The crowd erupted again, and I couldn't help but roll my eyes.

"Nice one," Vanessa said to me, and I laughed.

Hooks talked for a few minutes, almost every other line stopping to allow for more screams. Finally, he clapped his hands again and launched into another song, and then another. For a while, I was transported. I forgot about the phone, Keith, and everything else besides the music and the crowd and the excitement of sharing the experience with a concert hall full of strangers.

I was having fun.

I felt a tap on my arm, and then Vanessa leaned closed to me. "Be right back," she said.

I nodded. "Bathroom?"

She shook her head and winked. "Nope."

She slid past me and walked out of the aisle.

Jen moved closer to me. "She's trying to get us backstage, you know," she said.

I smiled and nodded.

Jen shrugged. "Hope it works."

I smiled again, surprised at how perceptive and composed Jen was for her age.

As Ryan Hooks continued to belt out song after song, I felt that he was looking through the crowds directly at me. I knew that it was impossible, but I watched him from our balcony and imagined that he could see me, swaying along in the background.

What the hell are you doing here, Paula?

As I listened to the next couple of songs, I stepped outside of myself and watched me, standing there swaying back and forth with Ryan's cell phone in my purse.

Like a creep. I'd officially crossed the line of pathetic. I'd once read a story about a fan who'd stolen a celebrity's burger off his plate at a restaurant, right after he'd taken a bite, and I remembered thinking it was an incredibly low moment for that fan.

I was just a step or two above the burger thief.

I'd take the phone back home and sell it online like I'd planned to. Ryan probably had another one by now anyway. The phone would be wiped clean and sold again. I would make a few bucks and treat the whole experience as a fun dinner party story to tell when the mood hit me.

That's what I would do.

But then, as if she could sense what I was thinking, Vanessa was back at my side, placing her hand on my back as she slid into the aisle next to her daughter. Even with the loud music and cheering fans, I heard Jen's squeal as her mother said something to her and then turned back to me.

"Wow, that's still as fun as it used to be," she said.

"What did you do?"

She winked and looked back at the stage for a moment, then lifted her hands high above her head and screamed.

"We love you, Ryan!"

It was drowned out in the roar of the crowd. She turned and smiled.

"We're in. After the show, we're going to see a cutie named Brien, with an *e*, and he's going to let us backstage."

"What?" I asked as a drumbeat started up for one of the final songs. "How did you—"

Vanessa shook her head and raised a hand.

"Don't ask questions you don't want the answer to," she said, then she took a peek over her shoulder. "But no, really, I'll tell you later."

When the lights finally came on, the massive crowds began to stream out of the auditorium. We grabbed our things and followed Vanessa as she moved out of the aisle and toward the exits.

"This way," she said.

Jen and I followed closely on her heels. We navigated the crowds of exhausted fans, and I pushed down the nerves that were coursing through my body. Were we really going to get to meet him? Would he recognize me, and if so, what would he say?

What would *I* say?

We took a long loop around the stadium, and I wondered if we were going in circles.

I looked up and saw that we were approaching the C wing, and there were a scattering of people standing next to the entrance, directing people back the way we'd come. Vanessa looked back at us and gestured with her head.

"Come on," she said and grabbed her daughter's hand.

I followed, my throat dry and hands clammy.

What are we doing?

Vanessa walked up to a tall, skinny security guard who looked like he couldn't have been more than twenty-two. He smiled as he saw her approach.

"Hey, the pierogi lady," he said. "Thanks for the recipe. I'm making it for my mom this weekend."

Vanessa peeked back at me with a smile, then turned to face the guard. "No problem. This is my best friend, Paula, and my daughter, Jen, who I was telling you about."

"Nice to meet you, ladies," he said. He looked down at Jen. "Your mom is awesome!"

We all laughed and thanked him before scurrying past him and down the long hall of the C wing.

"Pierogis?" I whispered as we walked along. "That was the super-secret thing you couldn't tell me about in front of Jen?"

"Figured I'd let your imagination have a little fun with it," she said with a smirk.

We turned a corner, and then we were walking through a large, open space that was filled on either side with concert equipment, chairs, and other supplies. There were a lot of people there, all moving around with purpose, and I waited for someone to ask who we were or what we were doing there. A tall man with a clipboard walked in our direction, and when he saw us, he smiled. "That way," he said, pointing around another corner.

Vanessa, Jen, and I looked at each other and then walked quickly in that direction. As we turned, we all groaned.

In front of us, there was a line of at least forty or so fans, standing in groups and pairs, leaning to look at the front of the room. We couldn't see what was going on at the front, but it was clear we were in the right place.

"Apparently, you weren't the only one with a recipe to share," I said.

"At least in my case, it really was just a recipe," she said, looking disappointed.

"I'm sure it'll move fast," Jen said.

I once again had to admire her determination.

We joined the back of the line and waited.

The line did move quickly, and in a couple of minutes, we were halfway up the wall. I stood on my toes and let out a gasp when I saw the scene at the front.

"There!" I said.

Vanessa and Jen craned their necks.

"Oh my God!" Jen said, clutching her heart.

He was standing there, right at the front of the room, taking a photo with a group of girls young enough to be his daughters. One was in tears, and the others beamed like it was their wedding day.

I couldn't believe it. In another few minutes, I'd be right there beside Lotti, with his phone in my purse.

Would he recognize me?

Did I even want him to?

The line moved forward again, and then again, and suddenly, we were next in line.

I had a brief moment of panic. What if I hadn't put his phone on silent and it rang? What if he recognized the ringtone? I'd never heard it before. Maybe it was something unique. I swallowed, resisting the urge to take it out and check. I hadn't looked at it since Vanessa and I had found it in the trunk; chances were the battery had died by now anyway.

Right?

"You okay?" Vanessa asked.

I looked over and nodded.

"Okay, next," the stern woman standing next to Ryan said.

Vanessa, Jen, and I stepped forward.

And just like that, I was face-to-face with Ryan Hooks.

He looked at us, and I held my breath. But he smiled, the way he had with everyone in the line, and then held up his hand for high fives.

"Hey, ladies," he said. "Thanks so much for coming to the show. What are your names?"

"Vanessa."

"Jen."

I swallowed. I couldn't very well lie in front of them. "Paula."

"Well, Vanessa, Jen, and Paula, did you like the show?"

"It was amazing," Jen said quickly, and she launched forward with her phone. "Could we get a picture?"

"Of course," he said. "In fact, I'll take it." He took the phone from her, and we all crowded around him. He reached out his hand to take the selfie, and I squeezed in close to him. He smelled good, like expensive cologne, and I was surprised he didn't smell like sweat after all the dancing he'd done for the past hour and a half.

"Thanks again," Vanessa said, and she and Jen both leaned over to examine the picture.

I was standing right next to him, and there was a line of fans just a few feet away from us, waiting for their chance to come up and get their selfie with him. I could've just ended it there, could have leaned in to look at the picture and then walked away, following behind Vanessa and Jen, as I was supposed to.

But as I stood there beside him awkwardly, I was overwhelmed with the feeling that I had to do something, to say something, or accept that I let the opportunity get away from me.

"Really great show," I said.

He smiled at me. "Thank you so much. You guys are the best," he said, the words falling out of his mouth quickly, and I knew he'd said the sentence a hundred times already that night.

I bit my lip.

Do it.

Just say it.

"Almost worth battling through the hordes of prepubescent fans."

He didn't respond immediately. He blinked, and the perfect smile fell from his face for just a second, and then, for the first time since we had walked up to him, he truly looked at me.

"Sorry?"

I smiled but didn't repeat myself.

He frowned, examining my face. "Do I know you?"

I shook my head a little and smiled, but now he was really looking at me, eyes locked, and he squinted as if that would help him out. I saw the recognition dawn, and then he spoke quietly.

"The DAC driver?"

I froze, and it wasn't until then that I realized that I hadn't really expected him to know who I was.

"It is you, isn't it?" he asked.

I saw something flitter across his face. Concern? Fear?

It reminded me of the night I'd dropped him off on Oak Street and the way he'd looked back at me to see if I was watching him as he stared up at Emma in the window. For a moment, I was transported, staring at him in the moonlight, Emma's silhouette looking down on us.

"How about that?" I heard Hooks say, and I was jolted back to the present. He was watching me with a slight, nervous smile. "I didn't think you recognized me! Were you just messing with me that night?"

"I…uh…"

He stepped closer and looped an arm around my shoulder, lowering his voice.

"Hey, quick question. I've been meaning to contact DAC. You

didn't see my phone, did you? I haven't been able to find it since that night."

"Oh...uh...well..." I fumbled and trailed off, looking over at Vanessa and Jen, who were still bent over their phones, examining the pictures we'd just taken.

The line of excited fans seemed to be growing, and they all stared at Ryan and me. I wondered what was going through their minds about why he had his arm looped over my shoulders.

"Uh..."

"Did you see it?"

My tongue was a big hunk of sandpaper, and I wasn't sure what to say, since I didn't know exactly what I wanted.

"Yes," I blurted out.

His eyes widened. "Really?" he asked. "That's awesome." He waited a moment, and when I didn't say anything else, he stepped even closer. "Uh, do you...have it?"

"Um, not with me," I lied, and I cleared my throat. "I guess I was wondering, is...is there any kind of...reward?"

It was as if I'd just picked up a brick, lifted it into the air, and smashed it into the side of his face.

He froze, his mouth wide open, and all the playfulness that had been in his eyes a moment before disappeared. He looked up to see who was nearby and then lowered his voice again.

"Are you kidding?" he asked. "No, there's no reward."

The anger was instant, visceral, and it made me take a step back. He covered it quickly, but I could still see it in his eyes. We stood there for a few moments more.

And then, something changed.

When I first asked the question, it really had just been a question, one that had been brewing in the back of my mind since Vanessa and I stood outside my car and held the phone in our hands.

It stayed there, festering as I walked in the park and shook the hand of his mistress, as I watched him swaying onstage.

But it hadn't really registered until now as I stood across from him, waiting for him to respond.

I didn't realize what I was doing until I held his gaze, my breath coming out in short, audible pants, my fists curled up at my side.

I wasn't asking him.

I was telling him.

I felt it, and I think he felt it too, because I stared at him steadily, and then his eyes narrowed.

"You sure about that?" I asked, feeling more in control of anything than I had in the past twelve months. "The woman you went to meet on Saturday—I'm guessing there are a few pics of her on there that you wouldn't want anyone to know about."

His eyes widened, and then he ground his jaw as he stared at me angrily.

"You bitch," he hissed.

I think he was about to say something else when the woman holding the clipboard suddenly yelled out, "Next!"

I backed up into Vanessa and Jen, and then we were being hurried away.

Ryan stuttered, as if he wanted to stop us, but then he looked out at the crowd of people watching us.

Watching him.

I could still see the fury in his eyes as we were ushered out of the room.

CHAPTER 9

I SETTLED INTO THE BACK seat of Vanessa's car as she pulled into line to leave the parking lot. The cars pointed in every direction, the headlights so bright, it felt like daytime. We inched along, one car at a time, and I was grateful that I was not the one driving. Vanessa was crouched up against the steering wheel, like usual, squinting at the back of the red SUV she was tailing.

"I swear to you, if anyone tries to get in between us, they're losing a headlight," she said, braking hard as the red car stopped suddenly.

I drummed my fingers against my leg. I had just done the most insane thing I'd ever done in my life—told someone, to his face, that I was blackmailing him—and now here we were, *stuck* in the parking lot where I'd committed my crime. I had visions of Hooks running clear across the lot, his security team in tow, and ripping open the door to drag me out.

I took a deep breath.

Certainly, any one of the fans in the parking lot would've held on to Ryan Hooks's phone if they had it. But would they be considering what I was considering—finding a way to force Ryan Hooks to pay me for what I knew?

I heard a giggle from the front seat, and then Jen squealed.

"I already have forty-seven likes on Instagram!" she said.

Vanessa braked hard again, turning to look at her daughter. "Do you even know forty-seven people?"

"Yeah, Mom," Jen said.

I zoned out and stared out the window. I could still see Ryan's face as I followed Vanessa and Jen out of the meet-and-greet area.

I'd lucked out with the element of surprise. He'd wanted to say something, to stop me, but there were just too many people around. Too much risk in calling attention to something that he didn't want anyone else to know about. As I'd floated away in the crowd, he'd watched me, the polished smile that he'd poured on his fans rusting over. The anger that had flashed in his eyes had sent a chill through my body, and I had the strong sense Ryan Hooks wasn't used to people not following his directions.

"Hello back there," I heard Vanessa say in a singsong voice, and I looked back toward the front of the car. She was staring at me in the rearview mirror with her eyebrows raised. "You alive?"

"Yeah," I said. "Sorry."

"It's okay. I think we're all a little spacey after that."

I thought back to the moment when Hooks and I had stood there, staring at each other, and the calmness I'd felt asking him for the reward.

I didn't know where the confidence had come from.

But I liked it.

I heard a noise, something loud and unfamiliar, and I frowned when I felt my purse vibrating. Unzipping it, I reached inside, my heart skipping a beat when I saw that it wasn't my phone that was ringing.

It was Ryan's.

Vanessa had finally reached the edge of the parking lot, and she turned onto the main road, which was packed, given the concert traffic. As she merged into the left lane to get on the highway, I heard Jen laugh out loud.

"You changed your ringtone to 'Love River'?" she asked.

I paused as I pulled the phone out of my purse. It took me a moment, but I recognized the melody as one of the songs we'd heard at the concert.

Ryan's wallpaper was a picture of himself and his wife.

Normal.

His ringtone was one of his own songs.

A step too far.

"Uh, yeah," I said. "Wanted to get in the right spirit before the show."

Vanessa was too busy merging into traffic, and she didn't seem to notice what had just happened. She and Jen had been so caught up looking at their pictures that she probably thought I'd given the phone back, and I wanted to keep it that way. No use getting her involved in my stupid decision. I turned the phone over and clicked the button on the side to shut off the ringer. Then I looked back at the screen.

The person calling was named Ray. I bit my lip, and my heart raced as I watched his name flash a few times before finally ending. A moment later, the phone lit up again, and Ray's name returned.

He was calling back. I swallowed. It had to be Hooks, calling from a friend's phone. Someone who was with him in the pavilion or on the tour bus, cursing the crazy fan who'd just quietly black-mailed him in front of a horde of people. I waited again for it to stop ringing and then tossed it into my purse.

"Which was your favorite song?" I heard Jen say, and she pivoted in her chair to look at me.

I blinked and then frowned, trying to rack my brain. "Uh, I don't know. It's hard to pick," I said, my mind racing. "What was yours?"

"Probably 'Out of Time.' I've heard it so many times, but it was so amazing to hear him sing it live." She squealed and put her head in her hands. "I just can't believe we met him in person!"

Vanessa pulled onto the highway, and we were finally on our way home. I let out a long breath. There was no caravan of police cars tracking us down and pulling us over to recover the phone. With the glow of the concert traffic dying down, the darkness descended on the car, and we were all silent for a few miles, lost in our own thoughts.

Vanessa was turning onto my block when I heard another noise from my purse. I winced and opened it, fumbling around with the items inside. After a few moments of searching, I recognized the noise as my own ringtone and let out a sigh of relief.

It didn't last long, though. As I pulled it out of my purse, I saw that it was a number I didn't recognize. A local number.

Could it be Hooks?

Could he have found a way to get my phone number that quickly? I silenced it so as not to disturb Jen, who'd been dozing off in the front seat. Then I stared at the phone number as it flashed over and over.

Please don't be him.

Please don't be him.

I answered the phone on the last ring, deepening my voice a little in case I needed to say "wrong number" and hang up.

"Hello?"

"Hi, is this Paula Wileson?"

Please don't be him.

Please.

"Yes, it is," I said slowly, and all the probable excuses began to float on the tip of my tongue.

My husband and I really need the money.

If you just pay it, I won't tell.

This isn't like me, I promise.

I wouldn't do this if I didn't absolutely have to.

"Mrs. Wileson, this is Dr. Jane Christensen at Northwestern Memorial Hospital. I am calling about your husband, Keith. There has been an accident."

And just like that, it was lights out.

I didn't really faint.

The breath was sucked out of my body so quickly that I gasped out loud. My vision blurred, and my stomach immediately cramped up. All these symptoms together made it hard for me to remain upright. I slumped to one side, my face pressed against the window, which was surprisingly cool given the warm air outside. The doctor continued to shell out words, so many *bad* words, that I wanted to fling the phone away in protest. Words like *collapsed* and *IV* and *monitoring*.

As I listened, I thought of the other telephone in my purse, glaring up at me, and I could almost feel the smugness that emanated from it.

You brought this on yourself!

You deserve it!

The doctor continued to speak for a few moments, and I listened, somewhere between defeat and disbelief. At some point, I forced myself to lean forward and speak to Vanessa, who was silently staring out at the road in front of her.

"Northwestern Memorial," I said softly, only because I had no energy to raise my voice. "We need to go there. Please. Now."

Vanessa jerked and looked up at me in the rearview mirror, a frown on her face. "What?"

"It's Keith."

She didn't say anything else, and a moment later, we were hurtling through the streets toward downtown Chicago. We hit a bit of traffic once we crossed into the South Loop, and that brought on a panic that burned deep down in my core. I watched the brake lights of the cars around me, and I *hated* them for standing in the way of me getting to the hospital. Vanessa did her best, dodging around cars and bikers like a pro.

We burst through the emergency room doors fifteen minutes later. As we walked inside, Jen's head was down, tears in her eyes. I walked next to her, my entire body shaking so hard, it hurt. Vanessa led the way, talking to the attendants at the front desk, finding a spot for Jen to sit down and wait, and speaking to the young doctor who came out to greet us.

"You can come with me," the doctor said to me.

Vanessa turned to look back at her daughter, who was sitting alone shivering in the waiting room.

"Do you want me to come too?" she asked.

I shook my head. "I'll be okay," I said, turning to follow the doctor. "Thank you, Ness."

It was all too much. It all seemed to be happening in slow motion, painfully reminiscent of the day when I'd been called in after the accident. I'd been in this exact position before—not the same hospital or the same doctor, but I'd been here. I'd been here before, once, which was one time too many. I didn't know if I could do it again.

Vanessa and Jen stayed back in the waiting room, and I followed the doctor down a long, sterile hall. She was walking quickly, with purpose, and I struggled to keep up, my legs feeling like jelly beneath me.

She stopped halfway down the hall and turned to look at me.

"Mrs. Wileson?" she said, staring at me. "Are you all right?"

She frowned when I didn't respond and then guided me backward toward a chair and helping me down into it. "Hey, can you do me a favor and grab me a bottle of water?" she asked a nurse walking by, and the woman nodded. The doctor leaned forward and put a hand on my shoulder.

I blinked and looked up at her. I wanted to scream that of course I wasn't all right. I was scared and tired and guilty, but I was not, by any stretch of the imagination, all right.

I didn't say any of that, of course, and just shook my head.

"Last time…" was all I managed to get out.

She stepped in front of me and looked into my face, realization dawning on her own. She spoke slowly, with what felt like trained patience, and placed a hand on my arm.

"Mrs. Wileson, you do know that your husband is fine, right? That he's absolutely okay?"

"What?" I said, my mind reeling back to the phone call in the back of Vanessa's car, the conversation she'd had with the nurses in the ER. None of the words they'd said had really sunken in after *hospital*, and I blinked, watching the woman in front of me.

"Your husband is okay," she said, and she turned as the other woman reappeared with a bottle of water. The doctor unscrewed it and handed it to me. As I took a sip, I suddenly had the feeling that someone had said those same words to me before in the past half hour, but it hadn't actually registered. She knelt down in front of me, and I suddenly felt silly, like I was creating a scene, another patient for them to take care of. "He lost consciousness at the swim meet, and we've determined that it was due to dehydration. He's okay."

"But last time…" I said again.

She shook her head. "I can only imagine," she said, her hand still on my arm. "But this is nothing like last time. Here, let's go in to see him. I think that'll make you feel a lot better."

She stepped back and allowed me to walk into the hospital room. It was small and cramped, and there was a curtain drawn in the middle of the room that hid a patient on the other side. Keith was looking up at the ceiling as I walked in, and he turned toward me when he heard the sound at the door. We locked eyes, and I knew instantly that what the doctor had said was both true and untrue.

He would be fine, but he was not okay.

I walked closer to the bed and swallowed, struggling to keep the tears in check. He looked so small, lying there in the hospital bed, barely filling it up. I hadn't noticed that he'd lost weight, but here, in this sterile, white space against the backdrop of equipment that kept track of his every breath, he seemed to get swallowed up, and I could tell that he'd dropped at least ten pounds.

I took his hand, and he looked up at me, the sadness in his eyes making my heart break.

"Are you okay?" I asked, and I leaned forward. He didn't speak. I could hear snoring from the other side of the curtain, and I leaned closer. "Keith?"

He opened his mouth, and then his face crumpled.

It took me a moment to react, because it wasn't something I'd ever seen before. Not once. At most, I'd seen a tear roll down his cheek and settle in the stubble of his beard. At his grandfather's funeral a few years back, he'd held his head in his hands for a long time and stared stoically at the floor while others sobbed around him.

"I'm not a crier," he'd said during one of our early dates, over drinks. "I guess it's just not how I process things."

"Did you cry as a baby?"

"Yes, Paula. I cried as a baby. I'm not a psychopath."

I had laughed and shrugged, twirling my martini glass between my fingers. "I'm just asking…"

Now, as I stood next to his hospital bed and his face scrunched up in the way faces do when they're about to explode into sobs, I was frozen, unable to process what was happening. I knew how much his return to the swim team had meant to him, but I didn't know how to handle his reaction. As the tears began to stream down his cheeks, I finally snapped out of it and moved closer, bringing my arms around his shaking body.

"Babe," I said. "It's okay."

And it was in that moment, as I quietly breathed in his sorrow in that shared hospital room, that I thought about the phone that was buried in my purse.

The one that might be dead by now but, if not, probably had several more missed calls from a famous pop star on it.

I thought about what Vanessa had said—there *should* be a reward for keeping quiet about what I'd seen that night. And for whatever evidence, given Hooks's reaction earlier that night, was undoubtedly on his phone.

A $180,000 reward.

I thought about Tiffane's promise that she would leave Ryan the minute she heard even a whisper about another woman. And I pictured the woman from the park—*Emma*—and her face when I'd mentioned that I'd be going to see Ryan Hooks.

It was right then that I knew what I would do.

"It's going to be okay," I said again, and I pulled back and looked into Keith's face. I cleared my throat. "Actually, I have some good news."

He looked up at me and wiped at his eyes before taking a few long, slow breaths. "What is it?" he asked.

"The la-di-d'artists," I said with a smile, swallowing as the lie began to form in the back of my throat. "They've decided to make you the primary recipient of the next Art Bowl. They told me yesterday, but I wasn't sure when to tell you."

The Art Bowl was an annual charity event that a few alumni from the School of the Art Institute of Chicago had been pulling together for the past five years. With contributions from the school, other former students, and community guests, it had become one of the largest crowd-sourced art fund-raisers in the city, raising money for a new cause each year. I'd talked to Tammy Davies, who led the effort, about the possibility of honoring Keith one year, and I'd never seen someone look more uncomfortable in my life.

"You know how much we feel for you and Keith," she'd said, her eyes darting around nervously as we sat in my living room a few months back. "But we can't make a habit of centering the Bowl around one of our close and personal friends. The optics of that... Well, you understand, right?"

Of course I did, but it didn't make hearing it any easier.

As the lie came out of my lips, Keith blinked and stared at me in confusion. Then his forehead scrunched up, and he pulled himself into an upright position and shook his head.

"What?" he hissed loudly.

I cleared my throat again. With him watching me so carefully, the lie was difficult to get out. "Tammy called me. They've all agreed. They want you to be the recipient of this year's annual benefit. Which means—"

"Paula—"

"—which means *we can afford it*, Keith," I said firmly. It was a risk, since he could easily call them to check, but then again, Keith hadn't been in touch with anyone from the la-di-d'artists in nearly a year. I knew he'd be happy to let me send thanks for both of us if I offered. "It won't cover everything, but it's a step in the right direction. We *will* be able to afford the surgery with Dr. Reveno. There's no sense in fighting this. They've already decided. I'm calling Dr. Bryant in the morning."

"I don't..." he started, but he shook his head again and dropped his body back onto the pillow. I could see that he wanted to protest, but behind that, I could see something else brewing. Something I hadn't seen on his face in a long time and that made me feel better about the lies I'd just told and the ones I would have to tell in the upcoming weeks.

Hope.

CHAPTER 10

OPENED THE SETTINGS IN my internet browser and deleted my search history.

Then I deleted the cookies.

Then I turned off the Wi-Fi and restarted my computer.

It was the third time I'd done it that night. It seemed that I couldn't be too careful when it came to searching for things like *how to blackmail someone* or *is all blackmail illegal?*

I've seen the movies where the criminal is brought to justice years later because of some file they opened on their computer back in the 1990s.

I'd be damned if I was going down like that.

Before tonight, the worst thing anyone would've found about me was a search about how many glasses of wine a night made you an alcoholic. Now, I was seriously contemplating doing something that was not only embarrassing—it was immoral.

Illegal.

I was sitting on the couch a little after 2:00 a.m. Keith was asleep in the bedroom. The doctors had let him go home with a prescription for a lot of rest and a lot of fluids.

The nondehydrating kind.

How to blackmail someone had produced more than *nine million* results. I couldn't believe the number of people out there who detailed exactly what was necessary to demand money from someone and get away with it. Some sites expressed that they were strictly designed for research; others stated that they in no way endorsed blackmail but wanted to provide the most comprehensive information about it. Why? Because that's what people do on the internet.

Besides the how-to articles, I'd found lots of pieces detailing the difference between blackmail and extortion. It was reassuring to know that what I was planning to do wasn't as bad as it could be. If anything, what I was doing could be called coercion.

The telephone and my silence in exchange for $180,000.

Hell, I'd call it a *suggestion*.

As I'd scanned through the pages, I tried to memorize as much as possible; there was no way I'd write any of it down. The articles all centered around a few key topics, which made it clear that there were three parts to a perfect blackmail.

One, I needed irrefutable proof of the deed.

In this case, the deed was Hooks's affair with Emma.

I'd seen the way they had looked at each other through the night, felt the tension between them, even as they stared at each other from afar. I'd seen it with my own eyes, so *I* knew it was true, but I didn't have proof. It had to be on the phone. Hooks's reaction backstage made it clear that there was something on it he didn't want me to see.

If only I could figure out how to access it.

Next, I needed to provide the subject (Hooks) with enough information for him to believe that I had the proof (whatever I found on the phone) and that I would be willing to give it over for the agreed-upon sum ($180,000). This meant that he had to believe that I wouldn't still tell his secret after he gave me the money. That his pesky problem would go away for what, to him, would be a negligible amount of money.

And finally, I would need an untraceable way to actually get the money. In some ways, that would be the hardest part, but I decided not to worry about it until I got past the first two.

Once I had the proof and his agreement to pay the money, I would figure out the rest.

I reached into my purse and pulled out the phone. I pressed the Home button and saw that the battery was at 43 percent.

Shit.

I could, of course, go out and buy a charger for it, but that seemed like overkill, especially since I didn't know what I'd actually find on it. I put it down on the couch beside me and started a new search on my computer: *most common phone pins*.

I scanned the results—all, of course, very appropriate articles about what to do if you forgot your *own* passcode. Unsurprisingly, the most common pins had to do with dates and numbers that meant something to people: birthdays, graduation dates, home addresses (past and present), area codes.

I'd already tried Hooks's and Tiffane's birthdays. It only took a few Google searches to find out that he'd graduated from high school in 1997, from college in 2001, and he'd once lived on a street named Parish in Cincinnati, house number 3882.

Thank you, internet.

I grabbed the phone and went to work.

Attempt four: 1-9-9-7.

Attempt five: 2-0-0-1.

Attempt six: 3-8-8-2.

Each time, I was met with a vehement no—the phone shook and alerted me that I'd used up yet another chance.

Four more incorrect entries, and the phone would be locked.

And then what?

Sighing, I put it back into my purse and picked up my computer again. I searched aimlessly for the next ten minutes, scanning articles about everything from his music to his relationships to his workout plan.

RYAN HOOKS AND TIFFANE SPOTTED AT COACHELLA
RYAN HOOKS: "WHY I DON'T EAT AFTER 6 P.M."
RYAN HOOKS ACCUSED OF SEXUAL HARASSMENT

I frowned, clicking on the last one, my heartbeat speeding up as I did. It was about a woman named Amanda Strager, who'd accused Hooks of coming on to her during a video shoot. She'd pressed charges and then withdrew them days later, with a statement released by her representatives: "Ms. Strager has decided that it is in the best interest of all parties involved for her to withdraw her former accusations so that she can move past this very troubling time in her life."

The same article quoted Hooks's attorney, Stephanie McClean of Baker & Pikensy Associates, as saying that "the accusations are completely unfounded, and that is all Mr. Hooks will say about the subject."

I realized there was a *lot* I didn't know about Ryan Hooks.

I cleaned my search history one more time before powering down and closing the laptop. I picked up my own phone and opened my Twitter app. I only had to type his first name for his account to show up.

@RyanHooksOfficial.

I took a deep breath, and before I could stop myself, I followed him. Then I took my time composing a tweet.

@RyanHooksOfficial: Nice meeting you tonight and
last Saturday, let's connect

I let my finger hover over the screen, closed my eyes, and tapped it.

I hoped it wasn't *too* vague.

I stood up and walked past Shelby toward the bedroom. This time, she wasn't pretending to be asleep, and in the moonlight, I could see her head raised as she watched me. She continued to stare at me for a moment, as if she knew I were up to no good, and then let her head drop back down on her mattress.

I watched her for a moment before walking into the bedroom and climbing into bed.

Whatever.

She couldn't be judging me any harder than I was already judging myself. '

The passcode came to me in the middle of the night.

I was dreaming about the two of them again. Ryan's back as he stood outside Emma's apartment building. Emma's face as she stared down at him. In my dream, I wasn't in my car at all but standing on the other side of the street, arms at my sides as I watched them. Suddenly, the scene in front of me became blurry, until just one element stood out clearly in the dark night—the address of the building, 115, the brass numbers clinging to the bricks.

0-1-1-5.

One of the most common passcodes is home addresses, past and present.
But not Ryan's address.
Emma's.

I sat up and crept out of bed, looking back at Keith as I did. He was on his back, his mouth open, his soft snores filling the room. I walked into the living room, where my purse was still sitting on the coffee table. I fished out Ryan's phone and then held my breath as I typed in the four digits.

0-1-1-5.

If it didn't work, I didn't know what I would do—

But then suddenly, I didn't have to think about that anymore. The keypad slid away from the screen, and just like that, I was instantly staring at the app-covered background of Ryan Hooks's cell phone.

You have got to be kidding me.

I sat there for a full minute, staring at it, the bright apps seeming to dance in front of my eyes in the dark room. I began to scroll through them. Ryan had all the usual suspects: Twitter, Instagram, YouTube, Snapchat. He also had a few games, more than one that looked like Candy Crush but were called something else.

I don't know what I expected to find—maybe a top-secret app called For Celebrity Eyes Only—but there was nothing out of the norm.

It was just a phone.

Only it was so much more than that. I swiped back to the home screen and let my eyes drop down to the icon for Messages. I ignored the slight trace of guilt that rushed over me as I clicked on it and watched as a list of names popped up. There was Tiff, Mom, and a long list of other names. I opened a few threads, but nothing seemed out of the ordinary.

His mother had asked if he was going to make Gary's wedding in October.

He'd texted someone named Sal a GIF of a penguin falling over. This was what celebrities did with their time?

Then I saw it.

A conversation thread with someone simply named "M."

I said it out loud in the dark room, and the realization made my pulse quicken.

Em.

Jackpot.

Yesterday, 6:17 p.m.

    M: What time u coming over?

    Ryan: Don't know, late. All clear?

    M: Yeah, tonight's good. Miss u. Sorry about yesterday.

    Ryan: It's ok. Miss u too.

July 28, 9:06 p.m.

    Ryan: I get into town Thursday night. Wanna see you.

    M: Can't always get what we want ;)

    Ryan: I tend to.

    M: Wow, lol. Think that attitude is going to work?

    Ryan: I do.

    Ryan: Am I right?

9:15 p.m.

    Ryan: Ruh roh.

    Ryan: Hello?

    Ryan: #toomuchconfidencefail?

    M: LOL

    M: Almost.

March 4, 2:39 a.m.

    Ryan: U up?

    Ryan: Sorry

    M: No, I am. Had a rough day.

    Ryan: I'm sorry. Want to talk?

    M: Are you at home?

    Ryan: Yeah. But Tiff's not. Now okay?

    M: Yeah, call me.

March 4, 4:03 a.m.

> M: I don't know what I would do without you. Good night.
>
> Ryan: Love you.

My heart was pounding as I pushed the button to return to the home screen.

Love you?

I damn sure hadn't expected that. Their relationship was cuter, funnier, more comfortable than I'd imagined it would be.

This was no celebrity hookup.

But that didn't change anything.

I had to do what I had to do.

With shaky fingers, I opened Twitter, which was already logged into his account. He wasn't following me back, so I couldn't message him directly from my own account, *but maybe…*

I opened his messages and began typing in his own username. @RyanHooksOfficial.

The message populated his name in the to field, and I let out a deep breath.

I could send a message from Ryan to Ryan.

I just had to pray he checked it on his computer, since he certainly wouldn't be doing so on his phone.

I thought for a moment and then typed out a short note.

> @RyanHooksOfficial: 115. Makes sense.

Before I could stop myself, I pressed Send.

I immediately pushed the button at the top of the screen to turn it off before tossing the phone into my purse.

I walked back into the bedroom to lie down, but I knew I wouldn't be falling asleep anytime soon. Around 4:00 a.m., I closed my eyes for what felt like nothing more than a long blink, but when I opened them, it was light outside. I'd underestimated how much of a toll the previous day had taken on me.

I got dressed and grabbed my purse before heading out. I completed a couple of rides, driving aimlessly, the information I'd read last night swirling in my mind. There was a part of me that knew the whole thing was ridiculous—I could never pull something like this off—but there was another part of me that knew I had to try.

We were running out of options, and this one had dropped itself into my back seat like a present.

I headed toward the Gold Coast. I picked up a few rides along the way, mostly as a distraction, but once I was downtown, I shut off the app. Soon, I was circling the blocks, moving closer and closer to the apartment building on Oak. As I drove past the dog park, I looked quickly for any signs of Emma and her puppy, but they were nowhere to be seen.

Of course they're not there, Paula.

Go home.

I continued down the block before turning to head back to the heart of downtown. I'd drive for another hour or so and then head home. I was in the left turn lane, waiting for a large crowd of people to cross the street, when something caught my eye.

It was a store, halfway down the block, with a large, red awning and a single word printed in curly letters.

Klein's.

I frowned and leaned forward to see what street I was on.

Halsted.

I thought back to the day I'd seen Emma outside the dog park as she spoke to someone on the phone.

"We're going to be at Klein's on Halsted."

It was the boutique she'd been telling someone about on the

phone. I wondered what kind of clothes would pass her muster, and on a whim, I pulled over into a parking space and shut off the car.

As I stepped inside Klein's, I couldn't help but smile when I saw how much the clothing fit Emma's style. There were at least four different versions of the jumper I saw her wearing at the dog park. Everything was modern, clean, and streamlined. Colorful but understated.

I walked around for a bit and finally picked up a scarf.

I'd gone so far as to come in; I had to buy something…

I stepped into line, resigning myself to paying for an item I didn't need, when I spotted the young couple in front of me. A moment later, I heard the woman speak.

"You can have it shipped to 115 West Oak."

My jaw dropped, and I stared at their backs. The woman had short, pink hair, and she stood next to a tall, lanky man who looked like he'd rather be anywhere else in the world.

"Sorry, I couldn't help but overhear," I said, trying not to wince. "Did you say you live at 115 West Oak?"

The girl looked back at me with a frown. "Yeah. How come?"

"Oh, it's a nice building," I said. "I actually met someone who lives there recently. Her name was Emma."

The girl's eyes widened, and she looked over at her friend.

"You know her?" I asked as casually as possible.

"Yeah, we—" the man started.

"She lives above us," the girl said, and I watched as she gave him a look. "How did you meet her?"

"Oh, just at the dog park nearby," I said. "She might become a client of mine. I'm an artist, and she said she's looking for some new work."

There was a chuckle from the boyfriend. "Of course she did," he said. The girl was shaking her head at him. "I told you, she doesn't have anything to do. She's in that damned dog park every afternoon."

"Shut up," the pink-haired girl hissed.

"Am I lying?" he asked. "Tell me where she is every day at four o'clock? Out there with that damned dog."

I cleared my throat. "Is something wrong?"

I'd taken one acting class in college—an improv comedy class, actually—and I'd been terrible at it. I'd dropped it after two weeks. As I stood there, I wished that I'd stuck with it just a little bit longer; it might have proven useful at a time like this.

Maybe then I wouldn't have sounded so damned suspicious.

Was I too interested?

Not interested enough?

The girl shook her head. "No, nothing's wrong," she said. "Emma is a friend of ours."

This time, the boyfriend laughed out loud.

"What?" she asked him. "If you have something to say, just say it."

"I don't," he said. "I would've said it if I did."

"Then you shouldn't keep making noises."

"It's just funny to hear you call her your friend…"

I swallowed. I had to push it. "Is there something I should know?" I asked. "I'm pretty careful about taking on new clients."

The girl locked eyes with me again.

"It's just no big surprise that she'd want you to paint something for her apartment after meeting her at a *park*," she said. "No offense. You seem lovely, and I'm sure you're very talented, but that's pretty random. Still, that absolutely sounds like something Emma would do, and God knows she has the money for it."

There was a bitterness in her voice, which she wasn't trying too hard to hide. "Just fair warning that Emma is known for being a little bit less than reliable, so I'd make sure you work out an agreement ahead of time," she said. "Something pretty concrete. Just my two cents. Trust me, I have firsthand experience."

I wanted to learn as much as I could. Every single detail seemed to count. If I could just find something, anything, I could go back to Hooks. I cleared my throat and tried to keep my expression as neutral as possible. "Are you saying she's someone I shouldn't work with?"

The girl shrugged. "I'm just saying she's a complicated person. I shouldn't really go into much more detail than that."

"What you're trying to say is that she's a nutso bitch," the man said. He turned back to face the clerk who was punching something into the register.

The girl smiled and began to turn back too but stopped and looked back at me.

"Don't listen to us," she said. "We're just being nosy neighbors. If she wants to hire you, I say go for it."

She turned her back to me, signaling that the conversation was over. I watched them finish up and leave the store before buying my scarf and heading back out to my car.

As I drove away, my phone buzzed, and my breath caught when I saw that I had a new Twitter notification.

@RyanHooksOfficial is now following you!
And a direct message.

Send me your number.

My mouth was dry as I turned the corner and began to head home.

CHAPTER 11

Claire
The Night in Question

CLAIRE WAS SITTING NEXT to Meggie Bentley on the couch in her sister's living room. She watched as an investigator bagged up the red shoe and carried it away.

"I need to ask you a few questions about what happened tonight," Claire said. "Is now a good time?"

With her bright-pink hair and small frame, the only clue that she was related to the tall, slender woman whom Claire had interviewed just moments earlier was the sparkle in her bright-green eyes. Meggie's gaze darted back and forth between the detective in front of her and her sister, who walked by and toward the short hallway that led to her bedroom.

"Okay," Meggie said slowly, crossing her hands in her lap. Where her sister had trembled with every breath and seemed unable to process what was happening, Meggie was calm, quiet, and collected. "What is it that you want to know?"

"You're the one who found Mrs. Brighton's body, yes?" Claire asked. "With your boyfriend?"

"Yes," Meggie said, and she exhaled through pursed lips. "I don't think I'll ever be able to get that image out of my mind."

"Where is your boyfriend now?"

"Patrick?" Meggie asked. "He's downstairs in our apartment. Emma asked me to come upstairs."

"Okay," Claire said. "Before I get into what happened tonight, can you tell me a little bit about your relationship with Mrs. Brighton?"

"With Bev?" Meggie asked. She spread her hands in front of her and took a quick glance at the kitchen. "I didn't have much of one. She was more Emma's friend, not mine."

"But she also was handling some of the legal work for your sister's clothing company, right? Have you been working with her on that?"

Claire tended to notice the little things, like the way people's voices changed when they were hiding something. Meggie stayed perfectly still for the most part, but her jaw clenched as she searched for the right response.

"Yes, I'm involved in the clothing line, since I'm the one who designs the clothes," she snapped, and then she put a hand on her chest. She lowered her voice. "I'm sorry. I'm just used to her doing things like that."

"Like what?" Claire asked.

"Like taking credit for things that she shouldn't."

Claire held the woman's eye for a moment before continuing. "Your sister owns the building, yes? How long have you lived here?"

"I moved in about two years ago," Meggie said.

"And your boyfriend?" Claire asked. "When did he move in with you?"

"Two years ago," Meggie repeated with a frown. "We've been together for four."

Claire nodded. "Tell me about what happened when you got home. What time was it?"

"About two thirty," she said. "Patrick and I decided to take a walk after the party and go down to Boxer's over on Walton. We left there at about two fifteen and came back home."

"Can anyone vouch for that?" Claire asked.

"Sure, the bartender, Kerry. She knows us, and she was there. Anyway, when we walked in, we saw the bloodstains on the wall and carpet and began walking upstairs. It was so out of place. Emma has this carpet cleaned every two weeks or something." Meggie shuddered, looking down at her hands. "You know how you just know something bad has happened? That's what I felt in my chest. But we kept walking up, because we knew the blood had to come from somewhere, and then we were almost up to the third floor when we saw her…" She stopped talking and then shook her head as if to get rid of the image.

"Did you see anyone else in the hallway? Or outside the building as you were walking inside?"

"No," Meggie said, shaking her head again. "There was no one."

"I need you to think about this carefully. The door to Beverly's apartment. Was it open?"

Meggie nodded. "It was. Not a lot. Just a crack. But I remember thinking that I didn't know what was inside. I was so scared. We ran back down into the apartment and closed the door before calling the cops."

Claire leaned forward. "We're asking all the tenants if we can swab their apartment for any evidence. Are you okay with that?"

"Yeah, have at it," Meggie said, and Claire got the sense that she was working hard at seeming unconcerned. Meggie dropped back against the seat cushion. "We don't have anything to hide. But you're barking up the wrong tree. If there's anyone you want to check out, it would be Beverly's husband, Andrew. He's a mess of a person, and honestly, I wouldn't put something like this past him."

"That's a strong accusation," Claire said. "What makes you say that?"

"First, he was wasted out of his mind tonight. He even got into it with Patrick at the dinner."

"About what?"

"Something about this real estate property they've been talking about investing in. I don't know. You'll have to ask Patrick. I think it's a bad idea, and Andrew's behavior tonight just proves it." She leaned forward and lowered her voice. "I think he has something of a drinking problem, to be honest. He's always really nice and calm on the surface, but when he drinks…it's a different story."

"Did you see him have any words with his wife?"

"No, but then again, he never did. She treated him like a sack of crap, and he always just took it. Didn't help that she held the purse strings in that relationship, and she talked pretty openly about their prenup." Meggie shrugged. "Maybe good old Andrew had one too many and finally cracked."

CHAPTER 12

―――――――――――――――――――
―――――――――――――――――――

Paula
Three days before

S *END ME YOUR NUMBER.*
I'd been checking my phone like a madwoman since Ryan had messaged me. I'd sent him the number right away, but then...nothing. I considered writing him again, but it seemed that the less information I put out publicly, the better.

So I waited.

I waited, and I read.

January 16, 11:13 a.m.

M:	I'm going to be in New York next week for work. Any chance you can be there too?
Ryan:	What days?
M:	Thurs-Sat
Ryan:	Pretty sure I was invited to a release party that falls during those exact dates, but not sure I can make it. It'll all depend...
M:	Oh ok. On what?
Ryan:	If you'll be packing that little lace thing I bought you.

M: 🙂

M: Can't wait. My favorite person, in my favorite city in
        the world.

I put the phone down and felt a familiar twinge of jealously rush through me. Keith and I had spent our honeymoon in New York, and it had been, without question, five of the happiest days of my life. Whenever we fought or argued, I sometimes went back to those days, remembering the carefree, infatuated way we'd roamed the city as we started our lives together.

I wanted that back.

I'd walked into the apartment after leaving Klein's and, for a reason I couldn't explain, had decided to change clothes. I pulled on my nicest pair of sweatpants and a tank top and brushed my hair up into a high bun. I grabbed my tube of root cover-up from the medicine cabinet and dabbed it on a few grays, added some concealer, and finally stepped out into the living room to face the afternoon's biggest challenge.

I moved into the living room and stood in front of Shelby. Keith was at the college again and wouldn't be home for another three hours. I wasn't scheduled at the diner that afternoon and could've picked up several more rides.

Instead, I was going to take Shelby to a dog park.

The girl with the pink hair and her boyfriend had said Emma went to the park almost every afternoon. Who was to say I couldn't go too? After all, it was a public park. And in a way, Emma and her friends had invited me back.

I swallowed.

If I didn't think it would one day be my downfall, I would've Googled *what's considered stalking*.

"Hey, girl," I said, kneeling down in front of Shelby.

She opened her eyes and then pulled herself up onto her feet, watching me warily. If Keith had so much as walked out of the bedroom, she would have been up instantly, spinning in circles and nipping at his pant leg.

Instead, she watched me, waiting, as if she could see through to the depths of my simple, terrible soul.

"Hi," I said. "How about we go for a little drive?" As the words came out of my mouth, I thanked my lucky stars that no one was around to hear me all but luring my dog into my unmarked white van. She continued to watch me without moving, and I straightened, walking over to the hook by the front door where we kept her leash.

I swallowed and walked back toward her, holding it in my hands.

"So…what do you think?" I asked. "Want to go to the park?"

Her back straightened a little at the word *park*, and I knew I had her. She continued to watch me, her big, brown eyes following my every move, and finally, she took a step forward.

"Yeah, cool, awesome," I said, kneeling down to put the leash on her. It had been a while since I'd done it, and I fumbled, but she just stood there, quietly watching me the whole time.

We left the apartment, and I followed behind her as she walked down the street. Keith shouldn't get home before we got back, but I had my cell phone just in case. If he did, I would have a hard time explaining my sudden decision to take Shelby to the park, given our mutual distaste for one another. As I opened the car door to let her inside, I prayed it wouldn't be an issue.

As I drove along, I put the windows down, and Shelby leaned her head out as she always did when she went for a ride. She looked content, but I knew that had nothing to do with me.

"I know you probably think I'm nuts," I said, and she pulled her head into the car for a moment. "I don't know what I'm doing, Shels, or what's wrong with me, but I just need you to work with me a little. Just for half an hour or so. Then we'll go home."

She'd already leaned her head back out the window, and I sighed and drove on.

Unlike the other two days when I'd been able to double-park for a minute, I actually needed to find a spot today. It was a small detail that had almost slipped my mind; parking in the Gold Coast on the best of days is a nightmare. It took more than twenty minutes to find a spot, and I winced as I paid the meter. Six dollars for the hour. I walked around and opened the passenger door, and Shelby hopped out gracefully. Grabbing her leash, I walked with her across the street and down the block toward the dog park.

On the way, we passed the apartment building, and I took a quick peek at it as we walked by. It seemed so ordinary in the daylight, just a normal building, like any of the others on the block. When we reached the gate of the dog park, I sucked in a breath and walked inside, and Shelby followed alongside me. I let the breath out when I saw there was only one woman in the park, and it was not Emma.

I bit my lip, walked over to an empty bench, and sat down.

Shelby stood in front of me, watching me for a moment, and then looked around the park for a moment before turning her attention back to me. I hadn't seen her like this, sweet and hesitant, and I wondered if she would have been as reserved if she'd been at the park with Keith.

"What?" I asked, and she continued to stare. "Go play," I said, pointing at a small sand pit in the middle of the park.

She turned and walked over to it, sniffing it for a moment. She circled it and then looked up at me, less interested than I'd hoped she would be. After a few moments, she walked back to my bench and sat down beside me, watching the other dog play.

"Yeah, this probably wasn't the best idea I've had in a while, huh?" I asked her. I'm not sure why I did it, but I reached out and touched the top of her head, reveling in the softness of her fur. She didn't move at first, but after a moment, she inched back a little. We sat like that for a while, and finally, I dropped my hand and stood up.

"Well, I guess that's that," I said.

I bent down and put her leash back on. The pink-haired girl's boyfriend had said that she tended to be in the park around 4:00 p.m. I looked at my phone; it was already 4:30.

It was time to go home.

As I stood, I felt something at the back of my legs, and I turned to see a small black poodle at my feet. It was the same dog from the other day, and I let out a small gasp. Looking up, I saw a tall woman striding toward me with a smile on her face.

Emma.

"Hi there," she said. "Chris, right? Looks like you came back after all."

She looked even more put-together than she had the first two times I'd seen her. She was wearing another jumper, this one bright pink. She was wearing a pair of tan flats, and she'd pulled her hair up into a high ponytail, which helped tone down the outfit. It didn't look like she was wearing makeup, but she had to be—nobody's skin is that flawless. I blinked a few times, shocked that this ridiculous outing had actually paid off.

"Yeah, I decided to see if Shelby likes it as much as I do," I said with a smile, and she nodded. My heart was pounding in my chest, and not for the first time that day, I wondered if I looked as suspicious as I felt.

"Did you walk here?" she asked. "You said you live around the corner, right? In those apartments on Elm?"

"Mm–hmm," I said. I couldn't admit to her that I'd searched for parking for twenty minutes and paid to come to a dog park that was nowhere near my house. As the lie came out of my lips, I tried to push down the guilt. I changed the subject quickly. "You weren't kidding when you said you come here every day."

She laughed. "Yeah, Dante loves it." She looked down at the small dog, who was peering at Shelby. Shelby was at least three times his size, but he didn't inch away, instead just standing there, watching to see what she would do. Dante finally walked to Shelby and nipped at her before taking off. Shelby looked at me for a moment and then turned to chase him.

Emma laughed. "I think they like each other," she said.

We sat down on the bench and watched the dogs playing for a few moments. There was something so normal about it, two wealthy women meeting each other in this carefully manicured dog park and watching their dogs play together.

Except one of us wasn't wealthy and was a complete and utter fraud. Part of me was appalled by the amount of information I knew about her and the fact that she would probably lose it if she knew that I had her lover's cell phone in my drawer at home at that very moment. That I knew her neighbors didn't like her very much, or that I'd come here today just to see her again.

"Chris?"

"Oh, sorry," I said, turning to her. "What did you say?"

"I asked how long you and your husband have lived in the area."

"A year," I said, the lie slipping easily from my lips.

"What does he do?" she asked. "Is he an artist too?"

"He is, but he's also a swim coach," I said, and then because I'd gotten so used to saying it over the past year, I continued without thinking. "He *was* a swim coach."

She sat there expectantly, waiting for me to continue, and I wanted to kick myself for oversharing. She didn't need to know too much about my real life. I spoke slowly, measuring my words.

"He was in an accident about a year ago," I said. "He isn't able to swim anymore."

I stopped, hoping she would let the conversation drop, but she held my gaze and nodded. "That must be very hard on both of you," she said. "I took care of my mother after her stroke a few years ago, so I know what it's like to see someone you love in pain."

It was a kind and oddly personal moment, and I could only smile and thank her before changing the subject.

"You said the other day that you were looking for some portraits," I said. "So, would that just be you or other people?"

Her eyes widened, and she laughed. "Oh, no, you must think I'm horribly vain," she said. "I don't want portraits of myself. I want them of some of the models in our show that's coming up."

I frowned, and she shook her head.

"Sorry, let me start over," she said. "We have a family business—a clothing line called Allure Apparel. Have you heard of it?"

I didn't know if I should've so I figured it was time to pull back on the lies. "No, I haven't," I said, shaking my head. "Sorry."

"Oh, don't apologize," she said. "It's up-and-coming. Anyway, we're having a few shows soon, and we're renting out a warehouse in the West Loop. I've been trying to think of some ways to decorate the space, and when you mentioned that you did portraits, I thought that might be a great idea—to have you do some portraits of the models in the clothing that they're going to be wearing on the night of the show! How amazing would that be?"

"Um, yes," I said, nodding. "That would be something else."

"Can I see some of your work?"

I hesitated.

She leaned forward. "Come on, just a couple."

It had been a while since anyone had been interested in my paintings, and I smiled a little before pulling out my phone. I opened my photo album and scrolled through to find a few shots of some of my work.

"You did these?" she asked, her eyes widening. "They're beautiful!" She tilted her head to one side. "Hey, I know this is totally random, but I'm having a little dinner party at my apartment on Saturday night. You should come! You could learn more about the line, see if it you're interested, no strings attached."

I smiled and shook my head slightly. "Oh, that's nice of you, but I couldn't…"

"Why not?" she asked. "I live right there." She pointed down the block, and I turned and squinted as if I didn't know where to look. "The brown brick one with the orange porch swing," she said. "Apartment 2. Eight o'clock. If you're not busy, I'd love to have you. You could meet the designer, the store owner, and take a look at some of the designs."

I didn't say anything.

She smiled. "I know. My sister says I can be a little bit impulsive about things. But when I meet someone who gives me good vibes, I tend to just go with it. And those paintings are truly impressive. Seriously, tell me you'll at least think about it."

There was no way in hell.

But I smiled and nodded. "Sure, I'll think about it."

"Here, take my number," she said. "I left my phone upstairs, but you can text me yours. And again, no strings. If you want to come, just show up on Saturday at…?"

"Eight o'clock," I said with a small smile. "I'll definitely think about it."

With shaking hands, I typed her number into my cell phone and saved it as Emma. Then I stared at my phone for a few moments and tapped around, just long enough to make her think I'd texted her my phone number.

Emma smiled and nodded. "There might be some major changes coming down the line for Allure, so this fashion show is really important to me. I hope you can make it Saturday. At the very least, come for the food. I'm ordering beef canapés from my favorite restaurant. If I can't sell you on anything else, trust me, you want to come for those."

We both laughed, and she sat up straighter. "Now, enough business. How was that concert you went to the other night? You said it was, um, Ryan Hooks, right?"

I watched her face, so innocent, and I wondered if I hadn't known the truth, if I would've been able to read her so easily. Her eyes were discerning as she watched me, and I knew she was sizing me up too.

"It was great," I said. "My friend surprised me with tickets at the last minute. It's not something I typically would've gone to. Her daughter is a big fan."

"But you're not?" she asked, again with an innocent smile.

"Oh, no, he's great," I said. "I'm just not much of a concert kind of person. I like his music, though. Don't you?"

"Yeah, sure," she said with a barely believable, disinterested shrug. I decided to push it.

"He's married to Tiffane, right?" I asked. "She's a lucky woman."

Emma blinked, and then her eyes narrowed, just a bit. "Yeah, she is."

"It must be amazing to be married to a man like that." I had a hard time saying the words, but I pushed them out, and as I expected, they hit the mark.

"I'm sure it is," she said softly, and then she leaned closer and put a hand on my shoulder. "But let me tell you a secret. For the most part, men are just men," she said with a smile, and I could tell she was trying to decide how much to tell me. "Rich men, poor men, attractive men, unattractive. They're all just men. Even *Ryan Hooks*," she said, his name rolling sharply off her tongue. "He's just a man, like anyone else...I'd bet."

I smiled but didn't say anything.

"In fact, I have a date tonight, with a very rich and important man."

I blinked and tried to keep my expression as neutral as possible. I was in the best possible situation; I was a stranger to her, nobody at all, and she obviously wanted to talk.

"Ooh," I said, leaning in. "A new boyfriend? How'd you meet?"

She blinked as if she hadn't expected the question, and then she smiled. "Through mutual friends."

I smiled, and then I just went for it. "Wait, *he's* not famous, is he?"

She frowned and shook her head. "No. I wish."

And then there was a secret smile on her face, and I wondered if she was enjoying the fact that she thought she had a secret that I knew nothing about.

I worked hard to make sure I didn't have the same secret grin on my face. I leaned in closer. "Because if you know somebody rich and famous, I hope you'll let me know if he has any friends," I said.

We both laughed, but it didn't reach her eyes any more than it reached mine.

CHAPTER 13

I GOT HOME THAT NIGHT and climbed into bed beside Keith.

I pulled out Hooks's phone and began to aimlessly scroll through the text messages. I felt bad—Emma was nicer than I'd expected her to be. It wasn't fair really; she was beautiful, wealthy, and she owned her own business.

She'd been charming and nice, and she wanted to hire me, of all things. It was almost laughable.

At the very least, she could be a jerk.

That would've made me feel better about what I was doing.

And there was something else.

It had taken me a few hours to connect the dots after I got home, but suddenly, something she had said jumped out to me.

There might be some major changes coming down the line for Allure, so this fashion show is really important to me.

I scrolled through the text messages until I found an exchange I'd read earlier that day, and when I scanned it a second time, I sucked in a breath.

June 12, 5:01 p.m.

   Ryan: Hey
   M: Hey you

Ryan:	So random question for you.
Ryan:	I'm going to be hiring a new assistant soon. What would you say if I asked you to take some time off from work and take the job.
M:	You're kidding
Ryan:	I'm not
M:	I can't just do that. You know I can't. Besides, I love my job
Ryan:	Wouldn't you love being able to travel with me?
M:	Of course, but...come on Ryan
Ryan:	Okay, never mind. We already have a ton of applications in. Forget I brought it up.
M:	Wait—let me think about it.

I felt a movement next to me, and Keith rolled over, pushing his face next to my own. "Hey," he said, his voice gruff and sleep-filled. "When'd you get home?"

"About ten minutes ago," I said. "Sorry, did I wake you?"

"No, I've been in and out of sleep, waiting for you to get here."

"Why?" I asked, sitting up slightly. "Is something wrong?"

"No," he said. "I talked to Randy today. He wants me to come along to the meet in Indianapolis next week."

I frowned in the darkness. Randy was the Morton College swim coach and one of Keith's best friends. "How are they getting there?"

"By bus."

"Okay," I said slowly. "You thinking about going?"

He didn't say anything for a moment, and then I felt him nod against my shoulder. "Yeah, I want to," he said. "I got really scared after what happened on Tuesday. But I was also so happy to be back. I don't want to give up on this, babe."

"Yeah, but maybe you should take it slow. An overnight trip so soon—"

"I can do it," he said firmly.

I nodded quickly. "Okay," I said. "That's great. When is it? I can let David know I need some days off so I can come with you."

"It's on Tuesday, and we get back on Thursday," he said. "But that's okay." He reached over and held my hand. "Believe me, I know I can do it if you're there with me, but I need to do this on my own. Randy is going to come pick me up, and he'll drop me off. I feel like it's something I have to do. For me."

"Okay," I said again, squeezing his hand. "That's great."

"I also started reading up a bit on Dr. Reveno."

I sucked in a breath. "Really?"

"Yes. And I just wanted to say thank you for pushing it, even when I gave you hell. And for everything you've done with the Art Bowl. I know they didn't come to this decision without a bit of convincing on your part. Not sure I ever told you how much I appreciate everything you've done for me."

I swallowed and tried to push the guilt away as he leaned in for a kiss.

I couldn't sleep, and I got up an hour later and walked out into the living room. I checked my phone and saw that I'd missed a call from an unknown number.

I also had a Skype message. I sucked in a breath when I read it.

> Mrs. Wileson. It's Dr. Reveno. Ruby Bryant gave
> me your phone number and told me about your

husband. I'd love to talk with you soon. You can give
me a call back here.

I pressed his name immediately to call him back.

I almost cursed out loud when a man answered the phone, his voice low and sleepy.

"Hello?"

"Oh, I'm so sorry. You were asleep."

There was a pause, and then I heard some shuffling.

"Hello?" he said again.

"I'm sorry," I said. "Is this Dr. Reveno?"

There was another pause, and I had to assume he was looking more closely at the screen, because a moment later, he spoke up, his voice a hair clearer. "Yes, it is. Mrs. Wileson?"

"I'm so sorry," I said again. "The time change didn't occur to me. I just called you back as soon as I saw your note. It must be, what, 4:00 a.m.?"

"Five," he said, but there was no annoyance in his voice. "I'm glad you called. Dr. Bryant told me about your husband and his case. Fascinating to hear. Have you heard much about what it is I do and the new procedure that we're working on out here?"

"Yes, Dr. Bryant told me about it, and I did some research online," I said, feeling the hope rise in my chest. It was surreal to actually be talking to him after all this time.

And for the surgery to be a real possibility.

"Well, from everything Ruby has told me, it sounds like your husband might be a great candidate. I would need to meet him in person of course, to know for sure, but in the meantime, I could make some assessments based on his charts if he agrees to have them released to me."

I nodded and then, realizing he couldn't see me, spoke. "Yes,"

I said. "You can email me whatever it is you need him to sign to release them, and I'll get him to do it. I know he'll be more than happy to get a review from you."

"Sure thing," he said. "I'm happy to do it. And then we'll need to work on getting you guys out here as soon as possible. I'm really excited about this. It could be a real game changer, not just for you and your husband, but for our field."

"As soon as possible?"

"Well, I'm sure you've read that the surgery needs to take place within the first eighteen months after injury. When did the accident occur?"

"A year ago," I said, feeling the blood drain from my face. "I must have missed that."

As I said the words, I felt any traces of the guilt I'd felt earlier disappear.

We were running out of time.

CHAPTER 14

Claire

The Night in Question

C LAIRE STOOD OUTSIDE THE second-floor apartment and watched as two men carried the covered body of Beverly Brighton down the stairs.

It was a painful moment, the narrowness of the staircase making it hard for them to turn the corner onto the second-floor landing. There were four other people in the hallway, but they all stopped talking and observed an unplanned moment of silence while the men completed their work.

As she waited, Claire thought about what she'd learned so far. There were a few things that stood out right away.

One, someone had broken the glass at the back of the building to make it *look* like an intruder had entered the building that way. That was the most concerning piece of evidence she had for one simple reason: the only reason to make it look like someone had broken in was if the person responsible for Beverly's death had already been inside the building.

That narrowed her suspects down to six people: Meggie Bentley and her boyfriend, Patrick; Emma Bentley; Andrew

Brighton, the husband; Joshua Burlap, the store owner; and the artist with the red shoe. They'd all left at different times. Any one of them could have waited in the building and confronted Beverly in the hallway.

But why?

The broken glass also told her that the murder hadn't been planned; the botched cover-up job would've immediately been ruled out if the killer had taken even a moment to think about it. No, it was a messy, last-minute attempt to cover up Beverly's murder, which only cemented Claire's suspicion that the crime was closer to home than the killer wanted them to think.

Was it a crime of passion?

An accident?

The interviews she'd conducted so far had been telling as well. Unless she was a great actor, Emma Bentley seemed truly shaken up about her friend's death. And she'd seemed a bit too eager to name Patrick as a potential suspect; Claire had the sense that the woman wasn't the biggest fan of her sister's boyfriend. Meggie Bentley hadn't done a great job hiding her dislike for the victim, but then again, she hadn't really been trying to. And then there was Andrew Brighton, who'd apparently spent the last hour hanging over a toilet bowl. Pretty accurate reaction for what he'd been through that night, but was there more to it than that?

The men had successfully navigated Beverly's body around the last corner and were heading down to the first floor. Claire closed her notebook and moved toward the staircase. As she did, she heard someone call her name.

"Puhl?"

It was Greg, and Claire looked over the bannister to see him peering up at her from the first floor. He waited for the two men to pass him and then jogged quickly up the steps toward her.

"Yes?" Claire said as he reached the landing.

"The building is locked up pretty tight. There are three ways to get into it. The front door, the back door, and up the back staircase, which takes you into the back door of each unit. That backyard has a locked gate, which requires a code to be opened up from the outside."

"Is there a way to determine if that system was used tonight?"

"Yep. We've already reached out to the landlord," he said. "Oh, and we found the brick that was used to smash the window. It was lying in a puddle of mud, so don't think we're going to find any prints on it, but we'll see."

"Good." Claire nodded her head up the stairs. "I'm going to go speak with the husband."

She walked just as carefully up the stairs as she had the first time. With the body gone, it was easier to see the splotches of blood that had seeped into the carpet and stained the wall near the top of the stairwell. Claire sidestepped each stain and frowned when he saw something on the carpet.

At first, it looked like blood, another one of the deep-red swipes that seemed to be everywhere in the staircase.

But she leaned closer and saw that the color was just a little bit off; the hue was darker and richer than the rest.

"There's something on the floor here," Claire said as she stepped into the third-floor apartment.

One of the investigators looked up and nodded before walking over to examine it.

Claire spotted Andrew Brighton right away. He was tall and stocky, with brown hair cut low to hide the fact that it was thinning at the temples. He was sitting by himself as the officers walked around the apartment looking for evidence.

"Mr. Brighton," she said, and he looked up. "I'm Detective Claire Puhl. I'm wondering if I could ask you a few questions."

Andrew blinked and stared at her for a few seconds before responding.

"Okay," he said robotically.

"I'm so incredibly sorry for your loss tonight," Claire said. "I can't imagine what you're going through. I just have a few questions to ask you so that we can do everything we can to figure out what happened to your wife."

"You want to question me because you think I might have done it." He said it matter-of-factly, with little emotion in his voice.

Claire swallowed. People reacted differently to tragedy, and while Andrew's response wasn't uncommon, it still made her raise an eyebrow. "I'm just trying to get the most information I can to find out what happened."

"They're all treating me like I'm a suspect," he said as if she hadn't spoken. "Like I could've done…" He trailed off and looked at the open door. After a moment, he swallowed and then looked back at Claire. "Like I could have done this."

"May I ask what you do for a living, Mr. Brighton?" Claire asked. "I know that Beverly was a lawyer."

"I'm a gym teacher at North Side College Prep," he said, looking down at a large class ring on his finger. He spun it around in a circle a few times. "That's where Bev and I met. High school sweethearts." He shook his head.

"Can you tell me about what time your wife left Emma Bentley's dinner party?"

"She left around midnight."

"And you stayed?"

"Yes," he said. "I was talking to the kid, Patrick."

"What time did you come upstairs?" Claire asked.

"Not much longer after she left. Forty-five minutes? An hour? I know I was up here by one."

"Patrick and Meggie say they were the last ones there. And they left at twelve forty-five."

He blinked and then shrugged. "So maybe it was less than that. I left right before them."

"Did you see what time the artist left? Chris?"

He frowned for a moment and then shook his head. "No, but I think it was before me. I went to grab one more beer, and when I came back into the living room, she was already gone."

"What was your wife doing when you got upstairs?"

"She was in the shower when I got home," he said. "She had this thing about showering before bed. She always thought it was so gross to get into the bed if you hadn't showered for the night."

"What happened after that?"

"Nothing," he said. "I was lying in the bed while she was in the shower. I remember that. I had a *lot* to drink tonight, as you may have been told. That's the thing about living in the same place where your friends live. You tend to overindulge because you know that you don't have far to get home."

He swayed a little in the chair, and I realized that he was still recovering from whatever it was he'd had to drink. The news of his wife's death had obviously been sobering but not nearly enough.

"The responding officer said that he had a hard time waking you up. Did you wake up anytime before he arrived?"

Andrew nodded. "Once. And I've been trying to rack my brain about it, but it's so damned fuzzy."

"What do you mean?" Claire asked.

"I woke up once because I heard Bev talking out in the living room."

Claire frowned. "What time was it?"

"I don't know," he said, and Claire could see the frustration on his face. "I don't know if it was as I was falling asleep or sometime later. But I heard her talking to someone."

"Was it a man or a woman?"

"It was a man's voice," he said. "I called out, and I think she said it was Emma, but looking back, I don't think it was."

"You sure you can't remember what time it was?"

He shook his head. "I'm sorry, I can't," he said, and his voice cracked. "I wish I could, but it's all so fuzzy. To be honest, there's a part of me that thinks I could've dreamt it."

CHAPTER 15

Paula
Two days before

RYAN HOOKS, THE VERY famous singer I was desperately trying to blackmail, finally called me at 3:34 a.m. on Thursday.

It took my brain a few minutes to break through the fog of sleep, recognize that the melodious sound filling my head was coming from my cell phone, register that it was from an unknown number, and understand that it might be him.

It might be him!

I bolted upright, my fingers fumbling over the small, screaming rectangle on my nightstand until I had it firmly gripped in my hands. I flipped the small switch on the side to silence it and rolled over onto my side, my back to Keith. He shifted too, either from the noise or the light, but a second later, I heard his deep, measured breaths as he settled back into sleep.

My chest was tight, and breaths flooded out of my body in ragged, unnaturally loud spurts. I stared at the screen as it lit up the dark room. I was used to getting unknown calls, but never at this time of night—it seemed that the telemarketers knew better than that.

They wouldn't call this late.

It *had* to be him.

I took a deep breath and swiped my finger across the screen to answer the call. With shaky hands, I raised the phone to my ear before whispering into it.

"Hello?"

There was silence, the quietest, heaviest silence I'd ever heard in my life, and I felt suddenly panicked at the void on the other end of the line. With all that open space pressed so close to my face, I felt vulnerable, exposed. When I spoke again, my voice sounded hollow and shaky to my own ears.

"Hello? Is someone there?"

Still no response, but I heard something, maybe the rustling of a headset or someone shifting in their seat. It was enough for me to know that there was indeed someone there, quietly listening to my frantic breaths. I opened my mouth wide in an attempt to silence myself.

With the phone still pressed against my ear, I rolled slowly out of bed and tiptoed toward the bedroom door. My legs felt wobbly as I crossed through the threshold and headed out toward the living room. Shelby stirred a little but remained quiet as I sat down on the couch.

And then I waited.

Or rather, *we* waited.

He was there—I knew it with every single bone in my body— yet neither of us spoke for ten seconds, and then another ten, and another. When it became clear that he wasn't going to say anything, that he'd called at three thirty in the morning and was just going to *sit there* in silence, I felt my breathing slow and my nervousness turn to annoyance, then anger. I cleared my throat and finally spoke again, my voice low, calm, and steadier than I expected.

"Ryan, I know you're there."

I heard him suck in a deep breath, and then he responded almost immediately.

"Okay."

That was it. Two syllables, his voice rough, gravelly, defiant. Then there was silence again.

I waited with the phone still pressed against my face, my chest rising and falling with each breath. I ground my jaw stubbornly, determined not to give in again, determined to sit there *all damned night* if I had to—

"You're going to have to start," he said suddenly.

I sat up straighter. It was just six words, but in them, I could feel all the anger and rage I'd seen on his face the night of the concert. I felt my stubbornness slip, if only slightly, as I tried to figure out what exactly it was that needed to be said.

I swallowed. "Okay," I said quietly. I shifted on the couch, folding my legs beneath me, and stared at a particularly shiny spot on the glass coffee table that was catching the moonlight in just the right way. The absurdity of the moment wasn't lost on me, but I forced myself to push forward.

"Well, thanks for calling," I began. "I know this is…crazy, and I appreciate you taking the time to talk to me. And I know this isn't an easy conversation to have, and I just want to say that, for the record, none of this is about judgment for anything that's going on or, you know, I can't speak to the, um, relationship that you have with Emma or your wife or anything like that, but it would be completely out of place for me to comment on that. That's not what this is about—"

"Hey," he jumped in.

I stopped speaking, grateful for the interruption. "Yes?"

"Let me start, since you've obviously never done this before," he said dryly. "How much do you want?"

I froze, my stomach turning over not so much at the words he was saying but how he said them.

"Sorry?"

"Money. How much do you want?"

"I—"

"Oh, come on, Paula. You have got to do better than this."

The first time he said my name, he'd been flirting with me, or so it seemed. He'd said it softly, seductively, and I'd played right into it, blushing like a schoolgirl in the front seat of my car.

This time was different. This time, he drew out my name, lingering over the syllables with purpose.

This time, he was sending a message—I know who you are.

"Well?" he asked. "How much?"

"I've never done this before."

"You've never done this before?" he asked with an incredulous laugh. That went on for a while, him chuckling loudly, and it was obvious he didn't actually find anything funny. "What do you think we're talking about, Paula? Skiing? A threesome? I'm sorry you've *never done this before*, but you really need to catch up quickly. There is, of course, the option of *not doing it*…"

We sat there silently for a moment, and finally, he spoke again.

"So, how much?"

I cleared my throat. "Well, I was hoping you would tell me how much you'd be willing to give me as a reward. You know, for the phone."

"Not one cent," he said. "But then you already know that, right? This is not about the phone. It's about you keeping your damned mouth shut about what you think you saw the other night, and—"

"I read the text messages," I blurted. "All of them, or almost all of them."

"And you had no right to do that," he hissed. "Those were private conversations between me and Em, and you had no right to read them, but I guess that's neither here nor there. So how much?"

"Well, I don't—"

"How much money, Paula? A number. You can't expect to—"

"A hundred and eighty thousand dollars."

It just fell out of me. It was the only number in my head, and I said it because I didn't know what else I was supposed to do.

If there had been silence before, it was deafening now. Maybe it was my imagination, or maybe it was quieter because I'd stopped breathing now that the number was out there.

When a full ten seconds passed without a word from Hooks, I spoke again. "Hello?"

"You really have lost your mind, you know that?"

"Is that...too much?" I asked, and I instantly wanted to kick myself as the question came out of my mouth.

He laughed, the same humorless laugh from before, and I shifted in my seat.

"I have to say, if you weren't blackmailing me, I'd almost find you cute. Endearing. That is, like I said, if you weren't such a horrible person. Does your husband know about this?"

The question caught me off guard, and I actually dropped the phone onto the couch. In the dark, I scrambled for it and put it back up to my ear.

"What?" I asked.

"Your husband. He's tagged in your Twitter photos, Paula. You *didn't think this through*. It's Keith, right? Does he know what you're doing?"

I was silent, completely frozen, and I realized that he was right—I hadn't thought it through, not enough. I'd just been moving forward, stumbling along. But the thought—the mere idea—of Keith finding out about what I'd done made it almost impossible to breathe, and I struggled to find the right response.

"I'm going to take that silence as a no," he said smugly. "So you think I have a lot to lose if my wife finds out where I was on Saturday. You have a lot to lose too. I'll get you your money, but I'll get it together when I can."

There was something about his final words that snapped me out of it. He was trying to bait me, to intimidate me, to make me feel that we were in this together, and I had to remind myself that *I* was the one who'd seen *him*.

I was the one who still had his phone with all the text messages.

And, most importantly, he wouldn't be calling me if he wasn't willing to pay.

"No, you'll give it to me in one week," I said. "Because if you don't, I'm posting screenshots online. No, I don't want my family finding out, but I'm willing to bet that you don't want yours to find out about Emma, or her little pup, Dante, or your midnight trips to Oak Street. If you want to take that chance, go for it."

He was silent for a long time. I was determined not to speak first, so we waited, and when he spoke, his tone had changed.

"You're fucking nuts," he said, surprise in his voice.

I was tempted to respond, but I still held myself back, and after another minute passed, he finally spoke again.

This time, he sounded tired and maybe…resigned.

"The crazy thing is that she doesn't mean anything to me," he said. "Emma Bentley is just some stupid whore, and I've never regretted hooking up with a fan more than I do now. I'll get you your money."

The line disconnected immediately, and I sat there in the dark, my heart racing, my stomach tied up in knots.

This is not your responsibility, Paula.

You have to let it go.

And yet…

Emma had mentioned that there were big changes coming for Allure. And judging by their text messages, she was going to sell her business for a man who'd just called her a "stupid whore."

There was a chance, of course, that he'd—very misguidedly—said that only for my benefit.

Maybe he thought that by expressing his loyalty to Tiffane, he'd get me to back off.

But his tone had been too callous for that.

No, he hadn't said it for my benefit.

He'd said it because he meant it.

Emma had opened herself up to me in the park the other afternoon. I owed it to her to at least let her know that her Prince Charming was a humongous piece of shit.

Besides, I'd always been a fan of canapés.

PART 2

❖
---

the night in question

CHAPTER 16

Paula

The Night in Question

FINISHED MY SHIFT AT the diner on Saturday and then hurried home to get ready for Emma's dinner party.

I think, deep down, there was a part of me that knew that I would go the moment she'd invited me that day in the park, that each one of my promises to myself that I wouldn't go had been as half-hearted as they'd been useless.

I chose my outfit carefully, settling on my favorite little black dress, a large, red-and-gold statement necklace, and my favorite pair of bright-red pumps with a little gold buckle on the back. They were my special occasion shoes, the kind that got you noticed, and even though I wanted to fly under the radar tonight, I couldn't resist. I combed my hair straight back from my face, just to test it, and then went for my usual side part, tucking one side behind my ear and fluffing the other side with my fingertips. Then I left the apartment, brushing Shelby's head with my hand before I walked out.

My excitement began to wane as I sat in my car outside Emma's apartment. I'd wanted to text her to let her know I was coming—it's what any normal guest would do—but then again, everything about me tonight was far from normal. I couldn't afford for Emma to have my cell phone number; it was just too messy.

Hopefully, she'd meant it when she said I could just show up.

I was sure that Hooks wouldn't be there, yet I was nervous about that too. What if, for some odd reason, he was the one who opened the door when I arrived? What if her small circle of friends knew about the affair and she'd invited him too? I knew it was close to impossible—Hooks wouldn't spend Saturday nights out in the open with his girlfriend and her friends—but I couldn't help but worry about it.

I checked my phone and saw that it was five minutes to eight. I took a deep breath and got out of the car, then walked to the building and up the steps. It was surreal; only a few nights ago, I'd sat in front of the same building tinkering with my DAC app as I watched Ryan Hooks walk up to greet the half-naked woman who had watched him from the second-story window.

Now, I was going in to meet the same woman, holding a cheap plant I'd bought at the grocery store. I'd picked it up at the last second—my mother was a firm believer that you never showed up at someone's home empty-handed—but now I was regretting it.

It's not a housewarming party, Paula.

I would be in and out. I would eat dinner, pretend to be interested in the designs, and find a moment to get Emma alone. I would convince her that she shouldn't sell the business to travel with Hooks, and then I would leave. She still didn't have my contact information, and I would keep it that way. If she pressed it, I would give her a fake number.

I took another breath, this one much longer and slower, before reaching up to push the button next to Emma's name. I waited, wondering what I was supposed to say. But nobody asked who it was; they only buzzed the door open, and a moment later, I was stepping inside.

THE NIGHT IN QUESTION

I was instantly awed by the simple, modern decor of the apartment building. I couldn't imagine how often they cleaned it, but there wasn't a speck on the plush, tan carpet under my feet or even a smudge on the cream-colored walls.

When I got to the second floor, I could see Emma standing in the door, though she was facing back into her apartment and talking to someone. She spun to face me when I was just steps away and then smiled, stepping back to let me inside.

"Chris!" she said, an expression of surprise on her face. But instead of asking me why the hell I'd shown up without confirming that I was coming, she reached forward and gave me a hug.

I was caught off guard for a moment and just froze, one arm cradling the plant, the other reaching around to pat her awkwardly on the back.

"I'm so happy you could make it," she said.

"Sorry I didn't call," I started.

But she shook her head. "Oh, don't worry about it. There's plenty of space and plenty of food."

I held the plant out, and she smiled and took it from me. "That was so kind of you," she said, and it sounded genuine. "Thank you." We walked inside together, and she set the plant down on a small table near the door.

The room was bright, large, and beautifully put together. There was a dining table against one wall, decorated so carefully that it looked like it should've been featured in an IKEA catalog. It was covered in a satin tablecloth that looked so soft, I almost reached out to touch it. There were eight place settings around the rectangular table, three on each side and one at either head of the table. Each setting contained a plate with a beautiful yellow-and-blue napkin folded delicately on top, a wineglass, and a bamboo place mat.

There was a man walking toward me, holding a glass of wine.

He was a few inches shorter than me in my heels, with thinning black hair and a huge, toothy smile.

"Chris, this is Joshua Burlap. He's the owner of Klein's on Halsted in Lincoln Park. We're planning on having our launch event there next week, which is just fantastic. "Joshua, this is the artist I was telling you about, Chris…"

Emma turned to me with a puzzled look and then a sheepish smile. She trailed off in a way that made it clear she was looking for my last name, but I played it off by reaching out quickly to shake his hand.

"Great to meet you," I said.

"Nice to meet you too," he said slowly and deliberately as he let his eyes trail from my head to my shoes and back up again. He smiled in a slow way that made a soft "Ew" fall from my lips, and I froze, my hand still in his. If he heard me, he ignored it and gripped my hand tighter, leaning in. "I love artists. The ideas that must go on in there…"

He used his chin to gesture up toward what I must assume was my head. Then he just stared at me and continued holding my hand. I pulled it away quickly and nodded.

"Uh, yeah," I said, watching as Emma turned to walk toward the kitchen, where I could see two women in uniforms pulling items out of large insulated bags. "Lots of thoughts and…things like that."

"Where do you get your inspiration?"

"Well, I do portraits for the most part, so…" He continued to watch me, and I cleared my throat. "My inspiration for those is, um, mostly the faces of the people…that I'm doing the portraits of."

A woman walked out of the kitchen toward us, with Emma right behind her, and I was happy for the interruption.

"Chris, this is Beverly, my friend and neighbor from upstairs.

You met Bev's husband, Andrew, on Monday at the park," Emma said.

"Nice to meet you," I said, shaking her hand.

"You too," Beverly said. She was shorter than me—maybe five foot six or so—and she had thick, dark-brown hair, which was pulled back into a ponytail at the nape of her neck. She watched me with something that felt very much like suspicion. "You're the artist, right?"

"Yes," I said.

"How long have you done that?" Her question came out abruptly—more interview-like than conversational—and I blinked.

"My whole life, in some way or another," I said. "But professionally, since I graduated top of my class from the School of the Art Institute of Chicago."

That came out more defensively than I'd planned, but Beverly didn't seem to notice.

"We'll need to talk about your rates," she said. My eyes widened slightly, and she continued. "I'm Emma's lawyer, and I've also been handling a lot of the finances for the company in the startup stage. No sense in beating around the bush. We'll want to get that part sorted out pretty quickly. Since I'm sure you're not here to do charity."

"Geez, Bev, let the woman have a glass of wine first," Emma said with a laugh. "I'll go get you one. Red or white?"

I considered turning her down, but I was too tense; maybe it would help. "White," I said. "Thank you."

Beverly opened her mouth to ask another question when I heard a man's voice behind me.

"Hello again!"

I turned to see Andrew, the man I'd met in the park with Emma, walking into the apartment. He was wearing jeans and a black T-shirt, and he had a smile on his face.

"Bev, this is the woman I was telling you about, the one who also takes the time to research dog parks before bringing her pup there."

"Oh," Beverly said, raising her eyebrows slightly, barely able to feign interest. "That's how you met Emma, right?"

"Mm-hmm," I said, suddenly aching for the glass of wine. I looked past them toward the kitchen.

Is this what people do when they meet for the first time?

Ask each other a shit-ton of questions?

"Hey, did you take Sammy out?" I heard Andrew ask his wife.

She frowned. "I got home from the office and came straight here. You were at a baseball game. You don't think you could've done that?"

Andrew glanced over at me with a sheepish smile before turning his back in an attempt to shield me from their conversation. He lowered his voice even further, but I could still hear him. "I didn't say you should've. I just asked if you did," he said.

"Like those aren't the same thing."

"They aren't," he said through gritted teeth.

Emma returned with the wine, and I thanked her before taking a sip.

There was movement by the door, and I watched as a tall man walked in, followed by a petite woman with bright-pink hair. The woman flew through the door and wrapped her arms around Emma, giving her a long hug.

"I've been waiting for this all week!" the woman said.

Emma stepped back with a laugh. She turned to look at me. "Chris, this is my little sister, Meggie, the wonderful designer I've been telling you about. And this is her boyfriend, Patrick."

The couple looked up at me, and I could see the recognition cross their faces at the same time. I flashed back to meeting them in

172

Klein's Boutique a few days ago, how they both had gone on and on about how selfish and cruel Emma was.

There was a long pause, and then Meggie stepped forward to shake my hand, her eyes narrow. "Nice to meet you," she said abruptly.

Patrick nodded his head toward me but didn't say anything else.

"You too," I said, combing my mind for something else to say.

Joshua Burlap walked back into the room at that moment, and he smiled broadly when he saw Beverly standing there.

"My favorite lawyer," he said. "Looking amazing as usual. Someone's been hitting the gym." He turned to Andrew and gave him a small smile and a shrug. "Sorry, man."

"Thank you, Joshua," Beverly said coolly. "But never apologize to my husband for making an inappropriate comment about me. He is my husband, not my keeper. You've offended me, and hence your apology should be directed my way."

There was a long, awkward pause, and then Emma stepped forward, breaking the silence.

"Well, since everyone is here, I think we can go ahead and eat," she said, walking over and placing a hand on the back of one of the seats at the end of the table. She waved a hand at the rest of the settings. "Please, everyone, take a seat. There's no assigned seating, so sit wherever you like."

We all hesitated for a moment, waiting for someone else to move, but finally, Meggie walked over and plopped down next to her sister. Patrick followed her, sitting in one of the middle seats, leaving one chair on the other side of him. Beverly followed Meggie's lead, sitting on the other side of Emma, and Andrew quickly slipped into the middle seat across from Patrick. Joshua and I settled into the remaining seats on opposite sides of Patrick and Andrew, leaving the other host place setting untouched.

"All right," Emma said with a smile. "Let's have a good night."

CHAPTER 17

LIKE CLOCKWORK, THE TWO members of the catering staff emerged from the kitchen, holding plates in their hands. They set the food down in front of Emma and then began to work their way around the table before hurrying back to get more plates. I looked down at the food—one small plate was the beef canapés that Emma had promised, and the other held a salad of microgreens, with walnuts and grape tomatoes.

"So, Meggie, how excited are you about having your first show?" Joshua asked, leaning forward to grab a piece of bread from the center of the table. He picked one up and examined it before tossing it back in the basket and grabbing another one. "Your work is really incredible, and I am absolutely honored to have the first showing at Klein's."

Meggie smiled. "I am excited," she said. "I will just feel a lot better once we figure a few things out."

She shot a glance at her sister before stabbing a tomato with her fork and putting it into her mouth. The answer felt abrupt, and there was silence for a few moments as everyone tried to decide if they should continue down that conversation path or pivot somewhere else.

"We should probably tell you a little more about Allure Apparel,"

Emma said, looking down the table at me. "We make shopping for clothes sort of like shopping for makeup. We recognize that different colors are more flattering for different skin tones, so once you find the piece you like, you can find the exact shade of that color for your skin tone. So instead of one pink pair of high-waist pattern shorts, we have thirteen."

"That's a cool concept," I said.

"After dinner, we can show you some of the books."

Meggie looked up at me, nodded, and then went back to her plate.

"Have you ever done something like this before?" Emma asked me.

"No, I haven't," I said. "But I'm excited to learn more about the line. I think, if done right, the paintings could—"

I was halfway through the sentence when Patrick said something across the table to Andrew, and they both laughed. It was something about the food, and I raised my voice a little to finish the conversation with Emma. But she'd turned to answer a question from Beverly, and suddenly, I was talking to no one, finishing my sentence only because it seemed silly to stop halfway through.

"—serve as a great complement to the clothes," I said quietly. I looked up to see that Joshua was watching me with a slight smirk on his face as if he enjoyed seeing my discomfort.

"I'm listening," he said softly with a wink.

The rest of the dinner was filled with several more awkward moments, and I wondered why Emma had invited me. Maybe she was just feeling in a good mood the other day and regretted the invitation this morning. Maybe she hadn't expected me to actually accept the last-minute invitation. I reached out and finished my glass of wine, smiling and nodding as one of the servers appeared to offer me some more.

By the end of dinner, I was feeling a lot better, thanks in large part to the three glasses of wine I'd consumed since I'd arrived. I wasn't alone in my revelry—the entire table, it seemed, was talking and laughing much louder than they had only an hour or so ago.

"I'm going outside for a smoke," I heard someone say at the far end of the table, and then Beverly stood and stepped around the table.

"I'll join you," I heard Meggie say, and the two women walked toward the kitchen. A moment later, I heard the sound of the patio door slide open. Emma stood and walked over to talk to the women from the catering company, who were packing up some of their bags. Patrick and Andrew were deep in conversation at my side, discussing something about real estate.

That left Joshua, who was staring at me from across the table. To avoid any more awkward conversation, I pretended to be listening to Patrick and Andrew, even though they barely seemed to notice that Joshua and I were still sitting there.

I continued to avoid the store owner's leering gaze and then finally stood and excused myself.

"I'll be right back," I said, deliberately looking at Patrick and Andrew, who nodded briefly and then jumped back into their conversation.

The wine made me sway, and I paused for a minute before hurrying off toward the bathroom. As I walked, I looked down the hall and saw that there were two more closed doors, one of which had to be the master bedroom.

I was about to step into the bathroom when I heard someone speak behind me.

"Hey."

I turned to see Meggie standing there.

"I thought you said you were doing some drawings for my sister's apartment!"

"That's what I thought at first," I said. "Turns out she meant portraits of the models of Allure. For the launch." I peered out into the living room. "You didn't mention Emma was your sister."

"I didn't feel I needed to," she snapped, and then she took a deep breath. "Sorry. Look, Patrick and I were just gossiping a little the other day. You know what I mean. Obviously, my sister has done a lot for me, so I'd appreciate if you don't talk about—"

"Oh, of course," I said. "I would never."

She nodded. "Good. In fact, no need for either of us to bring up that we've met before. Thanks," she said before spinning on her heel and walking away.

I stepped into the bathroom and closed the door behind me.

Don't forget why you came here tonight.

I just needed a few minutes alone with Emma to talk to her. To tell her that she shouldn't give up ownership of her business for Ryan Asshole Hooks. I washed my hands, then opened the door to the bathroom and stepped out.

I couldn't see anyone from the hallway, but I could still hear Patrick and Andrew talking from the dinner table. On a whim, I squared my shoulders and then took off down the hallway toward one of the closed doors. Pushing it open, I looked inside, my heart racing. It was a beautifully decorated room, with lavender accents on dark, wood furniture. I walked around for a few moments, but there were no pictures, no papers, nothing that would prove that Ryan Hooks had ever been there. I knew I was pushing my luck, so I turned and walked quickly toward the bedroom door. Stepping out and closing it behind me, I moved quickly down the hall back toward the living room. I'd almost made it back to the bathroom when Joshua appeared, moving in my direction. He frowned when he saw me.

"Doing okay?" he asked, looking curiously behind me to see where I was coming from.

I smiled. "Uh, yeah," I said, floundering for a reason why I was at the wrong end of the hallway. I looked over to see that the bathroom door was closed again and thought quickly.

"I was looking for another bathroom," I said with a shrug. "You know, all that white wine."

The door opened just then, and Bev walked out. She looked at us both with a frown and then walked past us.

Joshua watched her walk away and then turned back to me.

"I'll let you go first then," he said, stepping back to let me go in. "Then come back out and join the party."

I was sitting on the couch when I saw Emma walking toward me holding two glasses of wine. She held one out, and I took it as she slumped onto the couch.

"I'm exhausted," she said, and then she turned to me with a smile. "I'm so glad you came and stayed."

"Oh, no problem," I said. "It's actually been really fun."

"How is your husband?" she asked, sitting up.

I don't know why I was surprised by the fact that she remembered, but I felt a wave of emotion suddenly rush over me. "He's doing okay," I said. "Thank you."

"You know," she said, "I know it might sound weird, but the day we talked in the park, I felt like we had a lot in common. There was just something about you. And honestly, I could use some good friends in my life right now."

"You seem like you have a lot of friends," I said, gesturing around the apartment. "Well, good close friends, at least. Those are hard to come by."

"Friends, acquaintances, business partners," she said, shrugging. "Sometimes it all blends together."

I didn't know what she meant, but I nodded. I shifted in my seat as a thought came to me.

Maybe this was my chance.

"What about the guy you were telling me about the other day?" I asked, and I tried to keep my voice as innocent as possible.

Not too excited but interested.

She smiled, a deep, full smile that reached her eyes. "It was instant with him too. It used to be that I only felt like I could be myself when I was completely alone, like I had to put on a mask if there was anyone else around. But with him, it's not just that I can be myself. Sometimes I feel like I'm *more* the real me when he's around than when I'm alone. If that doesn't sound completely desperate." She laughed. "Who am I kidding? Of course it does."

I smiled. "It doesn't," I said softly.

She blinked a few times and then reached up and grabbed at her eye. "Oh goodness, looks like someone's had too much wine," she said with a sniffle and then pulled something away from her face. I was surprised to see that her eyes were red and she was holding a long, feathery strip of fake eyelashes in her hand.

"You know it's a good party when you've cried your lashes off," I said.

She laughed again. "Damn right."

I took a deep breath. "Can I ask—why wasn't he here tonight?"

She blinked and looked up at me. "Oh, um…he's super busy…with work and everything," she said. She leaned forward.

"But he's taking some time off next month, and we're going on a little trip."

"Where are you going?" I asked.

"To Sonoma. He has a little villa out there. We're just going for a long weekend, but I can't wait."

"That sounds great," I said with a smile.

And as I sat there watching her hold her eyelashes between her fingertips and talking to me as if we'd been friends for years, I felt a wave of guilt rush over me.

I cleared my throat.

Now or never. This might be my only opportunity to tell her that she needed to reconsider selling the business and taking Ryan up on his offer of being his assistant. I hadn't prepared well enough and finally just blurted out the first thing that came to mind.

"I can tell you really love Allure," I said.

It must have been too abrupt, because she frowned a little and tilted her head.

"Yeah, I do," she said. "It's brought Meggie and me closer together, so that's been great."

"What do you mean?"

She smiled sadly. "We've never had a great relationship, and it got really bad when my mom died seven years ago," she said. "Meggie is a strong, independent woman, and I'm so proud of her. We just operate so differently. I think she finds me a little controlling, which I can be, but I'm her big sister. I'm supposed to be. Before our father died, he asked me to watch out for her, and if that means being a little bit more controlling than she likes, so be it. But in the last year or so, the clothing line has been a real common ground for us."

"Where do you see the company in five years?"

Emma flinched, just slightly, but then the smile was back on her face. "Um, growing to have customers all across the world."

"Maybe starting in New York?" I asked.

She frowned. "Yeah, maybe," she said. "What's gotten into you? Is this an interview?"

"No, nothing," I said with a smile. "Sorry, it's just really inspiring to see someone following her dreams, that's all."

She smiled, and I detected a hint of sadness behind her eyes. "I think something has gotten into you all right," she said. "And we'll need to get some more in you." She stood up and walked over to the dining room table and picked up a bottle of wine. "Where's your glass?"

The next thing I knew, I was lying on my side, and there was carpet in my mouth.

Or maybe it was hair. I pressed my tongue upward and felt the grainy thread there, tickling the roof of my mouth. It took another few moments for me to realize that I was lying on the floor. I was still in Emma's apartment, but there was no one around me. And I was lying...

Behind the couch?

I clenched the carpet as the room spun around me again, and I wanted to cry because I should have been able to get up.

I needed help.

But I couldn't speak, the cries somehow lost in my throat.

I heard talking, and I tried to lift my head to see who it was.

I could see two figures in the kitchen. They were moving—first just feet, then their legs, and then their entire bodies.

A man and a woman.

They were talking quietly, and I couldn't make out any of their words. I had the distinct feeling that they didn't know I was there.

I strained upward to see them, but it sent a sharp pain down the side of my body, and I let myself drop as sleep, or something very much like it, took over.

CHAPTER 18

Claire
The Night in Question

THE SUN WAS COMING up by the time Claire walked out of
Andrew Brighton's apartment.

She knew she should call it a night. She was pushing her luck
trying to sneak in interviews so late at night. But she'd meant it
when she'd told Greg that she didn't want to let the dust settle.
People tended to stretch the truth when they had time to think
about what they were going to say.

She needed gut reactions.

She needed the truth.

Claire walked down to the first floor. She would wrap up the
night with one more interview. She'd go home and get some sleep,
then start all over again. Later that day, they'd have more information
from Dr. Ortiz about the exact time and cause of death, and they'd
know what the stain on Beverly and Andrew's carpet was. Claire
would also stop by to interview the store owner, Joshua Burlap.

Then she would dig a little harder into the artist, Chris.

If there was one piece of the puzzle that didn't fit, it was the
artist.

No contact information.

No last name.

No traces of her besides the fuzzy accounts of three party guests, who all seemed to have something to hide.

Claire walked over to the first-floor apartment and knocked on the door. It had been open when she arrived, but someone had shut it in the past hour.

It took a few moments, but then the door was flung open, and a man in his late twenties with shaggy, shoulder-length brown hair stood in the doorway.

"Seriously?" he asked, something close to a pout on his face. "Do we have to do this now?"

"I'd appreciate just a few minutes of your time," Claire said before introducing herself. "I spoke with your girlfriend, and she said you were down here. I know it's been a rough night, but this will only take a moment."

"A rough night?" Patrick asked, raising an eyebrow. "Is that what you call this?" He sighed and stepped back into the apartment, letting her inside. "This is just so completely fucked up. Where is Meggie anyway?"

"I think she's still upstairs with her sister." Claire stepped all the way into the room and looked around. Layout-wise, it looked a lot like the other two units, but the decor was much more colorful and crafty. They stopped in the living room near the couch, but Patrick didn't sit, nor did he invite Claire to.

"What can I tell you?" he asked.

"How about you start with what happened when you and Meggie got home?"

He frowned. "Didn't she already tell you?" Claire didn't respond, and he sighed. "Oh, I get it. You want to see if our stories match up. If this isn't the biggest crock of…" He took a deep breath and sighed. "We went to Boxer's, came home around two thirty, walked in, saw the blood on the carpet and the wall, and went upstairs to check it out. And when we got to the top, we saw her freaking *hand*." He swallowed and took a breath. "The blood on the carpet really stood out to us. I mean, that thing is always spotless. I think Emma has it cleaned every two weeks."

Claire frowned. Meggie had used almost those exact words, which made her wonder: Had they rehearsed their story?

And more importantly, *why*?

She made a mental note of it and moved on. "One of the other tenants mentioned that you've had some run-ins with Beverly in the past," she said.

He sighed. "One of the other tenants? You mean Emma? Look, Bev and I certainly weren't best friends after she accused me of stealing her necklace. Which I *didn't* do, if you're wondering. I'm a lot of things, but I'm no thief. Still, I wouldn't *bash* her over it. Not my style."

"What about anyone else at the party tonight? Anyone else have any issues with Beverly? Anyone you think could've done this?"

He shrugged. "Maybe that creepy store owner? He kept coming on to Bev all night, and she wasn't too happy about it."

Claire frowned. "Okay," she said. "And you were the last to leave?"

"Yeah, me and Meggie. Around one."

"What can you tell me about Chris?"

"Who?"

"The artist who was at the dinner party tonight?"

"Oh, Emma's weird friend?" he asked. "Not much."

"You know, we found one of her shoes underneath Emma's couch," Claire said.

Patrick let out a laugh. "Really? That's not a huge surprise, to be honest. She liked her beverage a little too much, if you know what I mean."

"I have an idea, but maybe you can elaborate," Claire said.

Patrick shrugged. "She was quiet at first, but after a few, she became very talkative. Talking about relationships and loyalty and stuff like that. It was weird and not a little awkward," he said with a laugh. "And then she was out of it. One moment, she was bouncing off the walls; the next, she was dead asleep behind the couch. So, like I said, I'm not surprised she left one of her shoes there."

"What time was that?" Claire asked.

"That I saw her knocked out?" he asked. "I don't know. Maybe midnight, maybe a little after that."

"And what time did you see her leave?"

"She must have left around twelve thirty or twelve forty-five or something, because, like I said, we left at one."

Something about the phrasing made Claire pause. "She must have?" she said. "Did you see her leave?"

Patrick started to nod and then he paused. "Well, no, I didn't see her walk out the door, but she was definitely gone before we left."

He said this last part slowly and tilted his head as he looked at his own couch, which was positioned in much the same way as Emma's upstairs.

He looked at Claire, then back at the couch, and then back at Claire again.

"Well, shit," he said with a small chuckle. "At least I *think* she was."

the week after
the night

CHAPTER 19

Paula

The day after

THE FIRST THING I noticed when I woke up was that my cheek was wet.

Everything hurt, and I do mean *everything*. Places on my body that I did not know could hurt throbbed—the joints between my fingers, the bottom of my tongue. It all *hurt so much*.

I took a few long, slow breaths to steady myself.

I was in a bed, which was a good start. The feel of the pillow beneath my head was familiar, the smell soothing.

I was at home.

Good.

Still, I couldn't grasp how I'd gotten there, what time it was, or, importantly, where Keith was. I only knew he wasn't there beside me.

I moved my head, my brain alert just enough to know it desired a dry spot. As I shifted, sunlight stabbed through the blinds, sending a sharp pain through my head. I winced and moved again, planting my cheek back in my own drool. I felt my stomach flip over in disgust. I needed to get up, to get away from my own filth, to take a shower and rinse away my shame and disappointment.

Instead, I flipped the pillow over and let my head drop back down.

The energy it took to lift and turn it drained everything out of me, and as I flopped down, I opened my mouth wide, breathing heavily as the room spun around me. I needed more air, and keeping my mouth open seemed like the most logical way to make that happen. I would drool again, there was no doubt about it, but that was something I was going to have to live with.

I didn't bother to look at the clock; the sun that snuck through the closed shades was the afternoon kind, not the morning. I'd slept a very long time, and still, I needed more. A lot more. I closed my eyes and thought the words I'd thought before and would think again:

I will never drink again.

I will never drink again.

As I lay there, the fuzzy memories from the night before came flooding back, and I reached up slowly and pressed a palm into my left eye. The embarrassment during dinner. I'd made a fool of myself because that's what happens when you're sad and angry and you drink more than you should.

And then there was Hooks.

Wait, Hooks?

Why could I see his face so clearly?

He hadn't been there—had he?

I started to sit up again, but the room spun quickly, and I let my body drop back down once again.

Vertical, bad.

Horizontal, better.

Not good by any means, but better.

I rolled onto my side and breathed out of my mouth again, since that seemed to help just a little. I tried to push the splotchy images together, and suddenly, I remembered lying, in much the same position as I was in right now, on Emma's floor, my cheek on the carpet, my eyelids heavy and tacky as I peered at the couple in the kitchen.

It all dissolved, and then I could only see Hooks's face, his jaw-line and his eyes. One moment, he was sitting in the back seat of my car, and then he was on the jumbo screen at the stadium. Next, he was in Emma's apartment, yelling at someone.

Was he yelling at me?

The images were a blurry, fuzzy mess, and trying to make any sense of them made my head hurt.

I saw two figures in Emma's kitchen, heard them whispering, saying words I couldn't make out, and then they turned—

Suddenly, I was right back in my own bed, and I heard a noise at the door. It was Keith coming into the bedroom, and he wheeled himself up alongside the bed. Through the slits in my eyes, I could see the concern on his face as he watched me, waiting for me to say something. After a moment, I let my eyelids flutter back down, the mere thought of keeping them open for much longer exhausting.

"Paula, wake up," I heard him say, and I was surprised not to hear any anger in his voice.

I blinked slowly and looked at him again. My mouth felt dry, and there were strands of hair covering my face, and through it all, I wondered what I looked like. If I looked as bad as I felt, and if, behind his concern, there was just a sliver of disgust there.

I wondered if he ever thought about how bad he looked when I had to clean the whiskey from his stubble.

Probably not.

"What happened to your face?" he asked, supporting my insecurities.

I cringed. It must be really bad. But then I saw his expression, and it occurred to me that he wasn't just saying that I didn't look great. He was talking about something particular. I tried to speak, but nothing came out, and my throat ached as I tried to form words. Summoning all the strength I could, I reached a hand up and touched the side of my face. I winced as my fingers connected with a puffy, tender part of my face, right below my right temple.

"Ow," I said, the first sound I'd made all morning, and it was a low, alcohol-laced growl of a word. I didn't have to see it to know that there was a sizable bruise there. "I don't know," I finally said, my voice sounding scratchy, deep, and nothing like my own.

Keith let out a long sigh. "You need to drink this," he said.

I looked down and noticed he had a glass of water in his hands. It fizzled a little in a way that plain water shouldn't, which let me know he'd added something to it.

"There's no way."

"Paula—"

"There's no way. Just give me a minute."

He sighed again and put the glass down on the nightstand beside me.

"Where did you guys go?" he asked. "Another one of Vanessa's parties?"

Through all my pain, I felt the immediate regret of my lies. There was a part of me—the good part of me—that wanted to tell the truth. To tell him that I hadn't been out with Vanessa, and that I hadn't actually lied about it, but that when *he'd* assumed it, I just hadn't corrected him. That same part of me wanted to say that I'd been with a new friend, at a party in the Gold Coast, and that I'd fallen asleep on her carpet and then been put in a cab to go home.

That's it.

A few pieces of the puzzle began to come together as I remembered stepping out of a cab in front of our apartment and falling onto the pavement.

I must have hurt my face then?

The driver had gotten out and helped me up. He'd actually helped me all the way to the front door and unlocked it. I remembered standing there with him on the stoop as he fumbled with my keys, unsure of which one fit the lock.

The embarrassment flooded over me, and I had a moment of thanks that there were still some good people in the world. The fact that I'd managed to make it to my own bed still seemed like a miracle.

"Paula?"

That part of me that wanted to tell him the truth, to tell him I was doing this all for us, was too tired, or maybe just too scared, and it curled up under the covers, away from the unforgiving daylight. I wanted to burrow down with it.

So instead of lying more, I avoided it all. I let my heavy eyelids droop some more, and a moment later, I wasn't pretending at all.

"Paula?" I heard him say tiredly. He waited a few moments, and then I was vaguely aware of him spinning around and moving toward the door.

As I drifted into sleep, I heard him speak again, the words barely making it into my consciousness.

"Oh yeah, you might not remember it, but you only came home with one shoe," he said. "That red pair you really like. You sat on the bed and cried about it for five minutes before you passed out. So…just so you know."

But I didn't know anything of the sort, because by the time he'd finished speaking, I was once again dead to the world.

I hadn't hurt my face when I fell out of the cab. That fall had given me only a slight scrape on my knee, which I would barely notice the next day due to my other ailments.

It had taken me drifting back into sleep to remember what really happened the night before to cause the massive, blue-green bruise on the side of my face.

Ryan Hooks's face appeared again when I dozed off.

One moment, he was in the back seat of my car, and I felt the same warmth I'd felt the night I'd picked him up. In the dream, he was a little more charming, a little more handsome, and even a little taller than he'd been that night, and I drove with both eyes on him in the rearview mirror, even though I knew I should be looking at the road. I knew there was another car coming—we were moments away from crashing, I could feel it—but I stayed focused on him, our gazes locked.

I could see the other car approaching the nose of my own, and right before the collision, it all disappeared, and suddenly, I was lying on the carpet in Emma's apartment again.

I could still see Hooks, but now he was pressed against Emma in the kitchen, and I couldn't tell if it was anger or passion that had his body so tense. He stood close to her, his body inches from hers, and she'd turned her face away so I couldn't actually see her.

She was backed up against a wall, and I couldn't tell if she wanted to be there or if she was trying to squirm away. I felt glued to the carpet, and as I watched them, I wanted to call out, but I couldn't move or speak. I wanted to get up to stop him, to hit him with something, to help, since I hadn't been a help to anyone that night, certainly not myself. As the pleas fluttered around my lips, I let my head settle just a little, since the plush carpet felt so soft against my cheek. I just needed to rest a little, and then I would get up to help.

I must have made a noise.

Suddenly, my eyes were open again, and they were both turned in my direction. I could only see Emma's face as she stared at me in horror, and then she pulled away from Hooks and rushed toward me. I'd been on the floor between the couch and the window, and they hadn't seen me all that time, and I should've kept it that way.

I wasn't hiding.

I wasn't spying on them.

I would've left if I could've, but I was just so damned tired.

They were both angry, walking toward me, and then they were pulling me up. Dragging me, their fingers gripped into my arms. I felt something cutting into my left arm, something sharp and bruising, and I cried out. Suddenly, I was upright. It hurt to stay up when everything around me was falling down, but they weren't listening to me, weren't understanding that I just needed a moment. I knew this was wrong, knew what I'd done was wrong, knew he would be telling her who I was and what I was doing there. But I couldn't get any words out, because the alcohol had clogged the back of my throat. And my feet weren't actually touching the floor...

They were pushing me.

They wanted it to seem like they were helping me, carrying me, but really, they were pushing me out of the apartment. Propelling me forward into the hallway, and then we were at the top of the stairs. Everything seemed so loud, and I wondered if we'd wake anyone else up. I was trying to get them to stop, but the words came out garbled and wine-laden. They were talking to each other in worried, fuzzy breaths. I could see Hooks's face clearly—he was the assertive one, taking on most of my weight. Emma was on my left, helping him, but her face was just out of view. My feet tapped on the padded stairs as they dragged me down, and all I could think was that I wanted to tell them I was sorry.

Sorry for what I'd done.

I was going down the stairs, fast.

Too fast.

The fingers cutting into my arm.

They were being careless, and I imagined their fingers slipping from my skin several seconds before it actually happened. Before anyone could stop it, I pitched forward, toppling the rest of the way down to the first floor, and the pain was simply just too much to bear.

When I woke up, someone was shouting.

"Paula!"

I was back in bed, and Keith was at my side again. The sunlight was gone, and in the back of my mind, I knew that I'd slept the morning away and part of the afternoon too. I felt sick, and my head throbbed, and I closed my eyes to feign sleep—maybe he would just go away.

"Paula!"

There were other words swimming in there too.

"I just got commission…art…"

I groaned and tried to pull the pillow over my face, but he pulled it away and kept talking.

"Art…wants a piece from me…"

I blinked, my eyes still tacky, the pillow wet again, and I covered my eyes with my hand.

"This week…Ryan Hooks."

I sat up too quickly, and the room seemed to turn over, a full forward flip, but I turned my body to stare at him.

"What did you just say?" I asked.

"I said that Ryan Hooks just liked three of my vases on Twitter and then sent me a direct message. He's interested in buying one."

The mixture of emotion was too much: his sheer joy, the excitement pulsing from his body. He was watching me expectantly, waiting for me to say something, to react in some way.

"Paula?" he said. "Did you hear what I just said? You just went to his concert, right? You and Vanessa? What, did you put in a good word for me?"

I watched him, the horror of what he was saying washing over me, and suddenly, my stomach lurched, and I jumped up from the bed and ran to the bathroom.

He wheeled back to let me by.

"Oh shit," he said as I ran in and made it to the toilet just in time.

When I was done being sick, I turned around, and he was sitting in the bathroom doorway, watching me.

"You okay?" he asked softly.

I nodded, standing and walking shakily to the sink to wash my mouth out.

"You have had a rough night," he said. "You need to lie back down."

I teetered back into the bedroom. "What happened?" I asked. "When did he contact you?"

"I guess he sent it early this morning, but I just saw it now," he said. "I can't believe it. I haven't felt this good since…I can't tell you the last time."

"How did he contact you?"

"Twitter," he said.

I nodded, looking around the room for my phone. It wasn't in the bedroom, and I walked past him again toward the living room. I saw my purse on the coffee table, and I picked it up, rifling inside for my phone.

"What are you doing?" Keith said, following me.

"Nothing. Just want to make sure I didn't miss a call from Vanessa."

"Yeah, she probably will want to know that you're okay. You guys have been pulling some nights."

I pulled my phone out of my pocket, and sure enough, there were several missed calls. I scrolled through them and felt my chest tighten when I saw the very last notification at the bottom of the screen.

Sent this morning, at 7:06 a.m.

From @RyanHooksOfficial on Twitter.

Truck stop. I-90. Today, 4:30 p.m.

CHAPTER 20

Claire

The day after

ON SUNDAY, CLAIRE WOKE up after only four hours of sleep and took a quick shower before heading out to Klein's Boutique in Chicago's Lincoln Park neighborhood. One of the store attendants went to get Joshua Burlap from the back of the store, and Claire watched as the neatly dressed man walked toward her with a frown on his face.

"What's going on?" he asked.

Claire filled him in, and the man's eyes widened.

"Beverly?" he asked. "But she was just… I don't understand…"

"What time did you leave last night?" Claire asked.

"I was the first one to leave, I think," he said. "Around midnight." He shook his head. "I can't believe it. I was really just doing Emma a favor. I didn't even know the lawyer that well."

Claire frowned. "That's not what the other guests told me," she said. "They mentioned that you may have exchanged a few words with Beverly last night?"

"A few words?" he asked. "I'm not sure who the 'they' is that you're referring to, but I can assure you that my interactions with

Bev and her husband are being taken grossly out of context. I'd met them a couple of times through Emma, but that's the extent of it."

"Did you see anything out of the ordinary last night?"

He shrugged. "Not really. Look, I was there because I had to be there. It's business. You think I wanted to spend my Saturday night socializing with a group of spoiled rich girls and their 'home business' clothing line? Spoiler, I didn't, but I had to show up with a smile."

"You mean you don't actually like the clothes in their Allure Apparel line?" Claire asked. "Then why are you hosting their show here?"

"Because it brings people into the store, and in this day and age, brick-and-mortar boutiques can use all the publicity we can get. Any more questions about my business model, Detective?"

Claire bit her lip. "Did you have any interaction with Chris? The artist who was there last night?"

Burlap's eyes lit up, and a smile crossed his face. "Oh, Chris. Yes, we got to chat a bit. Did she get home okay?"

"That's the question," Claire said. "We haven't been able to reach her, since Emma didn't have her last name or contact information."

Burlap frowned. "Well, that's odd, isn't it?" When Claire didn't respond, he shrugged. "I don't have much else to give you. She was nervous, but everyone else probably already told you that."

"Nervous?"

"Yeah, definitely. She was nervous from the moment she walked in. She was trying to pretend not to be, I could tell, but I'm a pretty good reader of people. The way she talked, the way she ate, the way she moved around—I could tell she was uncomfortable. That is, until she got a bit of drink in her."

Claire made a mental note and then thanked him for his time.

"One more question," she said. "When you left the apartment, where did you go?"

"I came back to oversee the night crew who were cleaning and stocking up for the morning. You can ask any of them."

Claire assured him she would, left the store, and headed straight to the station. When she got there, she sat down in front of her computer.

She didn't have much to go on, but it was worth a try.

She started by searching for *Chris, portraits, School of the Art Institute of Chicago.*

Nothing.

Christine, SAIC.

Nothing.

And then, out of pure desperation:

Chris, red shoes, School of Art Institute of Chicago, SAIC, painter.

Of course not.

Sighing, she sat back in her chair. It just wasn't enough.

They needed help.

It was time to go public.

Later that evening, she stood in a bathroom in the precinct, waiting to go outside to talk to a room full of reporters about the murder at the apartment on Oak Street. As much as she didn't want to admit it, this was the *only* other situation where she got nervous, besides online dates, the only other time when her mouth became dry and her palms began to sweat. She could talk to almost anyone about anything, but add a camera and a room full of people, and her entire body suddenly became a cottony mess of nerves.

She remembered the first time she did an interview on the job.

It was a domestic violence case, and a reporter had thrust a micro-phone in her face, the light of the camera blinding her.

"Tell me about what happened," the chipper reporter had said.

Claire had felt her blood run cold and her mouth become dry.

"I...um...I..."

Her partner at the time had jumped in, but she'd been called "I, um, I" for a solid year after that.

The bathroom in the police station felt small and confining, but Claire needed a moment to pull herself together. It was a single stall, unisex bathroom, and she'd stepped inside and locked the door before turning on the water and leaning over the sink.

Breathe.

She could ask Greg to do it, or her boss. But she wasn't the kind of person to ask for help, not for something like this. If she avoided it enough, everyone would pick up on it, and if there was one thing she had learned, people liked to see you uncomfortable. Whether they liked you or hated you, people enjoyed seeing you squirm.

"I, um, I" was proof of that.

So she acted like the press conferences didn't affect her at all, and she'd been able to ward off too many of them. When they came up, she did what she was doing now: walked into the bathroom, splashed a bit of water in her face, took a few long, deep breaths, and tried to psych herself up.

It was barely working this time.

The good news was, after this evening, they'd be getting tons of tips about the murder on Oak Street. Too many, really. They'd collected all the information they could before going public; they'd identified all the party guests except for the artist, Chris. They'd also talked to several of the victim's family members and coworkers. Now, it was time to announce it to the public and see what else came in. There'd be a flood at first, of course. So many people thought they had information about so many things; some even seemed to enjoy calling the tip line. Some people were lonely and just wanted to be a part of the action; others truly thought they had something that would contribute to the case. It would take time to sort through it all, but she knew that there'd be a gem in there. Something that would help them catch the person who had done this.

She gripped the side of the sink and looked into the mirror.

Get over it, Claire.

You have to do this.

She began to go over all the reasons that she should, starting with the image of the victim's bloodied face, which had been haunting her since she first saw it.

That was how it worked: she saw victims, and they stayed in her mind, just out of sight, until she solved the case. She knew deep down that was the reason why she'd never left a case unsolved; she feared that if she did, the image would eat her brain from the inside out and drive her insane.

Claire grasped the sink as she felt the anger rolling through her body, all the way to her fingertips. She could see the body at the top of the stairs, and she felt the fire rising. She had to solve this case, and if standing up in front of those cameras was the only way to do it, then so be it. She would have to get up there and describe the events that took place, answer a few questions, and ask the public for help in bringing justice. She'd have to be calm, show strength, and allow just the slightest bit of sadness to remain behind her eyes, for the family's sake.

But for Claire, she'd be talking to one person in particular.

One of the six party guests.

Meggie Bentley or her boyfriend, Patrick?

Emma Bentley?

Andrew Brighton?

Joshua, the quirky store owner?

Or the artist with the red shoe—Chris?

The murderer would be doing something mundane right now, watching television or eating a meal. Hoping that the day of reckoning would never come, that there was a chance in hell fate would pass over this one particular case.

Then Claire would appear on the television and make it clear that wasn't the case. Not with her in charge. She would stare into the camera and make it clear:

I will find you.

Her pep talk was working, and Claire felt her nerves subsiding just slightly. She splashed some more water on her face, careful not to wet her clothes. She straightened up and looked at herself in the mirror. Reaching into her bag, she took out a tube of lipstick and smeared on a deep eggplant color that was perfect against her dark-brown skin. She fluffed her curls a little bit and then took a step back from the mirror.

Go, go, you can do it!

It was silly, the little chant she sometimes said when she was feeling nervous, but it always helped. She'd been muttering it to herself when she walked into the restaurant to meet Bill. Claire bent her elbows, lifted her fists in front of her face, and punched the air a few times. She owned a kickboxing workout tape, which she did in her living room sometimes, and she ran through one of her favorite sequences.

Right hook, left hook, uppercut, jab.

You don't get to kill people, you motherfucker.

Right hook, left hook, uppercut, jab.

You don't get to take another person's life.

Right hook, left hook, uppercut, jab.

I'm coming for you.

Claire grabbed her purse and swung the bathroom door open, stepping out into the empty hallway.

"Go, go, you can do it," she muttered very quietly to herself, hoping that would help keep the nerves in check. She clenched her hands at her side. For good measure, she lifted her arms and did one more little punch, a right hook, followed by a left, and then quickly let her arms fall by her sides. She straightened her shoulders and continued walking.

"That's new."

Claire sucked in a breath and stopped before turning around to see Greg walking toward her from the other end of the hallway. She felt the heat rise to her face as he walked up, a small smile on his face.

"Moonlighting as a boxer?" he asked.

"Moonlighting as a stalker?" she asked, continuing to walk briskly toward the stairs to get to the press room. "Where are you coming from anyway?"

"Um, the other bathroom behind the storage room," he said, his eyes darting to the floor. He coughed uncomfortably. "No one usually uses it, but...well, this one was occupied for a while."

Claire's eyes widened, then she started walking more quickly. It was just Greg, and she realized that she'd rather him think she'd been on the toilet that long than know the truth.

As if he had his suspicions, he walked quickly to keep up with her. "You ready for this?"

"Yeah, of course," she answered quickly, maybe too quickly, and she forced a smile. "When have I not been?"

"Never," he said, and there was a confidence behind the word that made Claire uncomfortable. "I've never seen you not be ready for anything."

Claire stopped walking and frowned. "That sounds suspiciously like a pep talk," she said. "Are you trying to psych me up for this?" she asked.

Greg smiled, his brown eyes twinkling in the fluorescent lights of the precinct basement. "Absolutely not, Puhl, I would not dare—"

"Because if you were, I'd tell you I don't need your patronizing pat on the back to know that I'm going to crush this."

He nodded. "Absolutely," he said again, and then he lifted his hands in the air and made a quick jab with his right fist. "Go get 'em."

Claire grit her teeth as he chuckled again, then she turned and stormed up the stairs.

Go, go, you can do it.

CHAPTER 21

Paula

The day after

I ARRIVED AT THE TRUCK stop off I-90 just before four thirty. I walked inside, planning to launch into a speech or ask Hooks questions about the previous night, but he wasn't there. Instead, a tall man I'd never seen before walked over, asked me my name, and handed me a large duffel bag.

"The phone?" he said.

It was suspicious as all hell, but neither of the two customers nor the attendant at the small convenience store looked up.

I reached into my pocket and took out the phone, handing it to him. A moment later, the man was gone, and I sat there staring at the bag. I waited a few moments, gathering the courage to stand up and leave, the bag in my hand. It had to weigh at least twenty pounds, and I tensed my biceps to hold it and walk naturally back to my car. I left the truck stop and drove almost halfway home before I reached over and unzipped it with one hand.

And then I saw green.

I didn't know how much money it was, but it didn't seem to matter, since it was more money than I'd ever seen in my entire life. I felt a wave of guilt rush over me as the reality of what had just happened settled in.

He's the bad guy.

He's cheating, and he wants to hide it.

It's not your fault you saw him.

He can afford it.

I said it over and over to myself as I drove home, the duffel bag full of cash on my passenger seat. I felt sick but also a bit excited as I thought about what was inside the bag.

I was doing this.

No—I'd done it.

What had started out as just a ridiculous, passing notion had turned into a huge bag of cold, hard cash.

And as bad as I'd felt about what I'd done, I couldn't help but feel…giddy.

We could afford the surgery.

It was an odd and uncomfortable reality, one I'd wanted since Dr. Bryant mentioned it was even a possibility. Now it was actually on the table, and I had only two options:

Give it all back.

Or resign myself to move forward and live with what I'd done.

The answer seemed simple enough.

Who had time for a conscience when your whole future was on the line?

I walked into the house around 6:00 p.m. I knew Keith would be home soon, so I walked quickly with the duffel into the bathroom. I closed the door behind me and turned on the light.

There weren't many hiding places in the house. I'd found that out when we first moved in and I tried to hide a watch that I'd gotten Keith for his birthday. I'd bought it an entire month in advance and stashed it at the back of the coat closet. Keith had walked into the bedroom one night, holding it his hands.

"What's this doing in the closet?" he'd asked, a frown on his face.

"Uh, happy early birthday?"

I opened the closet door and got down on my hands and knees. The very bottom of the closet wasn't actually a shelf; it was just the floor of the bathroom. It was covered in bottles of nail polish remover and other toiletries. I began to pull the items out, lining them up on the floor in front of the vanity. When at least half the space was cleared, I pushed the duffel bag inside before placing each of the bottles back, one by one.

I heard a noise and the sound of the front door opening. I stood back up as I heard Keith's voice.

"Hey, you here?"

"Yep! One second!" I said.

I took a final look around and then opened the door, walking out into the living room. Keith was sitting on the couch, the remote control on his lap, and he smiled as I walked into the room. He already had a bowl of cereal in his hands, and he shrugged.

"Sorry, I was starving," he said.

I smiled. "I'm not really hungry."

I sat down on the couch beside him and watched as he shoveled the cereal in his mouth, his eyes glued to the screen. He was even eating his cereal in a different way since he'd been contacted by the wonderful and famous Ryan Hooks. I felt an overwhelming sense of guilt as I thought about how I'd dashed out earlier that afternoon and told him I would spend a couple hours driving DAC when, in reality, I'd gone to the truck stop. He hadn't even batted an eye.

There was a commercial on, and I watched as a family stood in the middle of a kitchen, drinking orange juice.

Keith had launched into another story about his upcoming trip to Indianapolis, but I found myself tuning out, my attention going back and forth between him and the family on the TV screen. The news returned, and the anchors began to go through their stories.

A car accident on I-94 that left two people dead and one in critical condition.

A jewelry store robbery up in Evanston.

"I'm glad I'm not going to share a room, though. We only had three rooms reserved, and there are four of us going."

"Mm-hmm," I said, still zoning out.

I sat up straighter when the anchor spoke again, and suddenly, a blue bar appeared across the bottom of the screen with the headline for the next story.

Body found in Gold Coast apartment.

It didn't really stand out to me, not more than any other "body found in X neighborhood" stood out to me these days. Terrible, sad, tragic, but sadly, far from unique.

I watched it with half my attention as Keith continued to talk.

"Luckily, Erin and Alison wanted to share, so the rest of us get our own rooms."

A body was found late last night in the 100 block of West Oak Street in the Gold Coast.

"I don't know what we would've done if they didn't, but I have a feeling I would've gotten my own room, no problem. There's gotta be some perks to this, right?"

The woman has been identified as a resident of the apartment building where her body was found.

"Paula?"

The television cut away to a woman standing behind a podium in a room full of police officers. She was African American and looked to be in her late thirties or early forties, with huge brown eyes and curly hair pulled tightly back from her face in a low pony-tail. She was staring out at the crowd in front of her, addressing them with a sort of ease that you had to be born with.

I watched as the detective linked her fingers, placed her hands on the podium, and stared assertively into the crowd.

"Thank you all for coming," she said. "We responded to the incident at three o'clock this morning. The victim has been identi-fied as Beverly Brighton, a Chicago-area lawyer. We are treating this as an open homicide. We're looking into all aspects of the case and would encourage anyone with any information whatsoever to come forward to help bring justice for Mrs. Brighton."

CHAPTER 22

I'VE NEVER BEEN SHOT before, but I have to imagine that the feeling that came over me as I watched the detective on the news had to be pretty damned close. I flopped backward against the couch as if I'd been struck and then sat frozen for a few moments. Keith was still talking, and the woman's mouth was moving on the screen, but my head was filled with a shrill, high-pitched sound that blocked everything else out.

She'd just said that Beverly...

...was dead.

Beverly.

The woman who I'd shared a dinner table with last night.

Not just dead.

Murdered.

I choked on my next breath and then coughed loudly, bending over at my stomach as I gasped for air. Keith stopped talking and frowned, concern covering his face, but I raised a hand and shook my head as the coughing fit consumed me. When it was done, I took a long, slow breath, and he smiled.

"You all right?"

I nodded, and he went back to his story. I pretended to listen, but my gaze was on the screen. The woman speaking to the small audience was Detective Claire Puhl, her name printed at the bottom of the screen for a few seconds before disappearing. She was dressed impeccably—a perfect-fitting navy suit over a patterned green shirt and dark-purple lipstick that was both stylish and professional. She was talking about the details of the case—the neighborhood, the building, and, of course, Beverly—and every word that came out of her mouth was measured and said with confidence. It sounded like she was reading from a script, even though I had a feeling she wasn't. Her face was made up of almost all sharp, angular brushstrokes, her eyebrows heavy and defined, her cheekbones high and pronounced. She looked like one of those people who meant every word they said and rarely joked around.

I swallowed.

"To anyone who has any information at all, I invite you to come forward using the tip line that's on the screen," she said. "The smallest detail can help solve this case and bring closure to the victim's family. We need the entire community involved to catch the person who did this."

The news then flashed to shaky footage of the apartment building, and my stomach sank further, even though I didn't think it had any lower to go.

I was just there.

It looked so different on the screen than it did in real life. Not just because of the haze of police lights in the frames and the buzz of activity as they showed the street I'd been on so many times in the last week. No, it looked different because it wasn't supposed to be real—just another blurry image of any Chicago apartment building that you see flash by on the news each night.

"We are doing everything possible. If anyone has any information on the killing of Beverly Brighton, please give us a call," the detective was saying, and they flashed back to her press conference.

"It's the eyes and ears on the ground that are responsible for solving most cases like this, and we're really looking for justice for Beverly and her family."

Detective Puhl stared into the camera, and I got the sense that she was sending a message. She was saying loud and clear that she—not the police department as an entity, but she herself—would get to the bottom of it.

And I'd be damned if I didn't believe her.

I leaned forward, engrossed in the report, when the picture suddenly disappeared, and I was staring at a familiar face. It was an actor, and it took me a moment to realize that Keith had changed the channel to an old episode of *Modern Family*. I turned to him in outrage and saw that he was leaning back on the couch, the remote control in his hand. He laughed out loud at something that was said, then turned and looked at me mid-chuckle. He stopped laughing and frowned when he saw my face.

"What?" he asked. "Oh, were you watching that?"

Beverly was dead.

"Yes!" I said too loudly, and I swallowed. "Sorry. I mean yes, I was. That sounded...horrible."

"The lady on the Gold Coast?" he asked. "Uh, yeah, it was super depressing. That's why I changed it."

I felt a surge of anger at his flippant attitude, but I held it back and spoke through pursed lips. "Do you mind turning back?"

"Oh, yeah, sure," he said. He raised the remote and flipped in the wrong direction, going up instead of down, and I honestly wanted to throw something at him. "Oops," he said with another chuckle, thumbing down back to the news.

He landed on the station again, but by then, the news had moved on to a story about a burglary on the train. I blinked a few times, staring at the screen, my palms sweaty.

"Guess it's done," Keith said. "Maybe it's on somewhere else."

He went back to flipping, and I continued to sit there, my entire body frozen, my mind reeling at what I'd just learned.

It didn't make any sense.

It had happened late Saturday night, which meant—

I stood up quickly, and Keith looked up at me, his forehead scrunched together.

"You all right?" he asked.

"Yeah," I said. "Be right back."

Shelby stood up as I walked by her and then settled back down as I walked into the bedroom and shut the door.

No, no, no, no.

I picked my laptop up off the dresser and carried it over to the bed before sitting down. I could hear Keith laughing at something in the living room, and I still fumed over how quickly the news of Beverly's death had gone in one ear and out the other for him. I wasn't judging him for it. I'm sure I'd done the same thing many times before—watched the news at night and seen horrible deaths and fires, then gone on to turn to whatever sitcom came on and cackled just as loudly.

But this time was different.

I couldn't accept that somebody had killed her, right upstairs, later that night, after I'd drunkenly made my way home—

I gasped as a thought crossed my mind.

Had it been after I left? I didn't know how long, exactly, I'd lain on the carpet in Emma's apartment. What if it had happened while—

I closed my eyes and put the laptop on the bed. Placing both hands on my knees, I forced myself to take long, slow, deep breaths until the panic subsided. Picking the computer up again, I navigated to Google and typed in her name. A handful of news articles popped up, all posted within the last forty-five minutes.

NIC JOSEPH

Woman's body found in Gold Coast apartment

Prominent Chicago lawyer found dead in apartment

One of the articles contained the same video I'd just watched of the detective. I played it again and watched as Detective Puhl stared out into the crowd.

The article went on to include a quote from Beverly's parents, who lived in Tucson.

"Beverly was the love of our lives, our only child," her mother was quoted as saying. "I ask you all to respect our privacy during this tragic period."

Then there was a person from her law firm, crying into the camera, which I'd missed when Keith flipped the channel.

"Beverly was one of the best of the best, a lawyer with the highest integrity. Beyond that, she was a great friend and person who really cared about people."

My hands were shaking as I read the same stories over and over again. Beverly's law firm would be holding a memorial at a local church the next day. I thought about the detective's words as she looked into the camera.

To anyone who has any information at all, I invite you to come forward.

I felt ill and put the computer down on the bed beside me again, lying back until the wave of nausea passed.

Detective Puhl could've been talking directly to me, but what could I come forward and say? What exactly could I tell them about that night? How much could I share about Hooks without giving away the fact that I had a duffel bag filled with his money sitting in my bathroom closet?

I sucked in a breath and tried to focus.

Think, Paula.

I picked up my computer again and navigated back to the

216

news article with the video of Detective Puhl. I started it from the beginning, watching as she stood behind the podium with her chin raised and shoulders squared. The expression in her eyes was sharp and discerning, but there was something else there too. Sadness? Compassion?

Maybe if I went and told her the truth, she'd cut me some slack for doing the right thing?

The video continued to play, and I watched with glazed eyes as the scenes changed in front of my face. Every time the report showed the picture of Beverly—a corporate headshot that appeared to be several years old—I felt my stomach turn over.

Then I saw something that made it drop.

The video had reached the point where Beverly's coworker was being interviewed. The woman appeared on the screen, and then the station flashed quickly to an image of the office building in downtown Chicago. The law firm loomed large on the city street, but it wasn't the impressive structure that struck me. The camera zoomed into the emblem of the company's name and logo emblazoned on the wall.

Baker & Pikensy.

I rewound it twice, watching for the moment when the camera zoomed in on the building, and I let the name of the law firm turn over in my mind.

Baker & Pikensy.

I repeated it again to myself.

Baker & Pikensy?

Where had I heard that name before?

When it hit me, I almost dropped the laptop on the floor.

I felt a lump growing in my throat as the memories from the past week flooded back. I opened another tab and typed in some of the terms I'd searched for the night after I found the phone.

But this time, I got more specific.

"Ryan Hooks sexual harassment case."

The long list of articles came up, and I scrolled through them, looking for one of the articles I'd seen that night.

It took me a few minutes, but I found it, the link still a dimmed-out purple from where I'd clicked it a few days ago. I gasped out loud as the article confirmed what I'd already known.

Baker & Pikensy.

It was an article about Amanda Strager, the woman who'd accused Ryan of sexual harassment four years ago.

Hooks's lawyer quoted in the article had worked for...

Baker & Pikensy.

I shut the laptop, breathing heavily.

I knew Bev was a lawyer, but it had never occurred to me to wonder what kind of law.

And it had also never occurred to me that Hooks might have known someone else at the Oak Street apartment that night.

Fuck.

CHAPTER 23

SPENT MUCH OF THE twelve hours after I got the news about Beverly pinching myself to see if it was all real.

It seemed that I should be able to blink a few times and wake myself up from this dark, shaky nightmare. When I finally accepted it, I felt an overbearing sadness for something so permanent, so *final*.

I didn't really know Beverly.

But she was a real person, with a real family, and real dreams, and a real life, and now...

She was gone.

I tried to make sense of it as I sat alone in the bedroom Monday morning. Randy had picked Keith up to go to a pre-meet practice, and Keith had kissed me on the way out the door. The feel of his lips against mine had been strange but comforting in a way he couldn't imagine, and I almost broke down in front of him right then. But I held it together and waved goodbye, then slumped back into bed after he left.

I lay back in the bed, opened Twitter, and searched for Ryan. He hadn't posted since last week. I wondered where he was and what he was doing right then. His show in Dallas was coming up in a few days... Had he left already? Was he still at his hotel?

I'd looked up everything I could about Baker & Pikensy.

Beverly had interned there out of law school and had worked at the firm for her entire career. I couldn't find any evidence that she'd worked on Amanda Strager's sexual harassment case, though I had found a picture of her smiling next to Hooks's lawyer. And then I found another article that made me pause.

LAW FIRM DROPS HOOKS FOLLOWING SECOND ASSAULT CHARGE

Another one?

That and the fact that he'd been at the apartment on Saturday night—somebody needed to tell the police.

But certainly not me?

That was problem number one. I couldn't very well go in and talk to the police, not after what I'd done. I had a *bag full of cash* in my bathroom, cash that did not belong to me, and only an idiot would walk into a police station to talk about it.

But could I keep quiet about this?

If only there was a way I could—

Of course there was a way!

I grabbed my phone and did a quick search for *anonymous tip Chicago police.*

The first thing that came up was TXT2TIP. All I had to do was compose a text, and it would be sent anonymously to the police. It was worth a try. Taking a deep breath, I typed out a message:

> Ryan Hooks was at 115 W. Oak Street on the night Beverly Brighton was murdered. He was also there one week prior. I witnessed this myself.

I hovered over the Send button for a moment before clicking it.

Problem number two was just as easy to solve but felt a lot more problematic. Dr. Reveno had sent over the confidentiality forms he needed us to sign, along with a bill to begin work.

So happy to be working with you, he'd written in the message. *We'll need to get moving if we're going to make the eighteen-month deadline.*

I opened the email and navigated to the payment link, my mind on the money in my bathroom closet.

Without giving myself time to think about all the reasons I shouldn't do it, I scrolled down to the bottom of the screen and clicked Pay Now.

I went to work a late shift at the diner. It was quiet, and I breathed a sigh of relief when I saw that Vanessa was out; I didn't know if I could continue to keep all this from her. I walked to the back of the diner and picked up the phone. I needed to talk to Emma, but I couldn't afford to use my own cell phone.

Not after everything that had happened.

I dialed her number, and it rang several times before going to voicemail. Sighing, I hung up and went back to work, focusing on the handful of customers who came in. It wasn't the best distraction, but it would do. When I finally left, it was dark outside, and I drove home slowly.

I pulled into a parking space and shut off the car.

It had been a long day, and I wanted to sit in the car for a while before heading in to talk to Keith.

I was about to open the door when I saw movement by the passenger door of my car.

I sucked in a breath, and suddenly, the door flew open, and a figure slid inside.

The doors had unlocked immediately when I parked, a feature that I was usually pretty paranoid about—I typically either got out of the car immediately or locked them again while I gathered my things.

My mind reeled back to when I was younger and first learning how to drive.

"Always look in your back seat before you get into the car," my father had said.

I remembered rolling my eyes and brushing off his warnings. "You don't think I would notice if someone was camping out in my back seat?" I asked.

"It's possible if you're not looking, especially at night," he'd said seriously. "Also, if you ever end up driving in a deserted place and a cop tries to pull you over—"

"I know, I know," I had said, exasperated, my hands on the wheel of his gray Buick Skyhawk, itching to end the safety lessons and just drive. "Put on my hazards and drive slowly to a crowded place."

"Exactly," he had said. "And—"

"Dad."

"One more thing," he had said, holding up a hand. "If you're ever sitting in your car for any reason, just do me a favor and make sure your doors are locked."

"Duh, Dad."

Whether it was the stress from the day or my general lack of focus recently, I'd neglected to lock the doors again when I shut off the car. As the man got in my car, I was so paralyzed with fear that I didn't move, didn't think to scramble out the other side, didn't think to do *anything*.

And then I saw who it was.

Ryan Hooks.

In my car.

Again.

He closed the door behind him and turned to look at me.

The scream was at the back of my throat when he put a hand up and spoke.

"I just want to talk to you," he said.

"How did you—"

"I went to see your husband."

"You what?" I asked, all thoughts of running fleeing. "Why did you do that?"

"I went to talk about the piece he's going to do for me."

"You *asshole*," I muttered, my body tense and ready to fight. "You had no right to do that."

"And you had no right to blackmail me," he spat back. He took a deep breath and pushed back his hoodie. He looked a lot different than he had the other two times I had met him; his eyes were tired, and his beard had grown in considerably in the last couple of days. "He was so upset that you weren't there to meet me. Nice guy actually."

"What the hell do you want?" I asked, cutting him off.

"I don't know," he said. "I was leaving, and I saw you pull up. I just want to talk."

"You already said that. What about?"

I still had one hand on the door, and I watched him carefully. I could make a run for it, but after an entire day of thinking about him, I found that I was interested in what he had to say.

Hooks stared back at me, and there was both anger and exhaustion in his eyes. "I want to know why you called the police," he finally said.

I swallowed and then slumped back even farther against the car door.

He knew?

A thousand thoughts ran through my head. Should I deny it?

Pretend I had no idea what he was talking about?

Admit it?

Clarify that I hadn't actually called them—I'd texted them?

I paused for too long, and he jumped in.

"There's no use in denying it," he said. "They called me and said that an anonymous tip had come in, stating that I'd been at the apartment building on the night that woman died. Emma's apartment building."

"I didn't specifically accuse you," I said, stumbling over my words. "But they needed to know you were there that night. And that Beverly worked at the same law firm—"

"I had nothing to do with her death," he spat out, the words clipped, the anger on par with what I'd seen the night of his concert. "And I can't believe you went to the cops. Since part of the reason I gave you that money was for you to keep your fucking mouth closed."

"About the fact that you're sleeping with a Chicago socialite," I snapped back. "Not about...not about..."

"About what?" he asked. He was staring at me with anger and disgust, and I suddenly felt scared again. "You don't know anything, so you should keep your stupid mouth shut. How is that so hard? I thought we had an agreement."

"That was before all this," I said. "I saw you there. You know I did."

He exhaled.

"So what if I was there?" he said. "That doesn't mean I killed somebody. Are you nuts? Calling the cops like that. It was the stupidest thing you could've done."

I frowned as I watched him. I thought back to the YouTube videos I'd watched where he'd been so charming, so funny, so put-together. Now, he seemed unhinged, his entire body shaking, his anger taking up too much space in the car. I leaned back against the driver's side door, wondering if I could open it and get out before he could reach across the gear shift and pull me back.

His hands were balled into fists on his lap, but then he reached up and slammed them down on the dashboard.

I jumped, my heart racing.

"You need to stop calling the cops," he said. "I thought we were in this together."

"In what together?" I asked. "I didn't have anything to do with the other night."

"I know," he said. "Not that, and neither did I. I'm talking about the whole thing with Emma. That's the only reason I'm not turning you in, because Tiffane can't find out about it. But if you keep doing stupid shit…I don't know what I'm going to do."

He seemed to be breaking down, his voice filled less with anger and now with desperation. I didn't know if I should be scared or feel sorry for him. I just knew that I wanted him gone. His chest was heaving, up and down, and I could see that he was struggling to regain control.

"I gave you that money, and the whole point was for you to keep your mouth shut." He opened the door and got out. Before he closed the door, Hooks dipped his head and leaned back into the car, staring me directly in the eye.

"I didn't do what you think I did, so stop calling the cops," he said. "We have a deal, Paula. I give you the money, you don't say anything, to anyone. That's how this works."

Something about the way he said it made me angry, and even though I knew I shouldn't, I leaned across the gear shift and peered up at him. "No, I don't say anything about the affair," I said. "That was the agreement. If you had anything to do with what happened to Beverly, I'll turn you into the police so fast, you won't know what hit you. *That's* how this works."

He stared down at me, and I could see the wave of emotions cross his face in the moonlight. Disbelief, desperation, anger.

"You really don't know what you're doing," he said. "But trust me, you'll learn."

He shut the door and walked away.

It was way too late, but as I watched him, I reached out with a shaking hand and locked the doors.

CHAPTER 24

Claire

Two days after

CLAIRE WALKED INTO THE station early on Monday morning, her eyes red from lack of sleep. She'd lain awake in bed the night before, Beverly's face crowding her mind the way her victims always did.

In the last day and a half, she'd talked to almost everyone who'd been at the dinner party on Saturday night, with the exception of the mysterious and elusive artist named Chris.

Emma had given her all the information she could—the woman's physical description (brown hair, with eyes that were two different colors—one blue and one brown), her profession (an artist), her demeanor (nervous, jumpy), but nothing of value like a last name or telephone number.

"Did you see her interact with Beverly at all?" Claire had asked.

Emma had shrugged. "Besides introductions and basic chitchat, not really," she had said.

Claire sighed and looked at the file folders spread out on the table in front of her, one for each of the residents of the apartment building on Oak Street. She had them all open, and they stared out at her, pictures pulled together from social media sites, driver's licenses, and the like. It was amazingly easy to find information on suspects these days with a few simple mouse clicks. As she looked at them, her mind went over the same question repeatedly.

Which one of you is lying?

Claire heard a noise behind her and saw Greg walking in with two cups of coffee in his hands and a file folder tucked beneath his arm. "I have so many presents for you this morning, I don't even know where to start," he said.

"Start with the caffeinated one," she said with a smile as he placed one of the cups on her desk. "Thanks. Okay, hit me with the rest."

"First, no fingerprints on the statue."

"None at all?"

"Nope," he said. "Wiped clean. Still some traces of blood and hair, which are a match for Beverly Brighton."

Claire nodded. "What else?"

"Got the results back on that red stain on the carpet next to the body," he said, dropping the folder on Claire's desk and then grabbing a seat beside her. Claire opened it as he continued to speak. "Definitely wasn't blood. It was lipstick, and very fresh. It was still tacky; the techs say it couldn't have been there for more than a few hours when we found it. We compared it to the lipstick found on Beverly and—"

"It was a match," Claire said, looking up. She frowned. "Doesn't make sense."

"What doesn't?" Greg asked.

"Why she put lipstick back on. According to her husband, she was in the shower when he got upstairs from the dinner party. Why shower and then reapply lipstick?"

They were silent for a few moments until Claire spoke again. "Okay, any other presents for me?"

Greg gestured toward the file folder. "It's in there too," he said. "So, remember I told you about the keypad lock on the backyard gate? Well, we checked the log, and nobody used it to get into the backyard that night."

"So nobody got in that way," she said, leaning forward and putting her head in her hands. "Damn it."

"What's wrong?" Greg asked.

Claire continued to stare at the desk, thinking as she spoke out loud.

"Since we first arrived at the scene, I knew that someone who'd already been in the building was responsible for Beverly Brighton's death. That was clear to me the moment we saw the broken glass with no evidence that someone had actually come in that way. A real intruder wouldn't work overtime to make it *look* like they broke in. So it had to be someone who was already in the building around one thirty or two o'clock, when Beverly was killed.

"So, imagine you're the killer. You strike Beverly on the back of the head, and as Dr. Ortiz said, she falls over and hits her head on the corner of the table. You're starting to freak out because you can see the blood spreading on the carpet. You're still holding the statue, but you can wipe that off. There's blood everywhere, and now you have to go back home. How did the assailant get inside one of the units without a trace? Maybe they ran downstairs and out the front door, washed off in the rain, enough so they wouldn't track blood through their apartment, and then return through the back. They grab the brick and bust out the window near the back door to make it look like someone came in that way, but instead, they run over to the staircase and go back to their apartment unseen. Only problem there is that you're telling me nobody used the gate code for the backyard last night."

Greg nodded. "What are we missing?"

"I don't know," Claire said softly. "Anything else?"

"Yeah, one more thing," he said. "We got the analysis on all the blood in the stairwell," he said. "Most of it belonged to the victim."

Claire froze. "Most?"

"Yes," Greg said. "There was a smudge at the bottom of the staircase on the first floor, on the wall, and a small chip in the paint. As if someone fell forward and knocked into it."

"But it wasn't the victim's?"

"No, it doesn't match."

"Can you tell how long it had been there?"

"Yes," Greg said. "Judging by how much it had dried—or, I should say, *hadn't* dried—it had to have happened earlier that same night."

Claire opened another file folder and pulled out some of the pictures from the scene. There were pictures of the first-floor hallway, of the third-floor landing, and of the outside of the building. She flipped through them mindlessly, searching for anything at all that would shed some light on what really happened to Beverly Brighton.

When she saw it, she stood up abruptly, knocking her chair back.

"What is it?" Greg asked, looking up.

"Of course!" Claire exclaimed.

"Of course what?" he asked.

Claire blinked at him for a moment and then finally responded. "I need to make a call."

An hour later, Claire was pulling up in front of the building on Oak Street. She rang the doorbell for the first-floor apartment.

"Hello?" Meggie Bentley said.

"Ms. Bentley, it's Detective Claire Puhl. Mind if I come in?"

There was a pause, and then the door buzzed, and Claire stepped inside. As she walked toward the first-floor apartment, she heard a noise. The door opened, and Meggie Bentley peered out.

"What's going on?" she asked.

"Do you mind if I come in?"

Meggie stepped back to let her inside. As Claire walked in, she saw that Patrick was sitting on the couch, his legs folded beneath him as he typed on a laptop.

"Good, you're here too," Claire said.

"What's this about?" he asked.

Claire cleared her throat. "I had a couple of questions about Saturday night. Namely, why you lied about what time you got home."

"Sorry?" Meggie said, her forehead scrunching up. "What are you talking about?"

"You told me that when you arrived home, you saw the blood in the stairwell and on the carpet and decided to go upstairs to make sure everything was okay."

"Yes," Meggie said with a frown on her face.

"I took a look at the photos of the entryway and first floor of your apartment building. And it occurred to me: there's no way for you to see the staircase when you walk in the door. If you walked in and went straight to your apartment, you wouldn't have seen the blood, and you would've had no reason to go upstairs to the third floor. I don't know about you, but I don't walk past my apartment and take a look around before going inside. So tell me: Why did you walk over to the staircase?"

"I don't know," Meggie said. "We just did. There wasn't a reason."

"Of course there was a reason," Claire said. "There's a reason for everything, and it is my job to figure out what those reasons are. Here's what I think. Actually, here's what I *know*, since I just made a call to Boxer's, and with a few threats of taking a closer look at their books, I got the owner, Kerry, to tell me the truth, not the lie you asked her to feed us. You two weren't at the bar until two fifteen, as you said earlier; instead, she said you left by one thirty. You went in, you met with someone, and then you left, according to Kerry. Which means you were in your apartment before Beverly was killed."

Meggie and Patrick looked at each other in an obvious effort to determine how much they should reveal. Claire jumped in again before either of them responded.

"I think you were here, and I think you heard something that concerned you. Something that made you scared. Maybe a yell, maybe the sound of someone running down the stairs. But you didn't open the door and call the police, because you were otherwise occupied. The report came back on the swabs from your apartment, and we found traces of cocaine in the bathroom. Is that what you picked up at Boxer's?"

Meggie slumped forward, and she rested her forehead against the palm of her head.

"You knew something was going on, but before you could call the police, you wanted to get rid of the drugs. So you finished up and then opened the door. You already knew something was wrong. You were going upstairs to see what happened and to make sure everything was okay."

"We didn't do anything to her, we promise," Patrick said.

"How about you tell me exactly what you heard from your apartment?" Claire said.

Meggie sighed, straightening up. "We heard the sound of someone yelling. We couldn't really make out who it was. And then we heard a loud thump, like something had fallen. We heard the sound of someone running on the staircase, and then that was it. We finished up, then called the police."

"Was the person running up the stairs or down?"

"I don't know," Meggie said. "It was hard to tell."

"Did you hear the front door open?"

"No, I don't think so," she said.

"You should've called the police right away," Claire said.

"We know. We're sorry," Meggie said, and there was something about the way the woman said it that made Claire believe her.

CHAPTER 25

Paula
Two days after

I COULDN'T BEAR TO GO inside.

I knew Keith would be upset, yet I couldn't bring myself to go home, to look him the eye, to not tell him what had just happened.

I couldn't lie to his face.

So I did it from the front seat of my car.

"Hey, I'm still at the diner," I said when he answered. I was leaning forward with my head on the steering wheel as I spoke. "I'm so sorry, but Vanessa needs me to work her shift."

"Are you kidding?" Keith asked. "What time will you get home? Randy is coming for me at three o'clock."

I took a deep breath before responding. "Probably not before then," I said. "I'll be here until six or seven this morning. I'm so sorry. Text me when you leave."

We hung up a few minutes later, and although he was upset, I knew he would get over it. I told myself that he was so nervous for the trip, not saying goodbye to me was probably just a minor disappointment in the grand scheme of things.

I pulled out of the space and headed to Vanessa's apartment. When I arrived, she took one look at my face and then stepped back to let me aside.

"Sorry for just dropping in," I said.

"No problem," she said as I walked over to the couch and sat down. She grabbed a blanket and tossed it over to me. "Is everything okay?"

I desperately wanted to tell her what was going on, but I didn't know where to start.

Hey, you remember when you joked around that I should try to get some money out of the whole Ryan Hooks thing?

Well, I did.

And now, I think he might have murdered someone.

Oh, and he just showed up in my car and threatened me.

So, no, not really okay.

How was your day?

"You look like you need one of those too," Vanessa said, pointing to the glass of red wine on the table in front of her. "Yeah?"

I sighed and nodded. Even though I'd promised myself I wouldn't drink ever again after Emma's dinner party, I couldn't help but say yes.

Vanessa left for a moment, then came back with the glass of wine. She handed it to me and dropped down on the couch beside me.

"Want to talk about it?"

"Would rather just watch TV," I said.

She nodded. "Done and done."

She unmuted the television, and we sat there for a while, watching the screen. Earlier, when I'd been at the diner, I'd been grateful that she wasn't there, because I didn't know how I could be in the same room with her and not let her know what was going on. But now, all I felt was exhaustion, and I appreciated the comfortable silence.

Three glasses of wine later, I stood up to leave.

"You sure you don't want to sleep here?" she asked.

"No, I have to go home and take Shelby out. Thanks, though."

I left, walking past my car and climbing into the DAC that I'd called to take me home. I'd come back for my car in the morning. There was something about leaving it at a place because I was too drunk to drive home that made me feel like I was in my twenties again, and I smiled to myself as the DAC driver moved through the streets.

"How's your night going?" she asked.

"Not too bad," I said as I leaned my head back. The car smelled like some sort of strong deodorizer, and I wrinkled my nose. "How about you?"

"Oh, not too bad," the girl said cheerily. She sounded young—she couldn't have been more than twenty-two or twenty-three, and she drove with both hands on the steering wheel. I wondered if she had a can of bug spray between her legs and considered telling her that she should, but that felt like it would be the wine talking. She looked up at me in the rearview mirror. "I just started, so I'm going to be driving for a while. You heading home or leaving home?"

I laughed. I tried to imagine who left home at three thirty in the morning. "I'm heading home."

"Oh, okay, cool! Well, let me know if the AC is cool enough for you."

"It is, thanks," I said.

We were silent for the rest of the trip, which I was grateful for. When she pulled up in front of the house, I thanked her and got out of the car. I made sure to leave her a tip in the app; I figured there was certainly bad karma for not treating other drivers well.

Not to mention the driver who'd helped me get home the other night. I owed *all* the DAC drivers *all* the tips for that.

I felt a chill rush over me as I walked up to my front door. When I opened it, I heard Shelby shuffle. I turned on a light and walked over to her. She stirred for a moment and then looked at me before lying back down.

I walked into the bedroom, the pull of the red wine making me tired but not sleepy. I lay back on the bed, fully clothed, spread out in the center of it, since I had it all to myself. I lay there for a few minutes, hoping the wine would lull me to sleep, but it didn't. I rolled over, stretching out, my hands sliding under my own pillow and Keith's—

I froze when my fingers hit something that felt like a small postcard. I pulled it out and sighed deeply when I saw what it was.

A scratch-off ticket.

One that I hadn't bought.

In any other case, it wouldn't be a big deal, but the single ticket told me that even though Keith said he was fine with accepting money from the Art Bowl, he was still looking for another way out. He'd been so upset when he saw that I was buying the scratch-offs, and here he was, sliding back into his old habits.

I'd have to watch out to make sure it didn't get any worse.

I put the ticket back and then rolled onto my back. My mind still raced, my thoughts jumping from Detective Puhl's face on the news to Hooks's face as he stared at me in my car.

I just wanted sleep. I needed rest so that I could get rid of the fog that seemed to be in front of my mind and wouldn't go away. Tomorrow would be a brand-new day; I would go to the diner and try Emma again and hope that she answered. I hadn't decided if I'd tell her about Hooks climbing into my car; that would require a lot of explaining.

After another twenty minutes, I finally sat up. Maybe if I took a shower and changed into pajamas—maybe then I'd start to feel sleepier. I got up and walked back into the living room. Shelby stayed in her bed and didn't lift her head as I walked by. I went into the bathroom and showered and brushed my teeth. As I walked past Shelby again, I saw her peek one eye open, but then I went into the bedroom and shut the door most of the way.

I lay down again, feeling more relaxed, more comfortable, but sleep still felt a million miles away. I punched the pillow angrily and flipped over, near tears for the need to let go of all this and just fall asleep. I was suddenly too hot, and I stood up on the bed and pulled the cord for the ceiling fan. The cool breeze brushed over me, and it was comforting, as was the loud white noise that the fan brought, blocking out almost everything else.

I lay back down and tried to count to one hundred.

I made it there easily and started another hundred after that.

I heard a tapping sound at the door and then the jingle of Shelby's dog collar. I sat up in the bed and looked as the door slowly swung inward. Shelby never came into our room, and I was surprised to see her trot up alongside the bed and stand there.

In the moonlight, I could see her eyes clearly, and we watched each other. She looked concerned, and I felt a lump rise in my throat.

In all the months of my insomnia, she hadn't once acknowledged that I was having a problem, and now here she was, her big brown eyes glistening. And all it had taken was me taking her to the park, for reasons she knew nothing about. As she stood there watching me, I put out a hand and rubbed her head.

"We don't deserve you, you know that," I said, the tears welling up in my eyes. She didn't move, and finally, I rolled over and patted the bed. She hesitated only a second before hopping up into the bed beside me. She held herself up for a few moments, but as

I settled in, she let her body drop down beside me, her head on her paws.

We lay there like that for a few moments, and then, out of nowhere, with her right there beside me, I felt a wave of sleep wash over me. I knew it wasn't actually tiredness; it was security. I was so grateful, I wanted to cry, but instead, I let myself fall under the spell of sleep, the softness of her fur the last thing I remember.

When I woke up again, it was still dark, and Shelby had gone back into the living room.

Or so I thought.

I was in that barely lucid state, halfway between sleep and being awake, where I knew that I was in bed, knew I was sleeping or dreaming, but couldn't bring myself to break out of it. My grandmother always said that moment, that feeling of being trapped, awake, in a sleeping body, only happened when there was another spirit in the room with you, holding you down. She also still displays all her children's baby teeth in glass jars on her mantel. I wasn't sure what I believed, but as I lay there, I could hear Shelby moving around in the living room, and I knew I needed to get up and make sure she was okay.

But I was just so tired…

Shelby made another noise, this one much louder than the rest, and I knew she needed to go to the bathroom. I finally broke through the sleep and pulled myself up onto one arm, coughing as I plunged face-first into a pile of fur.

Shelby.

She'd moved in the middle of the night and was no longer on the side of the bed where she'd leapt up earlier. She was on the other side, sprawled out asleep where Keith usually lay. As I sat up, she sat up too, and we both blinked in the moonlight.

Shelby was still here...

Wait. Shelby is still here?

I heard another crashing sound out in the living room, which made my heart nearly fall out of my chest, and Shelby jump straight up on the bed, her teeth bared and eyes alert as she breathed heavily into the dark.

CHAPTER 26

T HE FEAR THAT FLOODED through my body was unlike anything I'd ever felt before, and I lurched up in the bed, scrambling back against the headboard. I'm not sure why that was my first reaction, but it was the most distance I could put between myself and the bedroom door.

There was someone—or something—out there.

I thought about calling out to see if it was Keith—maybe he'd come home for some reason—but I knew it couldn't be him. He'd left hours ago.

I could hear the person moving around, but there was another noise drowning it out.

The ceiling fan.

With shaking legs, I pulled myself up and reached high, my fingers connecting with the cord that would turn it off. I pulled it twice, and the fan began to slow down. Once it was off, the silence seemed to be magnified, every creak clattering loudly in my head. I waited, my throat dry, and I suddenly tasted blood. It took me a moment to realize that I'd bitten my tongue.

Shelby was next to me, still on all fours, her eyes on the bedroom door. *We couldn't both be wrong*. We'd heard something. A moment later, we heard it again. Loud, rustling, deliberate movement, things being shifted around. There was someone out there, and I didn't have…

My phone.

It was on the coffee table, on top of the latest set of lottery tickets, where I always left it. We had never owned a landline, and for the first time, I wondered why we thought it was okay to give up on that small, simple standard of living. It could be burglars, of course, which meant that my best option was to burrow in the bedroom until they left—they wanted stuff, not people, right?—but the events of the past few days made me pause.

It could be a burglar.

But what if it wasn't?

I thought about Hooks's face as he sat in my car. Had Keith told him that he'd be in Indianapolis today?

Was it possible…?

Shelby jumped down and walked over to the door. I could see that her entire body was shaking as she stood there, snarling. I looked over to the small window, which faced the brick wall of the house next door and was covered by junk: an old massage cushion that didn't work, a box full of batteries, some books. We rarely used that window; in the summer, we either turned on the AC or the fan. I knew that chances of someone hearing me if I opened it were slim, and it would alert the burglars that I was awake.

If that's who they were…

The rustling started up again, and I walked close to the door. Shutting my eyes, I pushed as quietly as I could until the door was closed completely. It didn't lock, and I looked around the room to see what I could push up against it to barricade myself in.

Shelby remained next to the door, and I didn't realize what she was about to do until a minute too late. She growled lightly and then suddenly opened her mouth and barked, an angry, loud warning, which made my blood run cold with fear.

"No, Shel—"

She barked again, this one even louder, and then she let loose, a barrage of yelps exploding from her small body.

"Shel!" I hissed, trying to calm her down, but when I touched her, she flinched and kept her eyes trained on the door. She barked again, a loud, forceful sound, and I knew the person—or people—in my house had heard her.

Which meant they knew she was in the bedroom and anyone with her was awake.

She stopped, and then I heard a loud crashing noise in the living room. I swallowed, the blood pumping through my body furiously, and I felt both incredibly alert and dangerously close to losing consciousness.

Suddenly, I heard the sound of footsteps moving quickly toward the bedroom, quick and assertive, and I gasped.

Someone was coming for me.

Shelby barked again, and I stood by the door, ready to hold it back with all the strength I could muster, when it was suddenly flung open, the wood connecting—painfully—with my face.

The intruder had pushed hard, and the impact was enough to knock me straight onto my back. I moaned as my head connected with the floor. The person stopped at the door, but I could only see the ceiling right above my head. I heard Shelby barking loudly and frantically, and then I heard the sound of footsteps moving away from me and back into the living room. Shelby followed for a moment and then came back, and I was grateful to see her feet, just a few inches away from my face, as I lay there, stunned. She barked again, then spun around to look at the door, her tail hitting me in the face, as I struggled to find the energy to pull myself up.

But as I did, I felt a pain shoot through my head where the door had struck me, and that—combined with the fear that rushed through my veins—caused me to fall back. My eyelids fluttered a few times before drifting shut.

"You're a pretty lucky woman to have such a sweet and protective pooch," the cop was saying as she stood over me in the living room a few hours later, the morning light streaming through the window. "What's her name?"

I glanced up at her as I held the ice pack up to my head. "Shelby," I said, looking over at her. She was sitting on her mattress, and she snarled as she watched every person who walked past us.

"Are you sure you don't want to go to the hospital, Mrs. Wileson?" the cop asked. "It wouldn't be a bad idea just to go and get checked out, especially with a head injury like that."

"No, I'm okay," I said. "I think I passed out. I really just want to get some rest."

She stared at me. "Okay, but if you start feeling anything, you should go get it checked out."

I nodded.

My mind was still racing from what had happened a few hours ago. I'd come to on the floor in the bedroom with Shelby still standing next to the door. I'd been scared to go out, but I knew I couldn't stay in my room forever, and my cell phone was on the living room table. I'd opened the door slowly and had inched out with Shelby. She'd been quieter, which made me think the place was empty, but you could never be too sure. I had walked into the living room and grabbed my phone before darting back into the bedroom with Shelby right on my heels. I had shut the door and breathed heavily, my back against the door.

It was a silly move. I knew I should've left the house, gone anywhere else, but I didn't know where he was. He could still be inside or somewhere on the property. He could be anywhere.

I needed to call the cops and get someone there, fast.

They'd arrived less than five minutes later and combed the house from top to bottom while I called Keith to let him know what happened. He'd been completely silent when I spoke and then he'd said quietly, "I'm so sorry I'm not there."

"Is anything missing?"

"Hmm?" I looked up at the cop standing in front of me. They'd been asking me that question over and over, and I'd told them the same thing each time. "No, nothing is missing."

But that wasn't true at all.

The place had been ransacked—drawers turned over, couch turned inside out—and in the bathroom, all the bottles had been dragged out and scattered across the floor.

Behind them…

There was *nothing.*

No duffel bag.

No money.

And all I could think of was Hooks's face in the car.

You really don't know what you're doing.

But trust me, you'll learn.

"Mrs. Wileson?"

"Oh, yes?" I said, looking up at the cop who was staring at me.

"I said was it possible that you left the front door unlocked when you came inside?"

I racked my brain for what I'd done when I had gotten home

from Vanessa's. I'd been tired and more than a little drunk, but I'd locked the door, hadn't I?

Had I?

"I'm not sure," I said. "I mean, I think I did, but I don't really remember, to be honest."

"Okay. Did you see the intruder at all when he came into your bedroom? Anything you can tell us that might make it easier to identify him?"

"No," I said. "I didn't see anything. When he opened the door, I was standing right there, and it hit me in the face. I fell on my back, and then all I remember was being so thankful that Shelby was there."

"Okay," she said. "Well, we'll do another walk around the house, but he's gone now. So lock up tight, and then give us a call later this morning so we can finish up this paperwork."

"Okay, I will. Thanks."

After they all left, I went back into the bedroom with Shelby and closed the door.

This time, I had my cell phone with me, along with a heavy kitchen knife on the nightstand beside me. Shelby lay in the bed beside me, but her eyes were wide open, and she kept her eyes trained on the door.

"It's okay, girl," I said, stroking her head. "You need to get some sleep too."

But sleep wasn't going to come for either of us.

As I lay there, I couldn't help but wonder.

Had Hooks had a change of heart?

Was he the one who did this?

And most important of all, was he just after the money?

Or had he been after me too?

I crept out of bed and walked to the kitchen to grab a bottle of red wine and a glass.

When I woke up again, it was nighttime, and the wineglass was tipped on its side in the bed next to me, a single droplet staining the sheets near the rim.

CHAPTER 27

Claire

Three days after

CLAIRE WAS SITTING AT her desk on Tuesday night when the woman came in. Later, Greg would say that it was their lucky day, but Claire didn't feel like it was luck at all.

The woman was about five foot seven, with dark hair.

And she was drunk as a skunk.

"Hi, Detective Puhl," the woman said quietly, her hands clasped in front of her. She was shaking like a leaf, but she spoke assertively, as if she was trying to show that she wasn't nervous.

"My name is Paula Wileson. I saw you on television. I need to talk to you about the Beverly Brighton murder. I think I know who did it."

Claire blinked a few times and then let out a small gasp when the woman stepped forward and Claire saw that she had the most striking eyes she'd ever seen.

One brown and one blue.

"Okay, uh, yes, let's go find a room, and we can talk."

◆ ❖ ◆

Claire tapped her pen against the desk in front of her and listened as the woman detailed the most ludicrous story she'd ever heard in her life. She tried to keep a straight face while Paula—or Chris—went through her story.

She wanted to get as much as she could out of the woman before she let her know that the jig was up. With an amused Greg sitting beside her, Claire let the woman talk before probing for details.

"Thanks for seeing me," the woman said, her words slurring. "I hope you'll forgive me. After the break-in, I had a couple glasses of wine to fall asleep, and when I woke up, I came straight here, so I'll admit, I'm a little bit…"

Claire held up a hand. "What, exactly, can we help you with?"

The woman took a long, slow breath. "I left a tip about, um, Ryan Hooks, in relation to the murder that took place on Oak Street on Saturday. I have reason to think that he might be involved."

"Why do you say that?" Claire asked.

"Because I actually dropped him off there about a week ago. I drive for DAC, and I picked him up at the Renouvelle Hotel before dropping him at that same apartment." The woman shook her head. "But let me back up."

She launched into a long, drawn-out story about the elderly couple she had dropped off at Lurie Children's; her husband, whom she was taking care of; Ryan Hooks, whom she claimed to drop off at the Oak Street apartment without recognizing him; and a break-in at her apartment earlier that morning. When she was done, Claire leaned forward.

"Ms. Wilson—" she said.

"Mrs.," the woman said with a small shrug.

It was the fourth time she'd mentioned her husband since she'd arrived, and Claire made a note of it on the paper in front of her.

"Okay, Mrs. Wilson," Claire said, sneaking a glance at Greg. "Is there anything else you can tell us about what happened on the night you dropped him off? You said you thought Mr. Hooks seemed nervous when he got into your car. Do you still feel that way?"

The woman made a face, but she covered it quickly. "Yes, he was so…" She paused. "Fidgety. I guess you could describe it as nervous. I can't really explain it, but I could tell something was wrong."

Claire felt her anger rise as the woman stared at them innocently. She wanted to reach across the table to shake her, to demand that she tell the truth, but she also knew they had the upper hand by not letting on that they knew who she was. Not yet, at least.

They'd take their time, confirm she was who they thought she was, and get as much information out of her as they could.

"I really wish you could explain it."

Claire watched as the woman froze.

"So why exactly are you sharing this information with us?" Claire asked. "If you're insinuating that Mr. Hooks had something to do with the incident on Oak Street this past weekend, you must realize how serious of an accusation that is."

The woman still did not say anything; she just sat there frozen, looking back and forth between Claire and Greg.

"Are you okay?" Claire asked.

Still no response.

"Mrs. Wilson? Are you all right?"

Nothing.

"Mrs. Wilson?"

"Yes," Paula said, shifting in her seat. She cleared her throat. "Look, I think maybe we got off to a bad start. I'm not…"

"Not what?" Claire asked, leaning forward, and she watched as the woman flinched.

"I didn't..."

"Didn't what?" Claire said again, and she heard Greg chuckle, just slightly, under his breath.

"No, you don't understand," Paula said. "It's not what it seems like. I have a—"

"Husband?" Claire asked, and she watched all the blood drain from the woman's face. "I know you do, Mrs. Wilson," Claire said. "You've been saying that since you arrived."

The woman swallowed, a slow, nervous motion, and then her eyes darted up quickly to the clock.

"That's the reason we're supposed to believe everything you're saying, right?" Claire asked, and she couldn't help smiling a bit. "We should believe you because you have a husband, and let me guess—you love him very much?"

When she was gone, Greg walked with Claire back to their desks.

"Are you sure that was a good idea?" he asked. "Letting her go like that?"

"Yes," Claire said. "I don't think she's a flight risk. She seemed genuinely scared about this break-in, and that part can be corroborated pretty easily. For now, I need you to find out what you can about Paula Wilson."

Greg nodded and started to walk out. "Oh, by the way," he said, pausing to turn back. "I'm pretty sure she said 'Wileson' when she first walked in. Not 'Wilson.' I kept wondering if she was going to correct you."

Claire raised an eyebrow and then smiled slightly, shaking her head. "No, I don't think she was," she said softly. "Okay, Paula *Wileson*. I want to know absolutely everything."

CHAPTER 28

Paula

Three days after

A S I TOOK A cab away from the police station Tuesday night, I wondered if it was my imagination or if the two cops really had been incredibly suspicious of me.

Maybe that was just the way detectives acted?

Maybe I was overthinking it?

I tried to shake it off, but deep down, I knew going there had been a terrible idea.

For what felt like the tenth time that week, I vowed to lay off the alcohol.

Instead of going home, I had the cab drop me off at Emma's apartment building. I needed to talk to her, to get her to admit that Hooks had been at the apartment the other night, and to tell her about the break-in. I didn't know how much I would tell her about what I'd done, but I needed *somebody* to tell me I wasn't crazy.

I rang her doorbell several times. She wasn't answering, and it took all the willpower I had not to bang on the door or start to throw rocks at her window. I began to walk away slowly, aimlessly, when I came up to the dog park, and on a whim, I pushed the gate open and stepped inside.

I don't know why I was there; maybe I was too scared to go home and be by myself, too worried to call Keith to bother him with this. He'd wanted to cut his trip short after he found out about the break-in, but I told him not to, that this trip was a big deal for him, and there was no reason to come home early when I was perfectly fine.

But I wasn't fine. Not even close.

So I stalled. I walked farther into the park, the warm breeze tickling my face. As I stepped through the gates, I had the same thought I'd had the first time I'd visited the park: if I were coming here at another time, under other circumstances, maybe, just maybe, it could have been a place that Shelby and I frequented. I wondered what it would be like to be able to afford one of the luxury homes on the block, to spend my afternoons with Shelby tucked away in this perfect, manufactured space.

I sat down on the bench where I'd first met Emma and Andrew and listened to the leaves being pushed around by the wind.

As I sat there, I saw a flash of light out of the corner of my eye, and I blinked.

I brushed it off as nothing, but then it happened again, and I squinted, looking around the park. I looked up as it happened again, and I saw a small light coming from an apartment on the second floor of the building across the park. I squinted, standing up, and looked up at it in the dark.

The events of the past few nights had me on edge, and I felt my stomach flop over in fear. I should have been carrying a weapon with me, at least my bottle of bug spray. More than that, I shouldn't have been sitting out here alone. I was turning to head back to the street when I saw a figure in the window, and I realized that someone was standing there, holding the object that was being shone into my face.

A flashlight.

Again.

"What the hell?" I said out loud. The figure moved away, and I stood there for a few moments, looking up at the window. With the light gone, I could see that I was looking into a shadowy room that might have been a bedroom? A den?

I frowned and finally turned to leave. As I stepped through the gate, I saw a figure walking down the sidewalk toward me from the direction of the building I'd just been examining.

Sure enough, it was Reg, the man I'd met the first time I'd come to the park. He was walking toward me with the flashlight in one hand and something else in the other.

A flowerpot?

"Hello," I said as he walked up to me, but when he got close, I could see that his face was covered in a scowl, much like it had been the other time I met him.

"What are you doing out here so late?" he demanded.

"How is that any of your business?" I asked. "And what's with you pointing flashlights in people's eyes?"

"It's my business because I'm a resident of this neighborhood, and this is our park. Someone has been letting their dog leave a lot of mess out here every night, and I think it's you!"

"It's not," I said. "I wouldn't do that. Besides, do you see a dog?" I waved a hand around me.

He frowned, but the scowl didn't go away. "Where did you say you live again anyway?" he asked.

I folded my arms across my chest. "I live around the corner," I said.

"Where, exactly?" He peered at me suspiciously.

I swallowed. "It's none of your business," I said.

"Yeah, right," he said. "I know my neighborhood, and I know the people in it. I also know the people who couldn't afford to live around here if they sold everything they had."

I balled my fists up at my side but turned to walk away. I didn't have time for this.

"Maybe you didn't leave dog crap tonight, but I know you have been," he said. "And I have proof."

I stopped. "What?" I asked, turning back. "What are you talking about? You can't have proof, because it didn't *happen*."

"I've seen you driving around here," he said. "If you live around the corner, why do you always drive? It makes no sense. You should stop lying. Since I have it all on video."

I froze and watched the smug expression on his face as his words sunk in.

"What do you mean?"

He held up the flowerpot and spun it around so I could see a small, black square embedded in the side. It took me a moment to realize that it was a camera.

"This sits on my windowsill all day and night and feeds the stream to my laptop," he said. "I haven't gone through it, but I know I'm going to find you on it, walking your dog and leaving crap everywhere. You might as well just admit it."

I stared at the flowerpot, and an idea crossed my mind.

"Let me see that," I said, grabbing it from his hands.

I scrolled through the small screen and saw a list of four recordings, all exactly four hours long, and each one stamped with a different date and time.

"How long have you been doing this?" I asked.

"A couple weeks," Bolton said, narrowing his eyes. "Long enough to have captured you."

"What about the old ones?"

"I've saved everything from the past few weeks on my computer," he said.

"What time do you record?"

"Eleven o'clock to three o'clock."

"Can I come up and see them?"

"What?" he asked, and he looked at me as if I were a leper. "No!"

I rang Emma's buzzer once, and then again and then one more time.

I'd run all the way there from the park, leaving Reg standing there with his flowerpot, flashlight, and attitude in hand.

I could see that there was a light on in her apartment. After I pushed the buzzer a few times, I stepped back and saw that the light had been turned off.

Damn it.

I pushed it again, repeatedly now, and finally, I heard static over the intercom.

"Who is it?" she demanded, anger and exhaustion in her voice.

"It's Chris."

There was silence for a few moments, and then she spoke again.

"Go away, Chris, please. It's not a good time."

"I need to talk to you," I said.

I didn't hear anything for a moment, and then I laid on the buzzer again.

"Damn it, Chris!" I heard her say, and then she buzzed the door open. I pushed it and stepped inside.

As I walked in, the memories of the last time I'd been there came back to me, and I put a hand on the wall to steady myself.

I had a sudden image of myself walking down the stairs, Hooks on one side of me and Emma holding my elbow on the other side. I could only see his face; hers was just out of sight the entire time.

I walked up the stairs, and when I reached the second floor, I turned and headed toward her door. It was open, and Emma was standing there with her arms crossed in front of her chest, her face covered in frustration.

"What are you doing here?" she asked. "Do you know what time it is?"

"How can you keep avoiding me?" I asked. "You carried me down those steps with him."

She blinked and then shook her head. "What?" she asked.

I could see she was nervous. I could tell she was thinking hard, and I wondered what kinds of lies she was thinking about shelling out to keep me from knowing that I was right.

"You carried me downstairs—those stairs right there—with Ryan Hooks on the night Beverly was killed."

She stared at me for a moment with her eyes wide.

"What?" she said again, but I saw recognition dawning on her face. She looked around and then ushered me into her apartment. "What is wrong with you?"

"I know you were here with Ryan Hooks that night and that I fell asleep behind the couch. You don't have to protect him. I know how violent he is."

She still didn't say anything and just continued to watch me.

So I kept going. "He broke into my apartment and attacked me, Emma. He broke into my car the other day, too, to threaten me." The words were coming out in a rush now, and I just needed her to listen, to understand. "And if he's violent with me, he's probably violent with you too."

She swallowed and then spun around, her back to me. She was leaning forward with her head in her hands, and finally, she turned back around.

"What exactly is it that you want me to do?" she asked quietly.

"I want you to tell the police. I don't think they will believe me."

"Tell them what, exactly?"

I sighed. "About the affair, Emma. I know all about it. About the fact that he was in the building. And that he could've done this. Don't you think they should know?"

She spread her hands. "I don't know anything," she said, and she paused for a moment as if she was thinking about how much she should say. "Yes, we carried you out. You were so drunk, I honestly didn't think you would remember. But then he went home."

She shook her head, turned, and walked farther into the living room. I followed her, swallowing as I was transported quickly back to the night of the party. I looked at the floor where I'd lain, and it was pristine.

"Look," she said. "I will admit that we have been having an affair, since you seem to know that part already. But I can't do what you want me to do. I can't come with you to the police." Her eyes filled with tears, and she stepped back away from me.

"Why not?" I asked.

"For all the reasons you just told me," she said. "He is violent. Very. And we don't have any proof that he did anything to Beverly. Right? So we have to just let it go. I appreciate what you're trying to do here, but you have to remember that this is Ryan Hooks you're talking about. He has all the money in the world and twice as many connections. Unless you have some kind of proof...?"

I took a deep breath. "That's actually why I came here in the first place," I said. "I actually think I might have some, but I'm going to need your help to get it."

She frowned but looked curious. Before she could say anything, I turned and walked toward her front door.

"Come with me."

CHAPTER 29

S HE FOLLOWED ME OUT into the hallway, grabbing her keys from the hook by the door.

"Where are we going?" she asked.

I hesitated at the top of the stairs, torn between wanting to drag her down the block with me and knowing that I needed to take some time to explain. "We need to go next door," I said. "To see your neighbor, Mr. Bolton."

I was heading down the stairs but realized she hadn't moved. Turning back, I could see the confusion all over her face.

"What are you talking about?" she asked. "Why would we go see Mr. Bolton?"

I took a deep breath as a million thoughts rushed through my head.

We're running out of time!

We have to go now!

He has the proof if we could just get there!

"I just saw him, next to the dog park," I said. "You know how he's been worried that there's someone who's walking their dog and not picking up after it?"

"Yeah," she said slowly, and she still watched me as if she wasn't sure I wasn't crazy. "What's that got to do with anything?"

"Did you know that his apartment actually overlooks the dog park?" I asked.

"No," she said. "I mean, I know he lives nearby, but I didn't know he actually lived next door."

"Well, I was out there earlier, and I thought I saw something in the window. A moment later, he came outside and started yelling at me."

"Why?" she asked.

"Because he thought I was out there letting my dog crap in the park and not cleaning it up."

She didn't say anything for a moment, and then she shook her head. "Chris, what the hell are you talking about?"

I sighed again. "The thing is, he's really serious about it. So serious that he has been taping the park at night. Using a nanny cam in a flowerpot he leaves on the sill every night."

Emma blinked, and then her expression changed. She tilted her head to one side. "What do you mean he's been taping it?"

"He set up a camera," I said, trying to keep the impatience out of my voice. "He's had it up and running for the last couple of weeks. Long story short—"

"You think he might have proof that Ryan was here on the night Bev was killed." She said each word slowly, as if she was processing them while she spoke.

"I think it's worth a try," I said quietly. "I think it's our only chance. When he told me about it, I asked him if I could come up and see it. Let's just say he's not my biggest fan. Then I thought about you; he *likes* you. He'll let you up. Please, we have to get over there now."

Emma was on my heels as we walked out of her building. "You think that if Ryan left the apartment that night, it'll be on his video?"

"It's worth looking, don't you think?" I asked. She still looked hesitant, and I stopped. "We have to try. There has to be some way to prove that he was here, other than your word and mine."

She nodded, and we continued on, hurrying down the block and past the dog park. I looked at her and saw that she looked scared. I felt bad for her. She'd told me how much she was in love with Hooks, and I knew this couldn't be easy for her.

When we got to Bolton's apartment, I reached out and pushed his buzzer.

"Yeah?" he said. "Who is it?"

I looked over at Emma and nodded.

"Mr. Bolton," she said. "It's Emma Brighton from next door."

There was silence for a moment, and then he spoke again. "What do you want?"

She blinked and pointed at the intercom, but I shook my head.

"I was hoping I could come up for a minute to talk to you."

There was another moment of silence, and then he buzzed the door open.

We walked inside and took the elevator to the second floor. When we stepped out of the elevator, he was standing in a door-way on the right side of the hallway. He cursed when he saw us walking toward him.

"You've got to be kidding me. Not her again."

"We need to talk to you," Emma said.

But he shook his head. "She can't come into my home."

"I'll wait here," I said to Emma as we got closer to his door. "Just take a look at the videos."

She stared at me for a moment, then nodded. As she was walking inside, I had a moment of fear that she might see the evidence against Hooks and decide to delete it.

"Emma," I said, and she turned around. "Please, don't do anything…"

"Stupid?" she asked. She turned and walked inside.

Bolton slammed the door with a snarl in my direction. I paced in the hallway a few moments, and there was a part of me that considered checking to see if he'd locked the door.

You can't just barge in.

But a minute turned into five, and five turned into ten. I was seriously considering knocking on the door when it opened and Emma walked out.

"Well?" I said, stepping forward. "Did you see it?"

Her eyes were sad and tired, and she nodded.

"He's on the video," she said.

"I knew it!" I said. "Do you have it?"

"No," she said, spreading her hands. "Mr. Bolton is going to email it to me."

"He is?" I asked, frowning. "Are you sure?"

"Yes, Chris," she said. "We've imposed on him enough. If we push any harder, he might not send it."

I was silent as we walked into the elevator and then exited the building a few moments later.

"Are you sure—" I started, but she put up a hand.

"We have to trust him," she said. "And you have to trust me. He said he would send me the video tonight, and I promise, I'll give it to you."

The next morning, I got up and drove to the police station. Emma and I had agreed to meet there at 9:00 a.m. I was thirty minutes early, and I sat outside the station, gripping the steering wheel, my nerves making it hard for me to sit still.

If she didn't come, I was going to drive to her house and push the buzzer until she answered.

I didn't have to. At ten minutes to the hour, I saw a car pulling into the station parking lot and immediately recognized Emma in the driver's seat. She pulled into a space and sat there for a few minutes, a couple of cars down from me. There weren't many cars in the parking lot, and I watched as she scanned them until she saw me, sitting in my own car. She flinched, and I raised a hand and waved.

We both got out of our cars, and she walked toward me, her purse on her shoulder.

"Did he send it to you?" I asked.

She nodded. I could see that her eyes were red and puffy, as if she'd been crying.

"I can't go in there," she said, reaching into her purse and pulling out a jump drive. "Here's the video. And by the way, even though he was there, it doesn't mean that he actually killed her," she snapped. "I want to be very clear about that."

I frowned. "I never said it did." A thought crossed my mind, and I stopped walking. "Did you call him?"

"What?"

"Did you call Ryan? Did you tell him what we were doing?"

"No," she said, and when she saw my expression, she shook her head vehemently. "I didn't call him. I promise."

I walked into the station and asked for Detective Puhl. A few minutes later, she walked out the back of the station, looking incredibly put-together for so early in the morning.

She sighed when she saw me.

"What's this about?" she asked.

"I have something I need to show you," I said. "It's about Ryan Hooks."

A few minutes later, we were both standing behind Puhl's desk. She'd inserted the jump drive and was pulling up the file.

"There, that's the one," I said.

Puhl clicked on it, and suddenly, the video viewer popped up, filling most of the screen. It was slightly grainy footage of the dog park and the sidewalk beside it. We watched it for a few moments, then I leaned forward and clicked the mouse a few times.

We saw something like a figure move by on the sidewalk, and I pushed the space bar to stop the video.

"There," I said.

The video showed a man walking toward Emma's apartment building. We both leaned close, but it was clear that the man in the picture was the one, the only...

Ryan Hooks.

"See," I hissed.

Puhl had an expression of disbelief on her face. "He really was there, wasn't he?" she said, rewinding the video a couple of times. There was no mistaking that it was him. She dragged the video to the end, but there were no signs of him walking back the same way.

"How long did this record for?" Puhl asked.

"It stopped at 4:00 a.m."

"And we don't see him leave..." Puhl muttered quietly. It was more of a statement than a question.

The video stopped on the screen, a still shot of the park in the wee hours of the night.

Puhl was tapping her pen against the table, and she seemed to be mulling something over.

She leaned over and wrote something in her notebook. As she wrote, I stared at the image on the screen, the video stopped on the final, grainy image, and I tried to quell the voice that was rising in my head.

Something is wrong.

I leaned closer to the screen, trying to figure out what it was that was bothering me. There wasn't anything in the picture, nothing you could actually make out, but I stared anyway, pulled in by the image on the screen.

I was dragging my gaze back to Puhl when I stopped on one small piece of text on the screen and felt a chill run down my spine.

It was the time stamp for the video, which, since it was at the very end, showed the length of what we'd just seen.

3:58:48

I frowned when I saw that, instead of the solid four hours of every recorded session in the flowerpot camera, this video was just a little bit short.

There was a full minute and twelve seconds missing.

I decided not to say anything to Detective Puhl, not right away. I left the jump drive with her and walked out of the station. As I did, I saw that Emma was still sitting in her car. I walked up to her window.

"How'd it go?" she asked breathlessly. "Did they see him?"

I nodded.

"That was really tough," she said. "Thanks for encouraging me to do it, though. As hard as it was, I know it was the right thing to do."

I watched her as she stared at me, her face the picture of complete innocence, and I wondered if I could have gotten it wrong. Maybe I'd misread something; maybe I wasn't thinking straight.

"The video," I said before I could stop myself. "Did you notice anything about it?"

"What do you mean?" she asked.

I hesitated. "It seemed a bit short."

She blinked.

That was the mistake. I wouldn't have noticed anything, yet her eyes darted away for just a moment, and I saw her jaw clench just slightly. Other than that, her expression remained perfectly neutral except for a slight furrowing of her brow in confusion.

"What do you mean?" she asked again.

"The video, Emma," I said. "All the recordings were four hours long. Exactly four hours, because he set it for the maximum amount of time. How did we lose more than a minute?"

She continued to stare at me, and then I saw something on her face that I couldn't quite read.

"I don't know what you're talking about," she said, but there was something there that looked like…

Satisfaction.

"Thanks again for convincing me to come in," she said, and then she began to pull out of the spot. "It was the right thing to do."

CHAPTER 30

I WAS PARKED A FEW blocks down from Bolton's apartment, watching the building. It had only taken a few Google searches to learn that he was the "lead volunteer" at a local animal shelter. I'd called the shelter and spoken to Erica, a chipper veterinary student who'd been more than happy to tell me his schedule for the week.

"I'm so happy you were pleased with Reg's service the last time you came in," she had said. "He's one of our best. He's in every day except Mondays, if you want to come back on one of those days."

I drummed my fingers against the steering wheel. It was Wednesday, so he should be leaving soon, and then I was going to have to do something less legal than everything else I'd done in the past few days, which was saying a lot. I was going to have to go in and try to find the original footage of the recording from Saturday night. Emma had all but admitted that she'd cut something from the video because "it was the right thing to do."

What the hell did that mean?

About ten minutes later, I saw Bolton step out of his apartment, his dog trotting along behind him. I slumped down in my seat and hoped he didn't see my car; by now, I knew he'd recognize it, and that would be it. But he walked in the other direction and turned the corner.

Was he just walking his dog?

Or was he taking him to the shelter with him?

I knew how bad an idea it was. But I simply couldn't handle people acting like I was crazy any more. Like I'd made it all up. If Bolton had the evidence on his computer, I was going to find it. One way or another.

I waited a full ten minutes after he left before getting out of my car and crossing the street, careful to keep my head down.

You only look suspicious because you feel suspicious.

You only look suspicious because you feel suspicious.

I walked up to the door, took a deep breath, and pressed all the buzzers quickly.

Nothing happened right away, so I did it again.

In my very first apartment out of college, I lived in a building where the landlord constantly posted notices saying that we should not open the door when someone buzzed to get up if we did not know who they were.

Which meant there were people who did that.

I had to hope there was one in Bolton's building today.

I took a deep breath and did it again, dragging my finger along all the buzzers. Finally, I heard a woman's voice come through the intercom.

"Who is it?"

"Sorry, gas company," I said, thinking quickly. "I got locked out."

There was another pause, then the woman buzzed me in. It was a quick buzz—as if, by only pushing it for a second, she wasn't letting in a serial killer. I pushed the door open quickly, and just like that, I was inside Bolton's apartment building.

I rode the elevator up to the second floor, overcome by a sense of déjà vu after my trip there with Emma the previous day. I tried to think about what she must've seen when she went into Bolton's apartment. Something that incriminated Hooks? Something that incriminated her?

Was she trying to help Hooks or hurt him?

Whatever it was in that minute and twelve seconds she'd deleted would tell me the truth.

I stepped out into the hallway and walked down to Bolton's apartment. I hadn't heard anyone else inside, and I knew he'd taken his dog with him to work. Still, my heart was racing as I raised my hand and tapped lightly on the door. I didn't want anyone else on the floor to hear me knocking, but I couldn't very well break in if there was someone else inside. I waited a few moments and then tapped again. When nothing happened, I reached into my pocket and took out the ID card I'd put there.

I'd looked up how to break into an apartment on YouTube. Of course, the tutorials were designed for people who'd locked themselves out of their own apartments. But I'd studied how to open a door with a laminated credit card, and it was time to put my two-hour education to the test. I reached up to test the handle and let out a gasp as the door opened easily in my hand before I got anywhere near it with the card.

I paused, unsure if I should believe my luck. In my search, I'd read that most burglaries happened during the day, through unlocked front doors, but I couldn't believe that there were people who actually didn't lock their doors in the middle of Chicago. As I stepped inside, I let out a sigh of relief that Reg Bolton was one of them.

I closed the door behind me and leaned back against it, breathing heavily. I felt an immense amount of guilt wash over me as I stood in his apartment, his home. But I pushed it away and began looking around for the laptop where he'd said he stored the files.

I moved quickly through the living room and the kitchen, but there was nothing there. At the far end of the kitchen was the door to the bedroom, and I walked inside slowly, the weight of my intrusion on his personal space making my stomach turn. I was considering turning around when I saw the laptop, right there in the middle of his dresser. I walked over to it quickly and opened it, moving my finger across the mouse pad.

The desktop loaded almost immediately, and I thanked the password gods that he hadn't protected it. His background was a picture of his puppy, but it was absolutely covered in file folders and icons.

Shit.

I leaned closer to the computer and scanned them, looking for anything that stood out. I found the folder a few minutes later: *U-CAM37S.*

I opened it, and there was a list of recordings from the past two weeks. I wondered if he'd just started recording then, or if he'd been deleting them to save space. I scrolled through the list and found the one from Saturday. Sure enough, like the other recordings, it was exactly four hours long.

What did you cut, Emma?

I double-clicked it, and the video opened up. It was the familiar shot of the dog park, highlighted in the night by the large streetlights that surrounded it. I moved the video forward to the end, but there was nothing there in the last ten seconds, just more footage of the same. Which meant she'd cut from somewhere earlier in the video.

I began to drag the bar around to different portions of the night, but nothing changed. Just the same shot, every now and then showing someone walk by. Dragging the bar again, I searched for what she could've cut and felt myself start to get impatient.

What am I missing?

I needed more time. I could email the video to myself, but then there'd be a record of me breaking into Bolton's place. Taking a breath to calm myself down, I placed the video at the halfway mark and then fast-forwarded, watching as the image on the screen shook. I got to the part where Hooks walked toward the building as we saw at the station. The video wobbled for another minute or so as it sped through the night, and then suddenly—

I saw a figure move past the camera in the opposite direction.

I froze, reaching out and tapping the space bar quickly to pause the video. My heart was racing as I dragged the bar back and maximized the screen. When I saw the figure on the screen, I pressed Play.

It was a man, walking away from Emma's apartment with his head down and shoulders slumped.

Hooks.

Walking back the way he'd come, just a few minutes or so after he arrived.

There was a loud noise from the living room, and I gasped, stepping back. I froze for a moment and then closed the video screen and the laptop.

I was holding my breath and praying that I had made it up when I heard voices.

"I'm supposed to be at work. They really need me today," Bolton said. "I don't know why this couldn't wait until later."

"I know, and I can't tell you how much I appreciate this."

Emma.

"I'll give you a ride to the shelter. I'm so glad I ran into you, because this is really important. I need to see that footage you showed me yesterday."

"I sent it to you!"

"I know," she said. "I just need to check something out from one of the other days. Please. It will only take a second, and then I'll take you to work."

I stood there paralyzed for a few moments as I heard them walking toward the bedroom.

She was going to delete it.

I grabbed the laptop, raced across the room as quietly as possible, and stepped into Bolton's open closet. I pulled it closed just as the door to the bedroom opened and they walked inside. I opened my mouth and took in long gulps of air, certain I would pass out if I didn't just *breathe*.

I needed air.

Think, Paula.

I watched them through one of the slats in the closet door.

"Well, if it's so important, go ahead," Bolton said, gesturing toward the dresser. "Then we need to hustle. I don't want to be late."

"Where is it, Mr. Bolton?" Emma said.

I saw Bolton spin around, and he frowned. He turned to look around the room, first at the bed, then his nightstand, and then back at the dresser.

"What the hell?" he said, walking over to the dresser and putting his hand on it. "I left it right here."

They both spun in slow circles, then Bolton walked out of the room.

"Maybe I left it in the living room," I heard him yell.

Emma stood there silently in the middle of the room. For the first time, I saw something in her eyes that I hadn't seen before—a clear, quiet determination, and the mask of something that was almost...

Sinister.

She was still looking around the room, but I saw her stop, and she looked at the closet door. My heart almost stopped as she seemed to look right at me.

"Mr. Bolton," I heard her call out as she continued to stare at the closet door.

"Yeah," he called out from the living room.

"You said your computer was here when you left this morning?"

"Yes, of course," he said.

"And how long have you been gone?"

"I don't know, twenty minutes or so?"

"Can you come here, please? I need you to do me a favor."

I heard footsteps, and a disheveled-looking Bolton was back at the bedroom door, his eyebrows raised.

"What is it?" he asked. "I can't find my computer. I don't know what's going on."

"I think someone stole it," Emma said assertively. She reached into her pocket, took something out, and handed it to him. "I need you to call this number," she said, then she leaned over and said something else quietly to him that I couldn't hear.

Bolton said something back, then turned and walked away.

Emma turned to look at the closet door again, and in that instant, without any real proof at all...

I knew the truth.

I stared at her face, her nostrils flared, her gaze razor-sharp, and I knew instantly that I'd gotten it all wrong. I flashed back to the night of the dinner party as I lay on the ground watching Hooks pressed up against Emma in her kitchen, and I felt, more clearly than I had felt anything else in the last couple of days, that it *just wasn't right*.

The curves and lines of the woman's face in the kitchen, and the one staring at the closet door...

They weren't the same.

It wasn't her.

I'd gotten it wrong, so terribly wrong, but I didn't have time to think about what that meant.

Because a moment later, she charged.

CHAPTER 31

Claire
Four days after

C LAIRE WAS STANDING ON the staircase at the apartment on Oak Street when the call came in. She'd found that the best way for her to tackle a case was to go over all the things—big and small—that didn't make sense about a case until they did.

First, there was the blood in the stairwell. Most of it had belonged to the victim, except for one smudge at the bottom of the staircase, completely outside any logical place where Beverly's blood would have fallen.

Then there was the fact that everyone at the party had been wasted. Dr. Ortiz seemed to believe that the alcohol wouldn't have affected the ability to strike Beverly, but it would have severely limited the killer's ability to clean up after him- or herself. There wasn't a trace of blood in any of the units, which meant that the killer had to have been very skilled or left the building immediately after the murder was committed.

Then, there was this whole thing with Ryan Hooks. The likelihood of him actually being the person responsible seemed slim, but she couldn't ignore it, not after seeing him so clearly on the video. She'd called him but hadn't yet heard back.

And there was Chris, the artist.

Or better yet, *Paula*.

None of it was adding up.

As she stood in the stairwell, her phone rang, and Claire pulled it out of her pocket. She didn't recognize the number and frowned as she answered and put the phone up to her ear.

"Detective Puhl."

There was a moment of silence, and then a man spoke.

"Hi, uh, Detective Puhl, this is Reg Bolton from 218 West Oak Street. Um, down the block from where Emma Bentley lives."

Puhl's frown deepened, but she gripped the phone tighter and began to slowly walk down the stairs. "How can I help you, Mr. Bolton?"

"Well, I'm at my apartment now, and Emma is here. She asked me to call you."

"Is everything okay?"

"I don't think so," he said. "She's in my bedroom right now, and she told me to step out and ask you to send someone to my apartment right away. She said to tell you it's about Chris."

Claire blinked and then began to jog down the stairs more quickly. "I'm on my way."

She raced out of the apartment and ran down the block, her gaze scanning the apartment buildings as she walked by. She saw that 218 W. Oak was on the other side of a small dog park. When she got there, she looked for Bolton's name and pressed the buzzer. It sounded almost immediately, and Claire ran into the building.

As she walked out of the elevator on the second floor, Claire scanned the closed doors. She'd only taken a couple of steps when one flew open, and there was an older man with bright-white hair standing there.

"I think…they're in there," he said, stepping back to let Claire enter. His entire body was shaking, and he held a small puppy in his arms. His expression was a mixture of fear and confusion. "I don't know why, but they shut the door…"

With her hand on her weapon, Claire moved past him and walked toward the closed bedroom door. She swung it open and frowned as she surveyed the scene.

"You have got to be kidding me," she said, looking at the two women standing in front of her and dropping her hand from her holster.

It was Emma Bentley and Paula Wileson.

They'd obviously been in a fight of some kind. But they'd stopped and were standing at least two feet apart from each other, staring at something between their feet.

A laptop.

Shattered in half, keys scattered everywhere on the floor.

Claire heard Bolton gasp behind her, and he rushed forward.

"My computer!" he said.

The two women standing over it looked up at Claire, and then they began speaking at once.

"She smashed it!" Emma yelled, moving quickly toward the door. "She was hiding in the closet with it when we came in, and I asked Mr. Bolton to leave the room because I knew she was crazy. But not *this* crazy."

"What are you talking about?" Paula said, taking a step forward, anger covering her face.

Claire moved forward and stood between them, glaring at them both.

Paula kept speaking. "She smashed it! I was trying to *save* the video on it."

"What are you talking about?" Emma asked. "She was trying to delete it because she said there were videos from other nights that might incriminate him. She's been following me around because she thought that would help her get closer to him—when I don't even know him!"

"She broke into my apartment," Bolton said from the doorway, the shaking man from a moment ago gone and anger in his voice. "And she broke my computer!"

"I didn't break it!" Paula yelled.

"Enough!" Claire said.

"Mrs. Wileson, I'm going to have to charge you with trespassing."

"That's the least of it!" Bolton said.

Claire watched as the woman looked back and forth between her and Emma, protests on her lips. Finally, she nodded and began walking slowly toward the door.

"Everyone, please leave the room. I'll get someone here to get the laptop."

"You have to fix it," Paula said, looking up at Claire, and behind her crazed, frantic expression, there was something else there that Claire couldn't ignore.

Desperation.

"Yes, please," Emma said as they all walked out into the kitchen. "You have to find someone who can fix it. She's trying to delete evidence that proves she's the one who killed Bev."

CHAPTER 32

Paula

Four days after

DETECTIVE PUHL LET US go and told both of us to come to the station in the morning.

"Be there at eight o'clock on the dot."

She said it sternly, her gaze trained on me, and there was almost a challenge there.

I dare you not to show up.

"I'll be there," I muttered.

I walked into the house and stopped abruptly when I saw Keith sitting on the couch. He looked up sharply as I stepped inside. He was holding his phone in his hands, and his face was covered in a mix of concern and anger.

"Where the hell have you been?" he asked with more anger than anything. "I've been trying to call you all day."

I blinked rapidly, knowing I should answer his question, but the only thing that came to mind was another question. "What are you doing back?"

He stared at me for a moment with his mouth open, and then he shook his head and leaned back against the couch.

"What am I doing back?" he asked incredulously. "One of the coaches who drove separately came back early to bring me home because there was a *break-in at my house and my wife was attacked*! You'd know that if you'd picked up your phone. I was seconds away from calling the police! And all you have to say is 'What are you doing back'?"

"I..." I started, reviewing my list of excuses, but then I stopped and just stood there.

I'd been lying so much, so *easily*. I'd lied to Keith, to the cops, to Emma, to Vanessa. Whether by omission or outright, it had become second nature. And I needed it to stop.

No more lies.

"Paula?" I heard Keith say, and I blinked. "Are you okay?"

I was trying so hard to think of the right thing to say, and it hit me that I just needed to get started, to tell him something that would prevent me from lying again, to *force* myself to tell him the truth.

"I have to go to the police station tomorrow to give a statement," I blurted out. "I did something really, really bad."

He blinked but didn't say anything for a few moments. I finally walked over to the couch and sat down beside him.

And then, I began to talk.

We sat there for two hours. There were parts where the words seemed so absurd, I almost didn't believe they were true. I tiptoed around the word *blackmail* for as long as I could, but I finally said it, and once the details began to flow, I couldn't stop talking. I wanted him to understand why I'd done what I'd done.

I'd done it for him.

For us.

"You don't have to fix me," he said, and there was anger there that I knew I deserved. "I know it's been hard on you too, Paula, but this is my reality. Our reality."

I tried to cut in, but he kept talking.

"And a surgery is not going to 'fix' things. It never was going to. I've changed and you've changed, and I need you to understand that we can never go back."

I started to speak again, but he held up a hand.

"We can go forward, though."

We stared at each other for a few moments, and I nodded.

"I know that," I whispered. "I'm sorry."

I started talking again. I got through the rest of my story uninterrupted, and he watched me with an expression I couldn't read. He only flinched when I told him that it was Hooks who'd broken into the apartment, presumably to take the money back.

He stared at me, his entire body rigid, the idea that his new client and idol could've been responsible for the break-in seeming to jolt him out of the daze he'd been in for the last few hours.

"Are you okay?" I asked this time, and he shook his head.

"Hooks?" he said, looking around the room. He continued shaking his head and then lowered his gaze to his hands, which were nervously tapping on both thighs.

"Keith?"

He shook his head faster and then finally stopped and looked up at me. "Stop talking," he said. "My turn."

CHAPTER 33

Claire

Five days after

PART 1 OF RECORDED INTERVIEW:
EMMA BENTLEY

Interview duration: 24 minutes

Location: 18th District Police Department, City of Chicago

Interview conducted by:
Detective Claire Puhl, Detective Greg Kuchi

PUHL: This interview is being recorded. I'm Detective
             Claire Puhl. Also in the room with me is Detective
             Greg Kuchi. This interview is being conducted in
             relation to the investigation of the death of Mrs.
             Beverly Brighton, 115 West Oak Street in Chicago,
             Illinois, which took place on Saturday, August 8.
             Today is August 13. Can you please state your name?

BENTLEY: Um, Emma Bentley.

PUHL: And where do you live?

BENTLEY: 115 West Oak Street.

PUHL: You own the building, correct?

BENTLEY: Yes.

PUHL: Now, Ms. Bentley, I know we've already talked about this, but can you tell us how well you knew the victim, Beverly Brighton? She was one of your tenants, yes?

BENTLEY: Yes, she was. She lived upstairs with her husband, Andrew. I knew Bev very well. She's a close friend of mine. I mean, she was... *(inaudible)*

PUHL: Okay. Do you know this woman? Please let the record indicate that I am showing Ms. Bentley a picture of Mrs. Paula Christine Wileson.

BENTLEY: Yes. I only know her as Chris, though. We met about a week ago.

PUHL: Where did you meet?

BENTLEY: At a dog park near my apartment. She came there because she was looking for someplace to take her dog. I should have known something was wrong with her that day.

PUHL: What do you mean?

BENTLEY: She just seemed a little bit off, you know? Like she was there for a purpose and was trying to hide it. She didn't have her dog with her that day, which seemed a little weird. And she kept looking at me the whole time like she knew me.

PUHL: Did you ask her why she was looking at you that way?

BENTLEY: No, of course not.

PUHL: Did you interact with her?

BENTLEY: Just a little. She was talking to one of my neighbors about the park. Then she started talking about Ryan Hooks, and then she was gone.

PUHL: What did she say about Hooks?

BENTLEY: That she'd just gotten tickets to go to his concert the next day.

PUHL: When did you see her again?

BENTLEY: Um, I guess it would've been in the park again, two days later. I go out there almost every day, and she showed up. With her dog this time.

PUHL: Did you tell her that you would be there?

BENTLEY: No, I didn't, but I later found out that my sister did.

PUHL: When you arrived at the park the second time, did she approach you, or did you approach her?

BENTLEY: She came up to me. I was just sitting there, and she walked over and asked if I remembered her. She seemed to remember a lot about me, but I didn't really think too much about it. She told me that she was an artist and that she was looking for work. Said she was going through a really rough time because of medical bills for her husband, and she asked if I had any friends who might be looking for some artwork. She kept making comments about how she needed more clients "like me" and in my "world"—I wasn't really sure what that meant. Anyway, I'm actually looking for an artist to do some work for my company's fashion show, and after she showed me a few samples, I decided to give her a chance.

PUHL: Why? I mean, if she seemed a bit "off" to you, as you said earlier.

BENTLEY: I don't know. Believe me, I'm regretting it. My sister says I'm too trusting, and I think maybe I should start listening.

PUHL: Greg, we should… *(inaudible)* Okay, Ms. Bentley, so you invite Paula, or Chris as you know her, to your home. How did this happen, exactly? Did you give her your address?

BENTLEY: Well, yeah, and we were sitting just a few buildings down, so I was able to point it out. Weird thing is, I gave her my phone number and asked her to text me hers, but like I told you before, she never did. I thought it was just an oversight. I was a little surprised when she actually showed up for the dinner, but I'm not one to make a scene.

PUHL: What happened when she arrived?

BENTLEY: Everything was okay at first. You can ask anyone there. I mean, she was at dinner with a bunch of people she didn't know, so she was a little quiet. I thought it was just that. But then she started to drink. A lot. We all were: me, Meggie, Bev, Andrew, Patrick, and Joshua, and we were all having a good time, but Chris—she was going down fast. At some point, I remember wanting to ask her to leave, but you know, I didn't want to make her feel bad.

            Then she pulled me aside and started asking me all these questions about Beverly. If I knew if she was seeing anyone else, had I seen anyone around here that looked like Ryan Hooks. Thing is, I knew Bev was seeing him. I'd seen him around the building whenever he was in town. Bev all but told me that it was more than just a professional relationship without ever using the words.

            But I wasn't going to tell Chris that, so I just kind of ignored her. Then she sat down on the couch and started dozing off. I went out to the deck where everyone was smoking to try to get a few people to help me get her outside and down the block, but when we came back, she was gone.

PUHL: But you don't think she was gone, was she?

(Silence)

PUHL: Ms. Bentley?

BENTLEY: No. After talking to some of my neighbors over the last couple of days, I realize that nobody actually saw her leave. And that she may have been in my apartment still when I went to sleep. After Patrick and Meggie left, I knocked out. I don't know. I was really out of it. I guess in a way *(inaudible)* it was my fault.

PUHL: How so?

BENTLEY: Because I let a stranger into my home, and then I was so drunk, I didn't recognize that she was still there when I went to bed. That's what the video showed. That's what she's trying to erase. It showed that she left my apartment much later than she originally said. After Bev was killed, not before.

(Tape stopped)

(Tape resumed)

PUHL: One more question. In your honest opinion, what do you think happened that night, Ms. Bentley?

BENTLEY: Chris, or Paula, or whatever her name is, left my apartment that night, was wasted, got into some kind of altercation with Bev, and killed her. Thing is, it's not just what I think. She admitted it to me at Reg Bolton's house.

◆ ❖ ◆

PART 2 OF RECORDED INTERVIEW:
PAULA CHRISTINE WILESON

Interview duration: 39 minutes

Location: 18th District Police Department, City of Chicago

Interview conducted by:
Detective Claire Puhl, Detective Greg Kuchi

PUHL: This interview is being recorded. I'm Detective Claire Puhl. Also in the room with me is Detective Greg Kuchi. This interview is being conducted in relation to the investigation of the death of Mrs. Beverly Brighton, 115 West Oak Street in Chicago, Illinois, which took place on Saturday, August 8. Today is August 13.

Can you please state your name?

WILESON: Paula Wileson.

PUHL: And where do you live?

WILESON: 404 Parvis Road.

PUHL: Why are we here, Paula?

WILESON: Excuse me?

PUHL: When you last came in here to tell us your…theory… about Ryan Hooks, you said you'd never been back to the apartment on Oak Street. But that wasn't true, was it?

WILESON: *(Inaudible)*

PUHL: I need you to speak up, please.

WILESON: No, it wasn't true.

PUHL: Okay, from here on out, I need you to tell me the truth, the whole truth, not just bits and pieces. Can you do that for me?

WILESON: Yes.

PUHL: Okay. So, when did you first go back?

WILESON: To the apartment? The night of the party—

PUHL: Not just inside. Outside, around, down the block. Anywhere nearby. And I want you to be careful here, because I already know a lot.

WILESON: Oh, okay. Well, yeah, I went back a few days later, because I went to a dog park nearby.

PUHL: Why did you go there?

WILESON: Because I saw Emma Bentley.

PUHL: The woman who you saw in the window on Saturday, August 1.

WILESON: Yes. I was just driving by, and I saw her, and I stopped. I promise you, I can't really explain why. I just wanted to learn more about her. So I pulled over, and we got to talking.

PUHL: Then you went back to the park a couple days later.

WILESON: I did. She wasn't there when I arrived, but when she got there, she came right over, and we started talking.

PUHL: She says you approached her.

WILESON: That's not true.

PUHL: What did you talk about?

WILESON: I promise, I wasn't up to anything. I just wanted to meet her. And then I went back a few days later, and she asked me to come to the dinner party to learn more about the clothing line. I wasn't going to go.

PUHL: Had you already corresponded with Ryan Hooks by then?

(Inaudible)

PUHL: Louder, please.

WILESON: Yes, I had.

PUHL: What about?

WILESON: I asked him for money.

PUHL: Money in exchange for what?

WILESON: I'm sorry. I asked him for money in exchange for the cell phone. And for me not to say anything about what I saw that night. I saw him going into 115 to meet up with who I thought was Emma Bentley.

PUHL: You thought?

WILESON: I thought so, yes. And he let me think that, because he realized I didn't know the entire truth. But it wasn't Emma who he was having an affair with. It was Beverly Brighton. She worked at the law firm that's been representing him. I guess that's how they met.

PUHL: And how do you know this?

WILESON: Because I saw them. I saw them in the kitchen that
                   night. I thought it was Emma, but when I saw her face
                   in Bolton's apartment, it struck me. She wasn't the
                   woman I saw Hooks with that night. It was Beverly.

PUHL: In Emma Bentley's apartment?

WILESON: Yes.

(Inaudible—13 seconds)

PUHL: Okay, let's back up. So at first, you thought Ryan
                   Hooks was having an affair with Emma. Tell us what
                   you did then.

WILESON: I sent him a tweet, and then he called me, and we
                   arranged to trade the phone for the money.

PUHL: You do know that's illegal.

WILESON: Yes, I do, but I don't have it anymore.

PUHL: The money?

WILESON: The day he broke in, he took it back. I can't prove
                   it, but I know it was him. He's a violent man. That's
                   what I've learned over the past week. But he didn't
                   kill Beverly Brighton.

PUHL: What do you think happened, Mrs. Wileson?

WILESON: Actually, it's not about what I think. Emma Bentley
                     did it. She admitted it to me at Reg Bolton's, right
                     before she smashed the laptop. She killed her because
                     all this time, she's been seeing... *(Inaudible)*

PUHL: What? I need you to speak up.

WILESON: *(Difficult to hear)* The man she's been seeing. It was
                     Andrew Brighton all along.

CHAPTER 34

Claire
Five days after

CLAIRE AND GREG STEPPED out of the interrogation room where they'd been talking to Paula Wileson and walked over to their desks. Greg flopped down in his chair and crossed his arms in front of his chest, stretching as he leaned his head far back.

"Can you believe this shit?" he asked as he sat up straight. "Talk about a case of she-said, she-said. Where's Reg Bolton's nanny cam when you really need it?"

Claire didn't say anything. She paced back and forth in front of her desk; she was too on edge to sit down. After a moment, she leaned forward and placed her hands on the mound of file folders that she was accumulating for the Brighton case.

It all meant nothing.

The killer was sitting right there in one of those two interrogation rooms, and she didn't know who it was.

What was she missing?

As if she'd spoken out loud, Greg echoed her thoughts. "I can't believe one of them is just sitting there, lying to our faces," he said. "This isn't some kind of huge mix-up. They are both saying the other one *confessed*, which means one of them is full-blown lying."

Claire still didn't respond. She looked up at the two-way mirrors of the rooms where the two women still sat. The women couldn't see them, but Claire could watch their every move.

There had to be something she was missing.

The women couldn't be any more different. Emma Bentley was perfectly still, her hands folded in front of her on the table. She looked as if she'd stopped breathing, so motionless was her body, and she gazed out into the precinct as if she could see. Emma had spoken plainly and confidently during her interview, and it was hard not to believe her when Wileson had already admitted to lying about so much.

But there was something about Paula Wileson, something Claire couldn't put her finger on, that made her believable. She was a ball of nerves; she was trying to hide it, but she could barely get her words out, fumbling over sentences, mumbling her answers. She seemed desperate for Claire and Greg to believe her, which could be a sign of guilt or a sign that she truly had been in the wrong place at the wrong time.

"So, what do you think?" Greg asked. "I'm torn, but if I had to go one way, it would be the Wileson woman. She's too jumpy, too nervous, and she's admitted that she's been lurking around that apartment for the last week. Using different names, showing up unannounced, sneaking around. There's obviously something not quite right about her. And look at her. She can barely sit still in her seat."

"Would you be able to sit still if you were being accused of a murder you didn't commit?"

"So, you think it's Bentley?"

Claire pursed her lips and continued to watch the two women through the glass. "I don't know."

She went over the statements that both women had made.

The blackmail.

The affairs.

The dinner party.

The video.

The video.

Claire slumped down in her chair and put her head in her hands. "Of course," she said out loud.

"What's going on?" Greg asked.

She lifted her head and looked at him with a small smile. "I know how to figure out who's lying. I have an idea, but it's going to take a *lot* of convincing to get the help we need."

Claire's grandfather had always said that it was easy to tell who your real friends were when the shit hit the fan. "They're the ones that have to scrape shit off their face," he'd say seriously, much to Claire's mother's dismay.

"Dad, do you have to?" her mother would say as Claire and her grandfather collapsed in a heap of giggles.

When the shit hit the fan, Andrew Brighton went—no, he *ran*—the other way.

It had started with convincing Reg Bolton to tell a little white lie in exchange for extra surveillance of the dog park for violations.

"We can arrange that," Claire had said. "If you do what we ask."

"So, you want me to come back to the station and pretend that I have another copy of the video in front of each of the ridiculous women who destroyed my laptop earlier today," he asked.

"Yes," Claire said through gritted teeth, ignoring how happy he seemed to throw the words *ridiculous* and *women* together. "It would be a great help to the case."

Reg had reluctantly agreed, and he'd returned to the station where they handed him a jump drive.

He'd been shepherded past both rooms with the doors slightly ajar. Then Claire had gone in and said the same thing to both suspects.

"Good news. Mr. Bolton came in and dropped off a backup drive of the recordings," she'd said, holding up the jump drive that she'd fished out of the back of her desk drawer. "We'll be able to back up your story after all."

Emma Bentley's reaction had been immediate.

She'd launched her body across the table in a frantic, desperate attempt to take it.

It was all the proof Claire needed.

When Andrew Brighton heard what happened, he'd jumped at the opportunity to share his side of the story. He'd signed, sealed, and licked the stamp on his statement before he even had a chance to face Emma. He'd told them every sordid detail of their affair.

"She wanted me to leave Beverly, but I wouldn't do that to our families," he said. "Bev didn't want that either. We both had our…arrangements, but we'd decided to make it work. At the same time, I do care for Emma, a lot. That's why I helped her."

"What did you do?"

He swallowed. "I heard a noise outside the apartment and stepped out, and that's when I saw Emma standing there over Bev's body, holding the statue. I think she was in shock. There was blood splattered on her clothes. She told me that she'd woken up in her apartment to find the door open and that Ryan Hooks and Bev came back a moment later. They told her that they were help-ing the artist, the drunk lady, into a car to get her home. Hooks left, and Emma said she followed Bev upstairs, just to get her to talk. Said she asked my wife why she wasn't pushing for a divorce, especially since she was seeing Hooks."

"Why did you help her?"

"I was panicking," he said. "I know it wasn't the right thing to do. I told her to run all the way downstairs to the first floor and leave a trail of blood so it would look like the intruder left. Then she came back upstairs and took her clothes off. Right there at the top of the steps. I gave her a garbage bag to put them in. I wanted her to track the blood through the building but not into her apartment. After she went back home, I carried all her things through my apartment and took them out the back. I ditched them down the block. I left the gate propped open and went back up that way to get into my apartment. Emma and I both had a couple more drinks until we crashed."

"Did you break the glass on the way in?"

He hung his head. "Yes," he said, and he broke down and began to sob. "Like I said, I was panicking. I just wanted to help Emma. I don't love my wife anymore, but I didn't kill her. Do you believe me?"

Claire sighed. "Yeah," she said. "I do."

CHAPTER 35

Paula

Five days after

I WALKED OUT OF THE station around 2:00 p.m.

It was jarring to leave such a dark, depressing place and instantly be surrounded by so much…normality. All around me, people buzzed by carrying Starbucks cups and shopping bags as they enjoyed the warm August day without any thought of the darkness that lay just behind the glass doors of the 18th District Police Station.

Why should they know?

Why should they care?

A woman walked by me with her hands full of Macy's bags, her head angled to one side as she cradled her phone between her ear and her shoulder.

"I told you I left my headset at home, babe! No, I'm not going to just *hold* it. I'll talk to you later…"

Behind her, a family of four, presumably tourists, ambled by, their phones lifted in the air as they took photos of everything around them.

It was all so normal, so nice.

And so painfully oblivious.

It made me wonder how many times I'd walked or driven by this same building, lost in my own world, while somebody else's world was ending just out of sight.

Or, better yet, how many times had I laughed joyously in my own home while someone else sobbed a few doors down?

I'd seen Emma's face, just before I left, through the glass window of the interrogation room where she was still sitting. She was staring straight ahead, her gaze fixed on something or someone else in the room that I couldn't see. Her mouth was slightly open, and her skin was flushed, and she just sat there...transfixed. There were no traces of the woman I'd first seen just a week and a half earlier, standing proudly and confidently in her window. That woman was gone.

And I had to wonder. Had she ever been there?

Or was that just the woman I wanted to see?

I'd tried to tell the detectives everything, but the words and the stories had been jumbled in my head. I described my first meeting with Emma that day in the park—how she'd frozen up *not*, as I thought, because I'd mentioned the Ryan Hooks concert, but because Andrew had been there and he kept mentioning his wife. I explained that Emma had told me the truth right before she'd grabbed the laptop out of my hands and smashed it to the floor. That she'd opened up to me, with fury in her eyes, about her best friend Bev who seemed to have it all.

"She doesn't love him, you know," she'd said. "And she wouldn't let him go. She had Ryan Hooks hovering around all night, coming, leaving, coming back. *Ryan Hooks!* And she still couldn't let go of Andrew. I begged her. I said, 'Marie, you know how I feel about him,' but she was just so damned stubborn, so committed to this perfect image, she wouldn't dare get a divorce, and she'd sucked him into believing the same thing."

I'd frozen. "Wait. Marie?"

"Oh, only close friends and family called her that," Emma said. "It's her middle name."

Of course.

M.

Detective Puhl had made a point of saying she was letting me go, *for now.*

"We'll be monitoring your accounts," she'd said sternly, and I nodded. She seemed to believe that Hooks truly had taken the money back the night he broke in—but I understood why they had to check.

"No problem," I said. "Monitor anything you like. There won't be anything to find."

She stared at me for a moment. "And I'm assuming you're not going to press charges for the break-in, given..."

"No," I said quietly, measuring each word. "I don't have any real proof it was him, and...after everything else..."

Detective Puhl sighed. "I'll talk to him too. It's not just about giving the money back. He'll have the right to press charges too, though I have a feeling he won't as a matter of discretion. All that to say, don't be hard to get ahold of if I need to talk to you."

It wasn't the first time she'd told me that in the past week, and I nodded.

I began to walk, nowhere in particular, the sun bearing down on my face and warming my neck. At some point, I began to head east, toward Lake Michigan, and I walked until my breathing became labored and my back was drenched in sweat. It took me about twenty minutes to reach the pedestrian tunnel at Division Street that took me under Lake Shore Drive and out to the lakefront path.

In the middle of the warm August day, it was covered with

cyclists, runners, and toned women with high ponytails jogging behind expensive strollers. I waited for a break in the action and stepped onto the paved path.

Then I started to run.

I was already hot, tired, and sweaty, and I was far from dressed for it—I was still wearing the pair of jeans and simple flat shoes that I'd slipped on that morning. But I ran anyway. I ran because I had to, because my body craved it, and because my mind *needed* it. I could feel the sweat building under my arms, above my upper lip, and behind my kneecaps, but I pushed on anyway. I ran as fast as I could, the hot wind blowing into my face, the dust stinging my eyes. I felt my blood pumping through my body, heard it rushing in my ears, and I pushed some more.

I caught a few glances from people around me: other runners in their spandex athletic gear and proper running shoes; people dressed like me who were walking at a more appropriate pace. But I ignored them and pressed ahead, feeling addicted to the miserable, itchy feeling that was taking over my body as my blood vessels expanded and contracted.

I was a good person.

It wasn't something I'd ever questioned before, not really, not even during the past week. I'd seen what illness had done to my parents, and I'd wanted to avoid it by any means necessary.

But as I'd sat a room away from Emma and stared at a cop who seemed to very much put us in the same category, I couldn't help but wonder:

Did Emma Bentley think that she was a good person too?

It was a question that had bothered me from the moment I'd sat down, through the interrogation and my final conversation with Detective Puhl. If Emma came out of this thinking she was, deep down, a good person, she may be a bit more delusional than me.

But how much more?

I was panting heavily now, but I kept running, farther and farther and farther until I felt a pain in my side and my entire body cramped up. I veered off the path and raced toward a tree, placing my hand on the craggy bark as I leaned forward to gulp in the thick, hot air. My stomach turned over, and I thought I'd be sick, so I slumped down to the ground and waited a few beats.

"Hey, you okay?" a woman in a purple short set with a tennis racket asked, jogging over to me, but I put my hand up and nodded.

"I'm good," I managed to get out, and she jogged away. The nausea was subsiding, and I took a few deep breaths.

I was still a good person.

Emma had murdered someone in a jealous rage, for goodness' sake. I'd blackmailed someone for money, someone who (a) was not a nice person and (b) probably spent $180,000 a year on garage space for his cars.

I pulled myself up and then stumbled across the two-lane path, navigating around a pair of men jogging with no shirts and a biker who was bent forward as she barreled toward me.

"On your right!" she yelled, and I moved quickly out of the way.

I was breathing heavily as I walked away from the path and toward the street before fishing my phone out of my pocket and calling a DAC.

When I got home, I walked through the door, and the first thing I saw was Shelby standing next to her bed, watching me. I don't know if she could sense my despair, but she took a small step forward. It was all I needed. I rushed over and sank down on the floor in front of her, wrapping my arms around her neck and burying myself in her fur. She was stiff, only for a moment, then she relaxed against me, nuzzling the side of my face.

I heard a noise and looked up as Keith appeared, rolling himself into the living room. I hadn't let him come to the station with me; I'd needed to face it on my own. He looked at me expectantly, and I launched into a recap of the day. I told him everything that had happened—from the interrogation to Emma's ultimate confession.

He stared at me silently, the same tension on his face that had been there the night before. When I finished, he finally spoke.

"Did you tell them about the money?"

I nodded quickly. "Of course," I said. "I told them why I did it but that it was no excuse. And they said that they'll be monitoring our accounts for a while."

Keith opened his mouth to say something else, so I kept talking so as not to give him an opportunity to edge himself in.

"It was crazy, sitting there one room over from a murderer. You should've seen the way the detective was looking at me. It was horrible—"

"Paula," he said, cutting me off. "Did you tell them about the money? I mean, did you tell them everything?"

"I—"

"Did you tell them that it wasn't Hooks who broke in and stole the money?" he pressed. "Did you tell them what I did?"

I sighed and took a deep breath. I thought back to his words the previous night: *Stop talking, my turn.* I thought about the way he'd broken down and told me the truth.

I thought about my confession, and his.

And then I shook my head.

"No," I said. "I didn't tell them."

I was a good person.

Keith had told me that he was the one responsible for the break-in. He'd seen me storing the money the night I'd gotten it from Hooks and had arranged to steal it. The temptation for someone who'd struggled with gambling addiction had been too strong;

he'd hired a kid from the swim team to do it, one who hadn't traveled with them to Indianapolis.

"You told me you were going to be at the diner until seven that morning," he'd said, his voice cracking. "I'd been thinking about the money ever since I saw it, and I couldn't think of another way to take it. I'd talked to Jimmy about it, just in passing, but didn't really decide to act on it until you told me you had to work late that day. I texted him from the bus and told him to take some treats for Shelby, to tear the place up a bit before taking the money out of the bathroom. He didn't want to hurt you. He didn't even know you were there! He was just coming to the bedroom to try to calm Shelby down. I never would've put you in that situation. I'm so, so sorry."

Then, he opened up with one more confession.

"I've already gambled half of it away."

He'd stared at me, sadness, embarrassment, and disappointment in his eyes. I could tell he was holding his breath as he waited for my reaction. I knew I should scream, cry, or storm out of the room, the memory of the fear I'd felt that night washing over me in a wave of sickness.

But I reminded myself, it was just that.

A memory.

It was time we started to move forward.

"Half of it?" I'd asked levelly. "What about the rest? Do you still have it?"

Keith had stared at me for a moment, understanding settling on his face, and he'd nodded.

We'd have to be careful about how we used it, since Detective Puhl would be watching.

With or without the money, we would get past this.

We were good people.

But I'd be damned if the money wouldn't help.

READING GROUP GUIDE

1. What factors led to Paula's decision to blackmail Ryan Hooks? If you were in Paula's financial situation, what would you do with Hooks's phone?

2. Why do you think Paula jumped to conclusions about the relationship between Ryan and Emma? What clues did she miss? How did the memories of her mother's illness and her parents' relationship affect Paula's decision-making? How did it affect Paula and Keith's relationship?

3. Why do you think Keith was against having the surgery? Why was Paula pushing for it? What do you think caused this disconnect in their relationship?

4. Why do you think Emma fascinated Paula? How are the two women different? Similar?

5. After everything Paula did, Claire seems to trust her more than she trusts Emma Bentley, following the interrogations. Why do you think that is?

6. Describe Paula's relationship with the truth. How was she able to convince herself that it was okay to lie to her family and friends?

7. Do you think it's ever okay to lie to someone you love? Explain.

8. Is Paula a good person?

A CONVERSATION
WITH THE AUTHOR

Where did you get the inspiration for *The Night in Question*?

I take *a lot* of rideshares. One day, I was chatting with a driver about all the things he'd seen during his brief stint as a driver. He laughed and said I wouldn't believe some of the stories. He looked up at me in the rearview mirror as he said this, and that's a scene that made it into *The Night in Question*. I took out my phone during that ride and made a note to explore a story about a rideshare driver who saw something she shouldn't have seen. It spiraled from there.

I love writing and reading stories about good people who convince themselves that it's okay to do bad things. I think those kinds of stories are easy to relate to because we've all been in tough spots where we had to make a choice about what kind of person we were going to be in that moment. Paula makes a bad choice and must deal with the consequences of that decision.

Do you think Paula is a likable character?

I do! I think readers may vary in their reactions to her choices, but I think they'll see that she, at the very least, *thinks* she's doing her best. She's convinced herself that she and her husband need the money much more than Ryan Hooks does and that what she's doing isn't all that bad. Not great, certainly, but not *unforgivable*. That's important to her.

Why are so many of your books based in Chicago and/or the Midwest?

Chicago is a vibrant and diverse city with so much to do and learn every single day. It's also my home—I've lived here for all but three years of my life. I grew up in the south suburbs, went to graduate school in the north suburbs, and currently live in the city. While a little part of it is "writing what you know," it's no secret that Chicago has always been an amazing backdrop for crime, mystery, and suspense, and I'm happy to have the opportunity to add my voice to that.

Have you ever stopped writing a novel halfway through?

No, I haven't. That's because I rarely get halfway through a story without knowing where the rest of it is going to go. I am a heavy outliner, so I have a good sense of how a story is going to turn out by the time I've written the first chapter. I often put stories away for a while and come back to them, just to give them some time to breathe. But my unfinished manuscripts tend to be pages long, not chapters.

So how many (brief) unpublished books do you have in a drawer somewhere?

It's hard to say! Probably ten to fifteen, in various stages. I haven't given up on them yet!

When you develop characters, do you already know who they are before you begin writing, or do you let them develop as you go?

I know the basics about them when I start writing—their primary motivations, their backgrounds, their hobbies. But I definitely like to let them grow and develop along the way. A scene near the end of the book might give me a clue about how a character would react to something earlier in the novel, and I'll go back and add in a detail. It's fun to be able to watch characters come to life during the writing (and even editing) process.

What are some of the common themes in your work?

My suspense novels are *very* family-driven, with the major conflict often centering around relationships between parents and children, siblings, and spouses. I think that's because it's our deepest relationships that test us the most. Those are the ones we'll risk everything for and for which we'll put everything on the line.

What writing habits are you trying to break?

Writing stories in my head while I'm in the middle of a conversation...humor that borders on snark...oh, and overusing ellipses...!

ACKNOWLEDGMENTS

As always, I would like to thank my family and friends for their seemingly endless supply of love, support, excitement, and encouragement. Thanks, too, to my book family—Shana, MJ, Barbara, and the rest of the Sourcebooks and IGLA teams. And a special shout-out to The Book Cellar in Lincoln Square for supporting new authors and creating a space for people who love books to meet, mingle, and discuss.

To the many readers who have taken the time to reach out via email, social media, or at conferences and panels over the past two years—thank you for your kind words, your ideas, and, above all, your incredible imaginations.

ABOUT THE AUTHOR

© Damian Chaplin

Nic Joseph is fascinated by the very good reasons that make people do very bad things. She writes thrillers and suspense novels from her home in Chicago. As a trained journalist, Nic has written about everything from health care and business to aerospace and IT, but she feels most at home when there's a murder to be solved on the next page. Nic holds a bachelor of science in journalism and a master of arts in communications, both from Northwestern University. Visit nicjoseph.com or follow her on Twitter @nickeljoseph.